ISLES OF
STORM &
SORROW

VIPER

BEX HOGAN

Orion

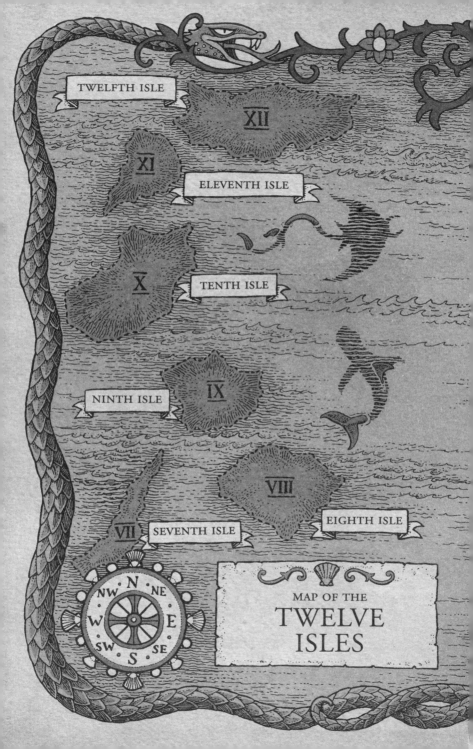

TWELFTH ISLE

XII

XI

ELEVENTH ISLE

X

TENTH ISLE

NINTH ISLE

IX

VIII

EIGHTH ISLE

VII SEVENTH ISLE

NW N NE
W E
SW S SE

MAP OF THE
TWELVE
ISLES

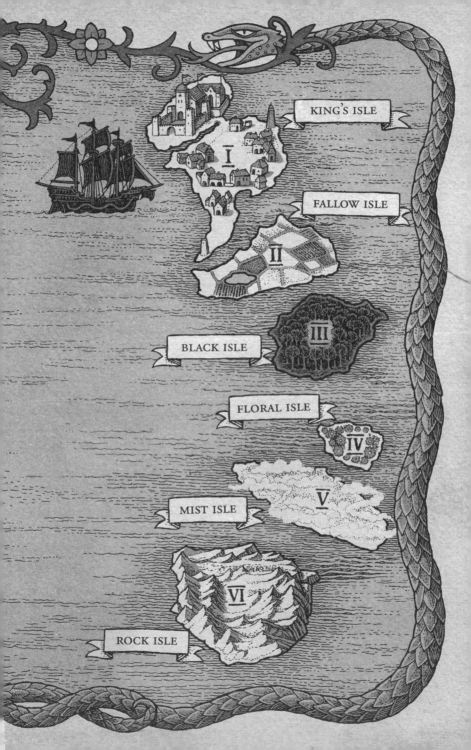

ISLES OF
STORM &
SORROW

VIPER

ORION CHILDREN'S BOOKS

First published in Great Britain in 2019
by Hodder and Stoughton

1 3 5 7 9 10 8 6 4 2

Text copyright © Rebecca Hogan, 2019
Map artwork copyright © Tomislav Tomic, 2019

A CIP catalogue record for this book
is available from the British Library.

ISBN 978 1 51010 583 6

Typeset in Adobe Garamond by Hewer Text UK Ltd, Edinburgh

Printed and bound in Great Britain by Clays Ltd, Elcograf S.p.A.

The paper and board used in this book are made
from wood from responsible sources.

MIX
Paper from
responsible sources
FSC® C104740
FSC
www.fsc.org

Orion Children's Books
An imprint of
Hachette Children's Group
Part of Hodder and Stoughton
Carmelite House
50 Victoria Embankment
London EC4Y 0DZ

An Hachette UK Company

www.hachette.co.uk
www.hachettechildrens.co.uk

For Kara and Odette.
We match, don't we?

I don't need to dissect the bird to know how it died. I watched it fly straight into the mast moments ago, its limp body falling to the deck, its fragmented skull rattling beneath my fingers as I picked it up. But its death isn't what interests me. I want to know how it lived.

At the first incision blood trickles down the black feathers on to my fingers. It's still warm. I wipe it away. Not because I'm squeamish, but because I want to see beyond, to the tiny organs hidden behind delicate bones. My previous attempts at this have taught me that my touch has to be gentle. One slip and the fragile body collapses in on itself, keeping its secrets buried within.

The knock on my door is unexpected and makes me jump. Cursing the unwanted interruption, I wrap the bird in a cloth and hide it in the nearby chest, not caring that the blood might seep out on to my belongings. Being discovered would be far worse.

Wiping my hands clean, I open the door as little as possible, in case I've overlooked any incriminating evidence, but it's just one of the crew, and his reluctance to be here is obvious.

'Captain wants to see you,' he says.

'Thank you,' I reply, and he hurries away.

Having learned a long time ago not to keep the Captain waiting, I give my clothes a cursory glance for stains, pause briefly to wash away the remaining traces of blood from under my nails, and make my way through the ship to his quarters.

Some of the crew greet me as I pass; a few don't acknowledge me at all, but it doesn't bother me. Respect has to be earned among Snakes, and I have done nothing to gain theirs yet.

Three of them are huddled together, whispering. They turn their backs to me as I pass, excluding me from the conversation, but their voices carry.

'I heard there are still Mages in the West that can melt the flesh from your bones with a single word.'

My own skin prickles at the mere mention of magic. Real or not, I think I'd rather be on my way to see a Mage than the Captain right now, however cruel the stories say they were.

Outside the Captain's cabin, someone is waiting for me. Bronn, the most lethal man on board, stands guard. His sleeves are rolled up and I try very hard not to look at his deeply tanned arms; they're strong and deadly, but I also know how gentle they can be. They once made me feel safe. Now they exist only to protect his captain and to carry out his loathsome orders. I swallow back the bitterness that is quick to rise.

When he hears me approaching, Bronn turns and nods in a barely perceptible greeting. 'He's expecting you,' he says, and opens the door, gesturing for me to enter.

The room is designed to intimidate captured foes, and I hate almost everything about it, especially the grotesque display of body parts exhibited in jars on a shelf. The smell of death lingers in the air, which, I suppose, is the intention.

Sitting at his table – surrounded by treasures and trophies that speak of his dominance over the Eastern Isles, his sea vulture Talon looming alert on a perch behind him – is the Captain.

My father.

He is not alone. Standing beside him is his first mate and oldest friend, Cleeve, whom I'm supposed to address as Uncle, but struggle to, because he's a bloodthirsty lecher and I detest him.

In front of the desk two members of the crew flank a woman who is in shackles and has been badly beaten. I recognise her as one of our newer recruits, although her name momentarily escapes me.

Bronn moves silently across the room to stand on the other side of my father. Sensing I'm not going to like what's about to happen, I dig deep to keep my voice steady as I speak. 'You wanted to see me?'

My father's solitary eye meets mine, a messy scar where the other should be. His heavily lined face reveals no emotion. 'Marianne, thank you for joining us.' He says it in a way that suggests I've been keeping them waiting, despite my prompt attendance. Typical. 'I want your judgement on a matter that has arisen concerning a member of our crew.'

He beckons to the men, and the shackled Snake is roughly shoved towards me, so I cannot help but smell fear mingled with her sweat and blood.

'This scum,' my father continues, 'was caught stealing water from the barrel.'

My heart sinks. Stealing from the rations is a grave offence, and I don't like to think of the punishments this poor woman has already received. Anders, that's her name. I feel relieved to have remembered.

'What do you suggest we do with this thief?' The question is so heavily loaded that the room begins to spin.

Aware all eyes are fixed on me, waiting for my response, ready to judge any sign of weakness, I take a deep breath. My eyes meet the accused's and I see the desperation in them, the hope I might be lenient. I cannot pardon her, that much is clear. It occurs to me that perhaps a thief should lose a limb befitting the crime – her hand maybe, or her tongue? I almost laugh out loud – the notion of me commanding such a thing is ludicrous. But this is no laughing matter.

'Her crime is serious,' I say, hoping my voice sounds as authoritative as I intend it to, 'and cannot be excused.'

I face my father and glimpse a flicker of triumph in his eye. 'Throw her in the brig, then leave her behind on the next sandbar we pass. Let her see how thirsty she is then.'

The spark of satisfaction seeps away from my father's face at the delivery of my sentence. I have failed. This isn't what my father wanted to hear. I glance across at Bronn, hoping to see something suggesting comprehension, admiration, respect. But his face is set like stone as always, revealing nothing, and anger simmers painfully inside me. Like I care what he thinks anyway.

Anders seems to sense her fate has been sealed and she begins to plead with my father, begging for forgiveness until one of her captors silences her with a harsh blow across the cheek.

Father turns to Cleeve. 'Do it.'

A cruel grin flashes across Cleeve's face as he steps out from behind the table. In no more than three steps he has reached the prisoner and slit her throat. Talon flaps his wings, though whether out of protest or approval it's impossible to tell. Such a quick decision – such brutality – makes me sick, but I force myself to watch. After all, that is why I am here. Death was always going to be Anders' sentence; it was just that my father hoped I would give the order. He knows this is not the first time I have witnessed the light diminish in someone's eyes as life drains away – he has made me watch countless times – but he believes forcing me to endure what he deems necessary will change me. What he does not comprehend is I do not wish to change.

'Clean this mess up.'

My father's men instantly respond, dragging the corpse from the room. It leaves a blood trail behind it as if the body is trying to send out one final message for help. It will be ignored, erased.

When only the two of us remain in his cabin my father turns to me, and I expect to feel the full force of his anger. Instead he says nothing, which is decidedly more sinister. I wish the others hadn't left. When he eventually does speak, his voice is dangerously soft. 'You knew what I wanted you to do.'

'I did.' No point in denying it.

'Then why, Marianne? Why do you continue to resist?'

How do I answer? I cannot admit the truth, not to him, not ever. Not if I want to continue breathing. So instead I give him an approximation of what he wants to hear. 'I am trying, Father. One day I'll be able to give the orders you wish.' My voice shakes slightly through the lie but he doesn't seem to notice.

He strides over to his window, staring out at the inky sea.

'Do you remember when you were young? You used to sit in here with me, lining up toy boats on my charts before sending them into battle. You would melt my sealing wax in the candle and pour it over them. For the blood, you'd say. I should have had you thrashed because you ruined so many papers. But I didn't. You showed such promise and I was proud.'

'I think my fingers still have the burn marks,' I say with half a smile.

'And yet you have allowed your potential to rot away, until nothing remains but your weakness. You know what this means, don't you? You know what you are forcing me to do?'

Of course I do. My quiet defiance has always come at a cost. My father holds out his dagger for me.

'Please,' I say, not wanting to do this. Not again. 'I promise. I'll try harder. Next time—'

'Take it.' It's not just an order; it's a challenge.

Still I refuse, desperate to talk my way out of this. 'If you give me another chance—'

My father is in front of me in a heartbeat, his face in mine as he roughly pulls me towards him, the blade too close to my skin. He's breathing fast, enraged by my insolence, and slowly he lowers the dagger to rest it in my hand.

I'm shaking as he takes a step back to perch on the edge of his desk. There's no escape. There never is.

'Do it.' His voices trembles with excitement.

Shame burns my cheeks as I raise the blade and bring it down into the soft flesh of my palm. Beads of blood rise quickly to the surface, before slowly tracing their way round my hand and dripping to the floor.

'It gives me no pleasure to see you do this,' my father says, though his sadistic smile suggests otherwise. 'But it is for your own good.'

He says this every time he makes me purge my body of frailty and indecision. I used to believe him. Now I simply do what I must to survive.

It doesn't hurt much, not really, as only a little blood is required. Just a small cut. Just enough to remind me of his authority. Just enough to humiliate. I listen as he gives me the usual speech about how he's only seeking to protect me, that I'm my own worst enemy, how if I only obeyed him I could save myself pain, before ending it with the same old words . . .

'We're warriors, Marianne. And warriors aren't weak.'

He walks over to reclaim his dagger and it sickens me how on some level I'm still seeking his approval, wanting to return to that time when I adored him, before I feared him. He steps back, turning from me, and I hate that he makes me feel so small. So nothing.

Reaching into one of his many chests, he pulls a pile of material from it and holds it out. 'This is for you.'

Slightly confused, I take it from him, careful not to get any blood on it. Silky soft and aqua green, this is no Snake garb. Shaking out the folded fabric I see that, though it's a gown, it couldn't be more different from the one I'm wearing: lines of embroidery mimic the ocean's waves, pearls embellish the cuffs and neckline. I cannot think of a more unsuitable garment to wear aboard a ship.

'We are soon to receive an important guest. I need you to impress him. Can you do that?'

'Of course.' Finally an order I can actually obey.

'Good. Go and get changed. I'll send for you later.'

And knowing I've been dismissed I turn to leave, taking care not to slip in the blood that precedes me.

Desperate for air, I head up on deck. As I weave between Snakes waxing the boards to protect them from decay, a gust of wind catches my skirt, sending it billowing in front of me. Wearing a dress is an impracticality I learned to deal with a long time ago, ostensibly an outward sign to all we meet that I'm not yet an official member of the crew. But as I've never seen anyone else be made to wear one, I'm inclined to think it's another of my father's torments. No one but me cares that it's forever dragging in the pools of water that naturally occur on board and is sopping wet most of the time. I can hardly wait to trade it for an even more impractical one. I stare up at the rigging, the light glinting off the harpoon mounted on top of the mainmast, and cannot tell from this distance the men from the women. How I long to shed these wretched petticoats and join them.

My palm stings, and I curl my hand into a fist, hoping no one will notice my latest shaming. They won't. The truth is, no one pays me enough attention to care; at times it's easy to believe I'm invisible on this ship.

Anders' death has rattled me, even though it's nothing new. I was six when I saw my first execution. Well, the first one I remember anyway. Everybody had congregated at the ship's helm, the atmosphere so menacing that despite my youth I sensed something was terribly wrong.

The man had been dragged up from the brig, where he'd clearly been for some time. He was in a wretched state: emaciated, beaten, filthy. The wind carried his stench to where I stood and made me gag.

The Captain had towered over the cowering man and told us all of his betrayal, how he'd failed to carry out an assignment entrusted to him. I hadn't really understood what was happening until the Captain grabbed him by the hair and slashed his throat. Always the throat. He likes a savage death, my father. The man had dropped to his knees before falling forward, blood bubbling from the wound to surround his body with a strange and deathly halo.

I didn't see a captain reprimanding a disobedient crewmember; I saw my father committing the murder of an unarmed man. And I'd cried.

It was the wrong reaction. My father was furious with me, both for disappointing and humiliating him.

Punishments had followed, the worst of which was having to clean the congealed mess left behind once the corpse had been flung into the deep waters. Who knew a dress could absorb so much of a man?

Perhaps that is why even now the memory lingers. Standing on the same part of the deck, I can identify the exact place where the evidence once lay soaking into the fabric of our ship, though there is nothing visible to the eye. I was made to scour and scrub until every trace of the crimson stain was gone, but that dress always bore the scar. Yet somehow the metallic smell of iron still reaches my nose, and I move slightly further away, wanting to leave the past where it belongs. After all, I have seen many men die since that day. Too many.

I look down at the freezing black waters, the grave of countless sailors, and wonder why anyone would prefer the unsettling waves to the solidity of the ground. My father's ship, *The Maiden's Revenge*, cuts through the water with ease, a silent predator feared by all in the Eastern Isles. She's untroubled by these treacherous seas, but I've seen what happens to those on lesser ships when caught in storms, and know the ocean to be as deadly as any assassin. Lurking in its depths is an army of its own, vicious killers hidden in the dark, waiting to strike at any opportunity. Merbeasts will hunt anything for prey, including humans, and more than one ship has been devoured by giant serpentsharks.

One of my earliest memories is of spiralling through the sea, my limbs tangling with the water as it filled my lungs. The weight of it. The unbearable, heavy darkness. I don't remember how I fell in, or who fished me out, but I do know the fear as if it were yesterday. My dreams remind me if I try to forget.

If the *Maiden* is my prison, then it is the ocean who is my gaoler.

For any Snake to feel this way is unthinkable. But for me – daughter of the Viper – to be afraid of the water? It is my greatest shame and my biggest failure. I have, after all, been born for this purpose.

Whether I like it or not.

I dig my nails into the splintering wood of the railing, wanting to inflict my pain on to the ship, willing her to suffer with me.

My only comfort is that, at seventeen, I'm yet to join official Snake ranks and am not required to carry out any acts of service to my father or my king. But my eighteenth birthday is only weeks away and once I'm of age I'll await Initiation, when I will be required to complete a series of tests before taking my place at my father's side. I'll become an assassin with a Royal Commission, just like the rest of Father's fifty-strong crew – each and every one a highly trained killer.

I'd laugh if it wasn't so horribly real.

It's not that I don't value the importance of the Viper and his crew. I do. Centuries ago the Eastern King created the first Viper in order to lead the King's Fleet in defending the Twelve Isles against the threat from the Largeland far across the sea. Answerable only to the King, the Viper became a presence so menacing, so terrifying, that no one in their right mind dared to challenge his authority on the waves, and though years of battle raged between the Isles and the Largeland, the Viper led the King's Fleet to ultimate victory and all was well.

Time passed, and with the threat from the Largeland extinguished, the Eastern and Western Isles turned on each other. The Viper became the Eastern King's most vital weapon, a means to eliminate those who threatened him. Though that war is long since done, over the generations the Viper has become a symbol of fear, his crew prepared to do whatever is necessary, however unpleasant, to keep the Eastern Isles peaceful.

So my father is cruel, yes, but for good reason. We keep the Isles safe. We keep the people safe. And I need to find a way to embrace the violence if I am to serve them, as I want to, as I must.

I just don't know how.

A movement in the corner of my eye makes me glance to my left, where I see the cabin boy, Toby, struggling with some rope. He is the only child currently living on the *Maiden*, having joined us when we last made port at the First Isle six months ago. My father rarely allows children aboard, and I'm not sure why he made an exception for Toby, who has no aptitude for sailing. I wander over to show him how to tie the knot he's after. He doesn't speak to me, but gives me a nervous smile before scurrying away. A boy of few words.

As I watch him go I notice Ren, the boatswain, staring at me. I smile in greeting, but he just grunts in response, before returning his attention to the mizzenmast. A man of few words.

A soft creaking on the boards causes me to look over my shoulder, and I relax when I see who it is.

Grace, the only Snake I'm ever happy to see, is approaching. Her uniform is closely fitted to allow her complete freedom of movement. There are no weapons on her person because her body *is* her weapon – agile, strong and deadly. She stands next to me, staring out to sea, her expression grim.

When she doesn't speak I fill the silence. 'Is something wrong?'

She tilts her head, panther-like, her astonishing black eyes locking on my own muddy-coloured ones. 'I heard about Anders.'

I shrug.

'You didn't make the kill.'

I wonder for the hundredth time what Grace thinks of me. Seven years my senior, and the most respected of all the women aboard, she knows me better than anyone, has trained me in combat over the years, knows exactly what I'm capable of, is perfectly aware how much I hold back – and yet she says nothing. Not once has she given me away to Father when I downplay my skills. Does she suspect I'd rather heal than kill? Can she sense the lack of murder in my heart? Or does she think, like my father, that in time I will learn to be one of them, a killer for my king? She is the closest thing I have to a sister, but as long as she answers to her captain, I can't entirely trust her. I can't trust any of them.

'I hear we're having a visitor,' I say, transparently changing the subject.

'We are. You should be getting ready.'

I hold up the hideous dress. 'Have you seen what I'm supposed to wear?'

She raises an eyebrow and takes it from me. 'Come on. I'll help you.'

As we make our way below deck I glance over at her. 'Who's this guest it's so important to impress?'

'The Captain didn't tell you?' She seems surprised. 'Apparently Prince Torin is gracing us with his presence. And, before you ask, I have no idea why.'

A royal visit? This is new. We always make port on the First Isle when Father needs to attend court or receive new orders. And he always goes alone. No one aboard the *Maiden* accompanies him, the King preferring to conduct business in secret. As far as I know, and admittedly my knowledge is limited, even the Prince isn't privy to his father's darker orders. I wonder whose idea this visit was, my father's or the King's? And why now?

No one seems to know much about the Prince, and so he's taken on quite an air of mystery. Some say he's a coward who's brought shame upon his father's name by hiding away, others say he's a scholar wedded to his books. I've even heard rumours that he's secretly fighting against his father under an alias and that they haven't even seen each other for years. Whatever the truth, one thing is certain: the Prince is rarely witnessed in public. And now he's coming here. I don't know what my father is up to, but it's unlikely to be good.

Once in my cabin I relax slightly, the door creating a false sense of security.

It's a poky space, my room: my bunk runs the full length of one wall and it's sparsely furnished. I can count the items in here on one hand: clothes, knife, chest, wash bowl and chamber pot.

And now a new gown.

I throw it on the floor and fling myself into my hammock. Grace bends to scoop the dress up and pulls a face.

'Where did the Captain dredge this up from?'

'I dread to think.' Maybe it belonged to a woman he entertained in his quarters last time we made port. Or maybe he prised it off a dead body. Either way I don't want to think about it too much.

Grace is shaking it out with a look of amusement. 'He knows it's going to take more than a new dress to make you respectable, right?' And she pokes me in the ribs.

I gasp with mock indignation, but swing my legs round and force myself to stand up. May as well get this over with.

Grace helps me into the gown – which we discover has several layers that create a full skirt and a low-cut bodice so tight I can barely breathe.

As she fastens the ribbons at my back, my mind wanders to the days when she spent more time alone with me here, when I was a child and she was one of the few who noticed me. 'Do you remember those stories you used to tell me?'

Grace pulls tight, winding me. 'What stories?'

'About magic. The Mages.'

I had wanted so badly to believe that they were true. Maybe I still do.

She pauses. 'I guess. What made you think about that?'

I shrug. Though the history books tell us magic left the East centuries ago, it may as well have never existed for all anyone talks about it. But I have always loved the merest mention of it, escaping into legends filled with mythical creatures as if they could somehow shelter me from reality.

'I'm surprised you remember.'

I fall quiet. 'I don't have many happy memories to choose from.'

Grace lightly touches my arm, and rests her chin on my shoulder. 'They were just fairy tales to help you sleep. Pay them no heed.'

My smile falters. I'd hoped she'd tell me one now, offer me some comfort, and her dismissal of them stings.

Wanting to move on from the topic, I clear my throat. 'Maybe I should do something with my hair?' My fingers pull at my corkscrew curls.

'Your hair's fine as it is,' she says, but I ignore her, attempting to make the matted mess cooperate as I pile it on top of my head, in what I suspect is an unflattering heap.

'What do you think?' I ask, but Grace doesn't answer. Though she's behind me, I can sense the shift in her mood, and I frown. 'What's wrong?'

'Nothing,' she says a little too dismissively. 'I just think you should leave your hair down. After all, your father prefers it that way and we don't want to give him cause to be angry, do we?'

It's true. Having my hair loose is like wearing a dress, another reminder that I'm not an official member of the crew. Only when I'm alone do I ever tie it out of the way and enjoy the relief of not having hair in my eyes.

Grace moves round to stand in front of me, and for a brief moment she has a distant look in her eyes, but then she snaps into focus. 'I'd like to see the Captain complain about this,' she says with an approving smile.

'Thank you.' Without her I'd probably still be lost in waves of material.

We sit on the hammock swinging gently, and she catches me off guard by taking my hand in hers. The gesture seems oddly maternal, and for one stupid moment I think I'm going to cry. I distract myself by mentally tracing the lines around the white patches she has in her skin, the lack of pigment creating mini islands on her hands. She has them on her arms too; I've seen them peeking out beneath her sleeves before. When I was younger I used to imagine she had a whole map over her body, a world entirely of her own.

'We should increase your training,' she says.

I say nothing, because all the training in the world isn't going to solve my problems.

'And, Marianne? There's no harm in believing in the magic.'

'Even if it's just a stupid story?'

Grace flashes me a wicked grin. 'No such thing.'

When she leaves and there's nothing to do but wait to be summoned, I dig out the dead bird from my chest, the smell clawing at my throat the moment it escapes. The body has started to decay already and the spark of life that lingered while there was warmth remaining has gone. It will teach me nothing now. Damn. I open my porthole, sea spray flicking up into my face, and drop the tiny corpse into the ocean. It may as well make a tasty morsel to some hungry creature down there so its death isn't entirely in vain.

I know why Grace wants me to practise more; she's thinking about my Initiation. Shrouded in secrecy, the ritual is different for everyone. I once asked Grace what to expect and she fell silent before answering.

You cannot ask. I cannot tell. You will pass or you will fail. That is the way.

That she seemed apprehensive of my Initiation did nothing to instil confidence in me. *She* fears nothing.

Personally I'm not sure what I'm more afraid of – Initiation itself, or what comes afterwards. How long will it be until I'm given my first assignment? And what then? Will I have to kill someone? I could. I'm more than capable. Grace has made sure of that. But should a life be valued so lightly? That it can end at the whim of one man?

However, it's one thing to avoid my father's requests now, and quite another to defy him as my captain, issuing orders from the King.

I look at the cut on my hand. Perhaps my father's right. Maybe I am just too weak.

My mind snakes away from such thoughts and instead returns to the imminent visit of the Prince. In all the vast expanse of the ocean, this particular location seems a strange place for us to meet.

We're close to the invisible divide that separates the Eastern waters from the Western ones. It's a line we never cross – the Western Isles aren't governed by the King or anyone else, and since the war that destroyed the unity between the Twelve Isles, the Western Isles have sunk into ruin. Now all that remains are stories whispered from generation to generation, of lawlessness, violent clans, evil creatures in the deep. It's said the last of the Mages still dwell in the West, fallen now to a crueller magic than in the days when they stood with kings. The legendary water raptors continue to strike fear into the toughest sailor's heart, though they are nothing more than myth. Everyone will breathe easier when we're a little further away from Western waters.

Apart from me.

I have long been drawn to what lies beyond the divide, as eager for Grace to tell me stories of the West as the East when I was younger. The mystery surrounding the forgotten Six Isles entices me as strongly as it repels others, and leaves me with a longing to venture to the unknown – a feeling that I suspect stems less from bravery than from my desire to escape. But given that I'm alone in these feelings, it occurs to me how calculating my father has been to lure Prince Torin into unsettling waters for our meeting. He's trying to intimidate the Prince. I hate to think what part I'm supposed to play in this visit.

It's several hours before someone taps on my door and rescues me from my thoughts. The *Maiden* stopped moving a while ago, so I know we've dropped anchor. When I open my door Bronn is standing there and for a brief moment he gives me a strange look, which is confusing until I remember I'm wearing different clothes. No doubt he's suppressing the urge to laugh.

'What do you want?' I can't remember the last time Bronn came to my quarters.

He finds his voice eventually. 'Prince Torin is close by. You're wanted on deck.'

'Lucky me,' I say, unable to hold back my sarcasm. When he doesn't move I add, 'It's all right. I know the way.'

Still he says nothing, just stands there with such bored indifference that I push past him, unable to contain my irritation. Since when have I needed an escort on board the *Maiden*? He follows right behind, but I ignore him, the wall of silence that has long existed between us thicker than ever.

Given that it's the first time we've entertained royalty aboard the *Maiden* I'm not sure what I was expecting in the way of a welcoming committee, but it wasn't this. As I reach the deck I see the crew standing row upon neat row dressed in full uniform: their black tops and trousers covered by equally dark cloaks that tie neatly at the waist, their hoods pulled over their heads. My father stands ready to welcome the Prince; Cleeve and Ren are just behind him, while Grace is off to their side. Though I live among them, the sight of them standing on ceremony in all their deadly glory allows me to glimpse the terror they must drive into the hearts of our enemies. And quite probably our allies too.

My father looks up as we approach and to my relief I can tell my appearance has pleased him. 'Ah, Marianne, here you are. You look beautiful, daughter.' He is speaking too loudly, and I understand his words aren't meant for me; they're for his crew.

I had expected my apparel to cause amusement, perhaps even raise a laugh or two, but the way several of the men gawp suggests I'm having the opposite effect.

'Thank you, Captain,' I say, trying to communicate that I'm on my best behaviour. And I need to be because there's a vast ship, almost as big as ours, pulling next to us, flying the royal banner of blue and green alongside the Eastern Isles' flag. It's so brilliantly vibrant it only serves to emphasise the shroud of darkness that permanently covers the *Maiden*. Apart from me. Tonight I stand out like a beacon in this stupid dress.

Ren and Cleeve step forward to catch the ropes thrown by the royal quartermaster, pulling the ships close enough so we can be boarded. Several royal guards come over first, their spears ceremoniously pressed to their chests. I can't help but smile because if it came to a fight between them and my father's elite killers there'd be no contest. I wonder if Prince Torin realises quite how vulnerable he is here.

And then he steps aboard. I had imagined someone older, wide around the middle from an indulged and sedentary life, arrogant perhaps. But the man approaching us is close to my age, impeccably dressed, and his strong, lean physique tells me he's far from an idle passenger on his ship. He walks with the confidence of his station, and though his handsome face is tight with underlying tension, I imagine he is very popular at court. Especially with women.

'Prince Torin,' my father says, stepping forward and crossing his arms over his chest by way of salute. 'Welcome to the *Maiden*.'

'The honour is mine, Captain Adler,' Torin replies and his voice is velvet and honey. 'It's not every day one receives an invitation to dine on the most feared ship in our waters.'

'We're glad you could come.' I've never witnessed my father using his charm before – I hadn't realised he had any. 'Allow me to introduce my quartermaster, Cleeve. My boatswain, Ren. And this is Bronn. My most valuable assassin.'

I glance at Grace to see how she feels to be overlooked so publicly. She is, after all, one of the most senior of the crew. Her face betrays nothing, and I suspect this isn't the first time my father has treated her as less than the others. For all her brilliance she has one fatal flaw. She is a woman. All the women on board have to fight faster and work harder to get the same recognition as the men, and I know better than anyone the low opinion my father has of us.

Prince Torin nods politely as the introductions are made. 'It's a pleasure to meet you, although of course your reputations precede you. But where is my betrothed?'

I stare ahead, expecting a woman to appear from his ship, someone elegant and beautiful, calling sweet apologies for her lateness. But no one comes. And as my father turns to face me, a false smile upon his lips, I realise no one will. Because he means me.

The meal may be going well from a diplomatic point of view, but I cannot enjoy the food set before me, no matter how lavish, and if I were to drink all the rum in the world it wouldn't be enough to still my thoughts. Not that I've been allowed more than the smallest sip. My father is keeping me on a tight leash, presumably to prevent me misbehaving. Because he must know how I'm feeling about this ambush.

Since the moment this noose was slipped round my neck I've fought to keep my composure. If I struggle, if I speak my mind, raise my voice, scream at my father that I'm not his bloody possession to trade, then the rope will tighten and squeeze my life away. And so I sit still, play my part, and all the while my rage burns so intensely it chars my insides.

I hadn't known what to expect of Prince Torin, and, as our empty dinner plates are cleared to make way for sweet pastries, I still feel no closer to learning anything about him. He's behaved precisely how one would want a prince to behave, speaking to everyone as equals rather than his subjects, and being suitably attentive to me. What a beautiful gown I'm wearing; how it complements my own beauty; how the First Isle will be thrilled with the impending nuptials.

But not one word he's said sounds sincere or genuine. It's as if he's playing a version of himself, and while he may fool the others, I'm not convinced for a moment.

The dull throb in my palm reminds me that my father is watching my every move, but even so it's taking all my control to keep smiling. Only one other person looks as unhappy as I feel and that is Prince Torin's personal guard, who despite being similar to the Prince in age and height has a true scowl for every one of Torin's fake smiles. I don't blame him – he must know how little protection he can offer his master here.

When there is no more food to consume and the flagons are filled yet again, it's clear my presence is no longer required. Making my excuses, I slip away. Between my rising panic and the constricting bones of my corset, I struggle to breathe as I clamber to deck, running to the bow and collapsing in a heap. My father has utterly blindsided me with this trap. How could he not discuss it with me first? Is it a punishment for my failure to order Anders' death? Or does he truly think so little of me that my future is of no importance to him? The path laid out before me may be fraught with difficulty, but at least I knew what it was, and I have spent my life trying to be good enough for it. And I'd always assumed that by the time it came to marriage I would at least have some say in the matter, given that I'll be captain one day.

I gaze over at the figurehead attached to the far end of the ship's bow. Carved from the blackest wood is a woman leaning out, her dress and cloak billowing in the wind, ropes tied round her waist. A scarlet bloom is painted on her chest, her heart bleeding. She is the maiden the ship is named after. She is my mother. Father never speaks about her; only once did he break that rule to tell me she was his great love. When she was murdered shortly after my birth, he had the figurehead made from the nightheart wood found in the black forests of the Third Isle, and renamed the ship. This act of devotion has always led me to believe he understood the power of true love and would wish the same for me. Apparently I was wrong, and I see the woman bound to the ship in a new light. I'm no more breaking free of the *Maiden* than she is. I have more in common with a lump of wood than anyone else. Great.

I look up as someone approaches. Bronn has left the celebrations. He stands at the railing, facing out to sea, deliberately distant but close enough to keep an eye on me. Presumably to make sure I don't do anything reckless. My father can't afford to lose his commodity.

'Did you know?' I ask him, unable to keep the accusation from my voice – though it's been a long time since we've been anything close to friends.

'Captain only tells us what is necessary.'

'And what about me?' I round on him. 'Will anyone tell me what's necessary? Will you?'

He says nothing, once more impervious to my pain, and I turn away in frustration. There was a time when Bronn would have told me anything, his silence now all the more hurtful because of it.

I was only five when he came to live on the *Maiden*. Father found him on the docks, an orphan surviving by stealing from the ships, brimming with raw potential, and saw an opportunity to groom a young thief into a killer. Father brought Bronn aboard as a cabin boy, where he quickly shamed half the crew with his ability to shimmy up the mast and swing from the sails. Though almost three years older than me, he didn't mind when I trailed around after him and he would sit for hours on deck patiently teaching me complicated knots. I adored him.

But the Bronn I grew up with is nothing like the man he has become: a man who can kill with effortless precision, as brilliant in that as in everything else. Of the two children who grew up on the ship, he should have been my father's heir.

Everything changed after his Initiation. He stopped speaking to me, going out of his way to avoid crossing my path – no easy feat when you live on a ship. The loss of my best friend without explanation cut me deeply, but what happened a few weeks later was so much worse. It took me a long time to recover from his treachery. I had no choice but to harden my heart towards him.

'I'm not going to jump if that's what you're worried about.' I don't bother concealing the venom in my voice, because he damn well knows it's not going to be an issue.

There's no reaction, though, not even a flinch of guilt as he turns to face me.

'Will you do it? Marry him?'

'What makes you think I'm being given a choice?'

We fall silent and, as the light fails, memories of watching the stars with Bronn creep into my mind. There was a time, years ago, when I trusted him with my every secret, including my fear of water. To lessen my dread we would lie under the night sky and he would tell me how the stars were like nautical charts, mirroring the seas we sailed. How if you were ever lost, the stars could guide you home. I had been confused because the *Maiden* was my home and if I were on it, how could I be lost?

I look up at him again, his betrayal as raw as ever. His face, which was once so open and warm, is now hard and unyielding. And utterly closed to me.

I turn away, pushing the memories back to where they came from. 'As if you care. Leave me alone, Bronn.'

The familiar thud of boots on wood makes me glance up to see who else has escaped the farce of a celebration. To my surprise Prince Torin has come looking for me. Feeling it's rude to sit in a heap while addressing royalty, I clamber to my feet, struggling not to trip over my own skirt.

31

'Ah, there you are.' Torin glances over at Bronn. 'Would you excuse us?'

But rather than leave, Bronn takes a step closer to me. 'I have orders to stay with her.'

I can't decide what's worse: hearing him admit he's only here at my father's request, or that he's dared to defy the Prince.

Torin's thrown too, I can tell. He didn't expect to be challenged. 'She'll be perfectly safe with me, I can assure you.'

I was perfectly safe without either of them, but they don't seem too interested in that right now.

Bronn folds his arms. 'Nevertheless.'

An awkward silence descends as the two men enter a stand-off. I look from Torin to Bronn and bristle with irritation. Who the hell do they think they are?

'The Viper answers to the King, so I ask again, would you excuse us?' Torin is polite, but firm, and I find it curious that he doesn't seem afraid. Especially as his sullen personal guard is nowhere to be seen. The rumour that he's a coward doesn't appear to be true.

'I'm a Snake, not the Viper. And you're not the King.'

I've had enough of this. 'Bronn, you can go. The Prince and I will be perfectly fine without you.'

Bronn opens his mouth to object, but I get there first.

'I don't need you. I want you to go.' It comes out harsher than I intended, laced with years of bitterness.

For a moment Bronn simply stares at me, expressionless, but then he blinks and nods his head. 'M'lady.' The word is dripping with sarcasm and I have to swallow down the retorts I want to fire at his back as he turns and leaves.

Instead I give Torin a weary smile, trying to convey my apologies for Bronn's behaviour.

Torin raises his eyebrows. 'That's your father's most valuable assassin?'

'Yes, I think being introduced like that may have gone to his head.' I'm hoping he might return my smile, but he doesn't. Like Bronn, he is impossible to read.

The man I'm supposed to marry comes and stands beside me and leans over the railing. Following his lead, I do too, listening to the gentle lapping of waves against the ship. I should probably try to talk to him, but can think of nothing to say.

It turns out I don't need to, because he speaks first. '*When the sky is dark, the moon lost to the world, the water lies still. Silent. All magic is paused, frozen, for tonight the Night Hunter hunts.*'

He's quoting one of the stories Grace used to tell me, one of my favourites.

'*His prey: a devil. A vast, fierce devil. And across the waves the raptor roars.*' I finish the passage for him. Perhaps the scholar rumour was right after all.

He nods his head appreciatively. 'So. We are to be wed.'

My breath catches in my throat. 'Apparently.'

I raise my head slightly to glance at him, only to find him watching me closely. He really is startlingly handsome, his skin gently sun-kissed so it's almost as brown as mine. I hold his gaze, and can't shake the feeling that he's doing precisely what I am: trying to read his opponent. Mistrust hums in the air between us.

'Will you miss this?' he says, gesturing to the ship, the sea, the life I live. 'Or will the luxury of the palace suit you better?'

There's almost a hint of contempt in his words and I resent any implication that I'm using him for a more comfortable existence when, as I see it, I'm simply being traded from one prison to another.

Squaring up to him, I say, 'I think it's foolish for either of us to pretend that what I want matters in the slightest, don't you?'

The smallest crease forms across the bridge of his nose as he weighs me up. It seems like he's about to say something, but then the moment passes as he steps away from me and I realise we are no longer alone. His bodyguards are congregating, as are some of my father's men.

'It's time,' Torin says to me, and I frown, unsure for a moment what he means. And then it hits me. No. Surely not. With my world capsized I hadn't even thought about what Viper tradition dictates would happen tonight. I'd always half thought it was a myth, made up to discourage Vipers from putting anything or anyone

34

before their kings. It can't be real. But for the first time the look on Torin's face is unmistakable, and I understand he's been warned. My stomach lurches in terror and I would run if there were anywhere to go.

My father is coming on deck, his cheeks flushed from rum, his eye bloodshot, and he beckons for us to approach him.

There's nothing to do but obey.

When Torin and I reach him, the crew lock into a circle round us.

The binding ceremony has begun.

I'm not sure where to look, so hoping no one sees the fear spreading across my skin like a rash, I just stare ahead until my eyes water a little from the effort. Because I know what's coming, and I know I can't escape, and perhaps my eyes aren't watering from the strain, but from the tears I'm fighting to hold back. Cleeve is approaching us now, holding a silver platter upon which lies a chain made of many links that glow with heat from the furnace. The very sight of it makes my heart scream with panic.

My father pulls on thick gloves as he asks me to raise my left hand and Torin his right. We press our wrists together and maybe the fact I'd rather run, plunge overboard and die the death I fear above all others than do this is transmitting through my skin, because to my surprise Torin turns to look at me.

35

'Breathe,' he whispers, so softly it's possible I imagined it. And for a split second there is no pretence in him, no insincerity. We are simply two people about to endure a shared pain, and I offer him a small nod in solidarity.

Father is holding the red-hot chain now, and with precision he wraps it round our extended wrists, binding them together. The pain is immediate and searing as the metal melts through flesh, eating into skin to leave its imprint. Clenching every fibre of my body I force myself not to flinch. I will not show weakness. I will not let my father believe he's won.

'Let you all bear witness to the marking of their promise.' My father's voice carries loudly into the evening air, though the solemnity of the moment is somewhat tarnished by the drunken slur of his words. 'Viper and royalty shall become one, their bodies carrying this brand as a symbol of the vow they have made.' And with that he lifts the chain, pulling ribbons of skin away with it.

The pain is a thousand knives slashing viciously and I lower my hand, not wanting to see how bad the wound is, how much of my raw flesh is now exposed. I swallow back a wave of nausea and the sob that accompanies it. If Torin is thrown by the barbaric ritual, he doesn't show it. He thanks my father for his blessing on our intended union and declares the future of the Eastern Isles safe in this momentous alliance of our peoples.

I am not required to speak, and though I usually resent my opinion being overlooked, for once I'm grateful. I have absolutely nothing good to say.

Rum is brought out, and the flagons are filled once more as everyone toasts our binding ceremony. Yet again I am not offered any, though it would help numb my pain. Instead I distract myself by focusing all my energy on avoiding Grace. I've felt her gaze fixed on me throughout this display, and I daren't meet it, because I fear her pity will undo me entirely. Losing my composure would only strengthen my father's hold on me, would only tighten the noose. He'd love nothing more than to have to castigate me for exposing my shortcomings.

My sight rests instead on Torin's glowering bodyguard, the only other person not drinking, who makes no effort to hide his displeasure at this whole spectacle. I imagine watching his prince get scorched, even willingly, must go against all his instincts, and though he's not offered me the merest hint of friendliness, I find myself respecting his devotion to duty.

Bronn, on the other hand, is drinking enough for all of us. He stands slightly apart from the crowd, and even from a distance I can see danger flashing in his eyes. No one will cross him tonight, not when he's so clearly looking for a fight, and I can't decide if I'm pleased he seems miserable, or resentful that he can sulk unquestioned while I daren't move, daren't speak, daren't breathe lest someone perceives my slightest vulnerability.

Eventually the rum runs dry and Prince Torin comes to bid me farewell.

'It seems it's time for me to leave,' he says, his face betraying no sign of the pain I'm certain he must be in. Nor is there any trace of the man I thought I glimpsed behind his royal façade during our shared torture. 'But I do hope you will be able to visit me at my home some time soon, perhaps when our fathers agree a wedding date, so I can return your hospitality.'

'Thank you.'

'Until then,' he says, giving me a little nod before turning to join his men.

Farewells are made and the royal party departs. Ren sets about weighing anchor and soon the Prince's ship is just a speck on the horizon, its lanterns glowing in the darkness. There are no lanterns lit on our deck, the *Maiden* choosing to be an invisible predator. My father returns to his cabin without saying a word to me, no explanation, no thanks, no apology. Not that I expected any.

The moment my presence is no longer required I head to my quarters, my wrist burning as fiercely as my father's betrayal. Only once I'm alone, away from scrutiny, do I start breathing too fast, the rush of panic taking over. But the waves of emotion that crash over me aren't familiar and it's then that I realise it's not panic. I'm seething. So angry I could choke. All the years of suppressed fury bursting the dam and flooding me.

Desperate to be free of my stupid dress, I claw it off, the struggle to get out of it almost as hard as putting it on was. When I'm standing in only my undergarments I snatch up my knife and, with a howl of rage, send it flying into the wall. It hits the centre of a small scrap of cloth that's been caught on a splinter of wood and, despite my mood, I smile. Years of target practice have paid off and there are few things I can't hit with pinpoint accuracy. Something my father knows nothing about. I walk over and pull my knife free, then try again, this time with my eyes shut. Again, again, again, I send the dagger into the wall, and every time the blade hits its mark. Satisfaction outweighs my other worries – for a moment at least. It's late by the time I finish, my anger still simmering but my body tired.

I need to speak with Father. I want to burst into his cabin, tell him exactly what I think of his plan to marry me off without warning, demand to be given the freedom to make my own choices. But I don't. Because I remember the last time I openly spoke my mind and challenged my father's schemes.

I was thirteen and sick of being trapped on the *Maiden*. Though I'd longed to go ashore my whole life, my father had made it clear that it wasn't safe for me off the ship given how many enemies he had, and I had only ever been allowed on land twice, both times to the First Isle, and both times under heavy escort. We were approaching the Fourth Isle, on some errand for the King, and in a wave of petulant madness I had deluded myself into thinking my opinion mattered to my father. Driven by a craving for power – and, if I'm honest, attention – I had marched up to my father and questioned his decision. Why wasn't I allowed to roam the islands freely? I was his heir after all. There should have been no illusion for me over what would happen – I had first-hand experience of the kind of man my father was, knew I was courting a thrashing – but for some reason I thought because I was his daughter I was beyond severe punishment. That he would never truly hurt his little girl.

I was right. Instead he ordered one of the younger deckhands to be tied to the foremast and had Cleeve flog him in my stead. Forty flesh-ripping lashes were given to that poor man on my account, each one serving to remind me to watch my mouth, know my place, respect my father. When it was over, the sailor was barely conscious, his lacerated back a pulpy mess. Though I was banished to my room I later sneaked below deck to the crew's sleeping quarters to find him in his berth where he lay on his front moaning. When I tried to apologise he unleashed a tirade of abuse that left me in little doubt exactly what he thought of me. He died not long afterwards, thankfully not from those injuries but on a mission for the King, and though it shamed me, I was relieved not to have to endure his contempt any longer.

In the years since then I have become guarded, learning the importance of keeping my mouth shut and my opinions to myself. I know it would be futile to go to my father now and beg him to reconsider.

I roll over in my hammock to face the wall. Maybe I shouldn't want him to anyway. Maybe marriage *is* my way out. But here at least I understand the game, know the rules to keep myself alive. Leaving the *Maiden* won't end the game, just alter it, and then how can I keep myself safe?

And if I run away altogether?

Well, desertion is equal to mutiny, and I would be hunted to my death.

The violent swinging of my hammock wakes me from a troubled sleep. A storm is raging, and above me I can hear shouting as the crew try to keep control of the ship. I screw my eyes tight shut, willing it to be over. My father's rules are clear. I am not allowed out of my room at night, for any reason, and each time a storm whips up while I'm sleeping I fear the ship will go down with me trapped and helpless below deck.

But as I lie there, determined to ignore the elements, another sound carries on the wind. The clash of steel on steel. Sitting bolt upright, I listen closely, and after a moment's hesitation I pull on my clothes before grabbing my knife and heading for deck.

Another of my father's strict instructions is that when we're carrying out a mission I must remain in my quarters. For my protection. But I know nothing about any current missions, so I'm guessing we're under attack – which never happens. I can't imagine who would be brave enough to take on the Viper and there's no way I'm going to hide in my cabin when our ship needs defending. And *technically* I'm not defying my father because he's never directly specified what I should do in this scenario. Not that I intend for him to see me.

I'm greeted with chaos. Another boat is alongside ours, grappling ropes preventing her from escaping, as my father and his Snakes wage their attack on her crew. My mistake is painfully clear. For some reason no one's told me about this mission, but there's no denying we are the ones doing the attacking.

I shouldn't be here.

Heavy rain blocks the light from the moon and we are pitching so ferociously I can barely keep my footing, but those locked in battle seem oblivious.

My father is on the quarterdeck fighting three men simultaneously, easily parrying their blows with his cutlass. He towers over them, his bald head gleaming even on such a black night. He's never looked more alive. He's toying with those poor lads, making them think they stand a chance, and before I've even glanced away he's dispatched them all with efficient brutality.

Cleeve is pinned against the mainmast, weaponless, his captor raising his sword for the fatal blow. But Cleeve has no intention of going without a fight, and leans in to rip a chunk of flesh from his enemy's throat with his teeth. The blood sprays so far it almost reaches me.

Horrified at such savagery, I recoil. I don't want to be anywhere near Cleeve, and if my father catches me out here, then I might meet a similar fate. I'm about to escape back to my quarters when a flash of lightning illuminates a stack of crates, revealing a pair of wide eyes peering out from behind them. Toby. What is he doing out here? Waves crash on to the deck, mingling with blood to make it slippery, and I struggle to stay upright as I hurry over to where Toby's concealed. Crouching down, I hold out my hand for him to take.

'Come with me.' I shout to be heard over the storm.

He shakes his head, too frightened to move.

'It'll be OK,' I say. 'I promise.'

For a moment I think he's going to stay, frozen to the spot, but then he reaches for my hand and I'm able to help him out from his hiding place. We run towards the hatch and I use my body to shield him from the carnage around us. Toby hurries below deck and I'm about to follow him down the ladder when someone grabs me from behind. Strong, unfamiliar arms pull me backwards, and I kick and struggle to escape my assailant's iron grip. From this angle I can't get enough leverage to break free, but my knife's still in my hand and so, bending my wrist, I slash it through the artery in his arm.

He immediately releases me and I spin to confront him. I find myself staring at his middle and swallow hard as I look up. He's one of the biggest men I've ever seen, his bulging muscles solid as rock. Blood spurts from where I've cut him open, running down his arm to fall from his fingertips on to the deck, but despite the damage inflicted he seems unconcerned. He just looks angry.

He lunges towards me, and I dive between his legs, slicing my blade through his massive thigh as I go. He groans, but doesn't falter, just turns round, swinging his sword at me, which I duck to avoid. My dagger can't match the sword; I need him rid of it. And so this time when I strike I target his hand, landing a harsh blow on his knuckles. The sword clatters to the deck and I strike again, but he catches my wrist in his vast hand and holds me still. I try to free myself, but my feet won't grip the boards, making it hard just to stay upright. Though my left hand is weaker, I swing it round to punch him, but he catches that wrist too and the pain of pressure on my burn almost causes me to black out. He has me trapped, the two of us suspended in a temporary stalemate, and though I'm the one holding a weapon, considering how much stronger he is than me, I know I'm going to lose.

The *Maiden* lurches in the high winds and a pile of barrels we're standing close to catches my eye. The storm has loosened the ropes holding them and I can tell that they're going to come undone any minute. Gritting my teeth, I use all my strength to maintain our deadlock, keeping us where we are so that moments later when the barrels break free from their restraints they hurtle in our direction. My attacker is distracted long enough for me to pull my right hand away but his grip over my burnt wrist is too strong, the pain too great for me to pull free, so I'm still standing beside him as the barrels plough into

45

us, smashing us against the railings. This side of the ship is tilted so low in the water that momentum propels us further and before we can grab hold of anything we're flung overboard.

The force with which I'm thrown crushes the air from my lungs and I can't even scream as my body is tossed over the side. I steel myself for the icy embrace of the ocean, but it doesn't come. It takes me a moment to orientate myself and realise what has happened. I am upside down, crashing against the side of the *Maiden*, held in place by my dress, which has caught on the rigging. My attacker wasn't so lucky – the ocean has already devoured him. But my relief is short-lived as I hear fabric tearing under the pull of gravity and my weight. I frantically try to turn myself upright, but the ship is still tossing in the storm and the barrage of fresh waves pummelling my face threaten to drown me without my body actually being in the sea.

Panic rises in my throat alongside the salty water I cough up. No one knows I'm here. I gave no cry to alert anyone to my danger. And I realise that I only have moments before my dress fails to hold and my reprieve is over, the death I've always feared awaiting me. Making one last desperate attempt to grab hold of something, I only succeed in smashing my face hard against the *Maiden*, and blood mingles with the water forcing itself into my lungs.

Half blinded and choking, I barely hear the voice shouting my name and think I must be imagining it until there is a sharp tug on my dress, a hand clutching my leg, and still the voice is calling. With an enormous effort I twist my body up and see Bronn reaching down for me, his words drowned out by the pounding water in my ears. I stretch my arm out as far as I'm physically able until my skin touches his. It's all he needs to haul me back up and in moments I am huddled on the deck, his arms round me. For a second everything is still. Then I remember myself and push him away. He lost the right to touch me a long time ago and despite the fact he just saved my life, I'm furious.

'What the . . .?' Bronn says, nearly losing his balance. Clearly he was expecting a little more gratitude.

'I don't need your help.' Unfortunately this is blatantly untrue, which annoys me further.

Grace swoops in beside me, stemming the flow of blood from my nose, which I'm certain is broken. 'What are you doing out here?' She's as surprised as she is concerned to find me in this mess.

'Are you insane?' Bronn pays no attention to Grace, his anger entirely reserved for me. 'I just saved your life.'

'Is that why you did it? To have me in your debt? How did you know I'd fallen overboard?' I feel guilty even as the words are coming out of my mouth, but of all the people who had to save me why did it have to be him?

47

'You're unbelievable!' he shouts at me. 'Would you rather I'd left you to die?'

Well, it wouldn't be the first time, I scream in my head.

But all I can bring myself to say is, 'How about you just stay away from me?'

Bronn grunts. 'With pleasure. Your prince is welcome to you.'

Grace clears her throat and fixes me with a look that perfectly combines her worry and frustration as she helps me to my feet.

'Is now really the best time?' she says, and she has a point. Between the fighting and the storm, there are more pressing matters at hand. 'You, come with me,' she says, before hurrying me towards my quarters.

I glance back to glare at Bronn, but he's already gone, lost in the sea of people. Instead my gaze falls on the body of a fallen sailor – not one of ours. Lying face up on the deck, his shirt exposed, I'm sure he's wearing the emblem of the King's Fleet. But that doesn't make any sense. They're our ally, not our enemy – even if that relationship isn't always friendly.

It's been a long time since the Viper headed up the King's Fleet. Now we work alongside them to protect the Isles; they uphold the King's honour, while we deal with the less palatable side of things. Mostly we keep out of each other's way, our missions never overlapping. When the King sends us orders, we obey, and in exchange we are free to do what we want – and what my father wants is to be feared. The Fleet would rather we didn't exist at all, but the King likes having someone prepared to do his dirty work. We may not use the same tactics, but our overall purposes are aligned: protect the King and the peace of the Isles.

The question is, why is one of them dead on our deck?

Only once we are safely in my cabin does Grace speak again. 'What were you thinking?'

'I'm fine, thanks for your concern.' I grab a cloth and press it hard to my nose.

'Let's see,' she says, leaning in to inspect the damage and sighing. 'Well, it's broken, but it could have been worse. If Bronn hadn't seen you go over . . .'

She trails off. We both know I was lucky.

'What's going on out there?' I ask, still trying to make sense of what I saw, hoping she'll explain everything.

'Orders from the King,' Grace says. 'The Prince delivered them earlier. Some thieves who needed to be taught a lesson. We caught up with them sooner than expected or I would have told you.'

I can hear the lie even as it sits so effortlessly on her tongue. Because clearly the Prince wouldn't have asked us to attack his own father's fleet. I can think of no good reason why we would. Swallowing hard, I push back my fears, not wanting to think about what her deception means, what my father might be up to. And it hurts more than it should that Grace isn't telling me the truth. 'Shouldn't we get back out there?' It surprises even me how easily I can hide my emotions from her.

'I should. You're staying here. What would Torin say if you got murdered on your day of engagement?'

I roll my eyes, but don't argue. We both know I shouldn't have been there in the first place, that I defied my father's orders.

Once she's gone I slide into my hammock, but with the storm still throwing the *Maiden* around with alarming force and the awful sound of men and women dying carrying on the wind, sleep eludes me. I hate that I'm so powerless down here. For all the danger, at least when I was fighting I had some control. My father's orders don't make me feel protected. They make me isolated. Helpless.

Whenever I close my eyes I see the dead man, so clearly a member of the King's Fleet, and though I try to explain away his presence I struggle to come up with an answer that's in any way reassuring.

I keep my knife by my side, clenched in my fist. I am trapped. Caught in a war I hadn't even known was happening. There is no one I can trust – I'm completely on my own.

By morning all is calm and while the crew revel in their spoils I make an early visit to Milligan, the ship's surgeon.

My nose has swollen to unpleasant proportions and I am hopeful she can help, though she's more in the business of breaking bones than mending them. Her understanding of anatomy and her skill with a blade make her an excellent doctor and an even better inquisitor. Not many withstand Milligan's torture.

It's been a long time since I've ventured to her quarters, though I used to while away more hours there than I care to remember. The stench of the room reaches me long before I arrive, a combination of brewing tonics and rotting flesh.

When I appear at her door, Milligan grunts her indifference, barely looking up from what she's doing. I am not the only one seeking her remedies – many of the crew sustained injuries in last night's fight and Milligan has her hands full.

'Oh. It's you, is it?' I can tell she's overjoyed to see me. 'Well, don't just stand there – make yourself useful.'

When she says nothing more, just continues to stitch up a large gash in a crewmember's thigh, I reluctantly make my way in. It's strange to be back here again, having avoided it for so long. But despite myself, I'm drawn to the simmering pot on the fire, and breathe in the fumes. Barkwood and coralpine – a tonic for pain. One Milligan clearly hasn't given to her patient judging by the look on his face.

'Don't hover, girl,' she snaps.

Realising I'm going to have to earn any treatment of my own, I offer to help a man called Amos, who's badly broken the little finger on his left hand. The bone has pierced the skin, and infection will be quick to settle in unless it's treated soon.

Tearing some cloth, and grabbing some kindling for the fire, I set about creating a splint. If I can push the bone back in, treat the wound with some ointment, then set it straight, it should heal without complication.

'It's going to hurt,' I warn Amos, as I explain my plan. I avoid asking him how he sustained the injury in the first place. The less I dwell on the details of last night, the better.

But as I clean the skin around the wound with salted water, wanting it free from dirt before I replace the bone, Milligan shuffles over and pushes me out of the way.

'What are you doing?'

Again I outline my proposed treatment, and Milligan narrows her beady eyes.

'Did I teach you nothing?' she says in disgust.

And without another word she clasps Amos by the wrist, pulls him towards her filthy workbench, slams his hand on to it, splays his fingers and brings a cleaver down, removing the offending digit in one vicious movement.

Amos shrieks with pain, but Milligan holds him still, grabbing the poker resting in the fire, and pressing it hard on the stump to cauterise it.

I can't move, frozen in shock. There could be no better reminder of why I stopped coming here.

'Go,' Milligan says to Amos, ushering him out of the room. I suspect he'll pass out the moment he returns to his bunk. If he makes it that far.

Now she turns her attention to me. Milligan's face is sallow from lack of sunlight as she virtually never surfaces from her quarters, always preoccupied with some unpleasant experiment. She insists on drinking rum while she works, the smell of alcohol permanently heavy on her breath. Thankfully my injury means I can't detect it today.

'What is it you want?'

'Something for my nose.'

Milligan grabs my chin, and turns my face one way, then the other, before she grunts. 'Broken.'

'Yes, I know.'

She spits on the floor. 'Nothing to be done. Just wait for the swelling to go down.'

'I'm not leaving until you give me something for the pain.' She forgets I know her well. Her desire to have me gone will outweigh her indifference to helping me.

'You know where the second-salve is,' she says eventually. 'Get it and get out.'

I do as I'm told, grabbing a pot of the ointment from one of the cluttered shelves and fleeing before she can change her mind.

Not wanting to be the subject of prying eyes, and sick to death of the suffocating four walls of my cabin, I make my way to a favourite hiding place down in the hold where the spare sails and rigging are kept. There is a nook between the beams just large enough for me to squeeze into and remain undiscovered.

Second-salve is made from extracts of the peculiar black brambles indigenous to the Second Isle, and when I rub some on my nose, cold instantly penetrates deep into my face, numbing the pain. I spread some over my burn as well. It's heavenly. Relieved from my discomfort, I take a needle and thread from my pocket and set to work repairing the tear in my dress before it catches on something else.

It's a shame Milligan is so utterly vile, because of all the people aboard the *Maiden*, she's the one with the knowledge I crave. When I was younger and found my first injured bird on deck, I took it to my cabin and attempted to nurse it back to health. My ignorance killed it. But it awoke my desire to discover the secrets of the body, to heal, to save.

For several years I spent more hours than I care to remember alone with Milligan in her dank and foul quarters. To start with I worshipped her as she showed me how to mix tonics and remedies for various ailments, how combining silverbud and swampnettle aids healing or how blending earthenwort with ground mettleroot mends wounds. She's nothing like the Mages of old, whose magic merely began with potions and then stretched without limit, but she knows enough of the alchemy to make decent medicine and I was quickly enchanted by the art.

But of course I learned the hard way that Milligan isn't driven by a thirst to heal – all her skills exist to hurt. My lessons began to change from herbal remedies to basic anatomy – but these were practical lessons, not merely theory from books. Prisoners caught acting against the Eastern Isles, or crew who had misbehaved, were brought in for my studies. I remember those lessons with horrifying clarity, especially the ones when Milligan sought to teach me the fundamental pain points on a human being. She showed me how the simplest of things could undo a man – flaying the skin from the soles of his feet, for example. That produced a sound that haunted me for weeks.

She didn't teach me any of this because it was necessary. She showed me to scare, to impress, but most of all – because she enjoyed it.

Soon after that I pretended to lose interest in her lessons. Milligan had succeeded in teaching me how stupid I was to believe a healer could be nurtured on a ship of killers. And more importantly, I realised that if my father discovered my fascination with how bodies work then he would force me to become Milligan's successor. I'd rather be an honest assassin than have to torture anyone.

Since then I've had to make do with occasional explorations of dead birds or rats, but they haven't taught me nearly enough, which is frustrating. I've learned no new potions, nothing of the alchemy that bewitched me most. And Milligan's barely acknowledged my existence after what I think she perceived as my abandoning her – and she's not someone you want as an enemy.

'There are more comfortable places to be, you know.'

I hadn't heard him approach and I jump, stabbing the needle straight into my finger. Filthy and glistening with sweat, Bronn's clearly been hard at work repairing storm damage to the ship, his ripped shirt revealing glimpses of scars on his otherwise perfect body, and I'm suddenly absurdly self-conscious. My hair is a tangled mess and I'm about to flatten it when I realise his black mane is equally wild. I'm startled by a sudden urge to run my fingers through it. I shake the thought away, mortified at the desire stirring in the pit of my stomach. I search his face for any sign he feels as conflicted as I do, but his flint eyes betray no emotion. As always. Suddenly I want him to go away, resenting him for the way he makes me feel, hating him for discovering my secret sanctuary, but there is the small matter of his saving my life last night.

'Listen, I should thank—' I begin but he cuts across me.

'The Captain sent for you.'

Of course he did. Why else would Bronn come looking for me?

My father is the last person I want to see today, not with the evidence of my disobedience all over my swollen face. And yet I can only think of one reason why I'm being summoned.

'He heard about last night?' Even as I ask I know the answer.

Bronn nods. 'We shouldn't keep him waiting.'

Like I don't already know that. I climb out from my cosy hiding hole and together we make our way up. The ship is bustling with activity as the crew go about their duties, and I walk slightly ahead of Bronn, taking care not to get in anyone's path, half hoping to lose Bronn in the crowd, hating being escorted by him as if I'm a prisoner.

Errant water seeped down to the gun deck last night during the storm, making the steps here slippery, and when several men rush past me, shoving me out of the way, I slide and lose my footing. I expect to fall, but before I can, hands slip round my waist, steadying me. On reflex I try to break free from Bronn, but the stairway is narrow and I only succeed in turning, forcing our bodies together, his chest pressed against mine so that I can feel his heart beating in time with my own, his breath warm on my forehead. He's staring down at me with unnerving intensity and I lower my eyes, furious with my blushing cheeks and racing pulse.

Of all the ways Bronn could have saved me last night it had to be from drowning, didn't it? The very reason I hate him so much.

Because ignoring me after his Initiation wasn't enough for Bronn. It was as if the boy I knew disappeared the day he left to undertake the challenge, and in his place returned a cruel man who seemed to delight in causing me pain.

A man who one wet day shattered years of trust like a mallet on bone.

I had gone searching for him, tired of his silence, determined not to give up on him. On us. I'd found him on the quarterdeck, taking some shelter beneath the sails, gambling with a group of the crew, drinking rum as if it were water. I'd asked him if we could talk, and when he ignored me I'd tried to order him, unwisely attempting some sort of authority as the Captain's daughter. The others had started to laugh, called Bronn my pet, said he'd better go when whistled for. I remember the look he had in his eyes; it was pure rage.

I would have gone then, left them to it, and found somewhere private to cry, but Bronn wasn't about to let me embarrass him like that.

'I'm surprised you're even out here,' he'd said to me, his voice sharper than his blade. 'Given it's raining.'

My blood had run cold. The edge to his words told everyone that they meant something, and the deck seemed to fall silent with anticipation.

I'd feigned innocence. 'I don't know what you mean.'

But Bronn was on his feet, his companions following suit. Frightened, I'd tried to sidestep, but they moved to surround me until the railing was behind me and they were a wall of flesh preventing my escape.

'I mean, given your fear of water.'

He'd held my gaze unflinchingly, driving the words like a weapon hard into my chest, my secret laid bare and bleeding all over the deck.

The others had started to laugh again, but this time with the unspoken promise of menace. They almost couldn't believe their luck.

'You?' one of the men had said. 'The Captain's daughter, afraid of water?'

The hilarity of such a notion had them all in stitches again, until their laughter faded into gleeful anticipation.

'Think it's time she learned to swim, don't you, Bronn?'

The challenge was unmistakable, and I'd stared at Bronn through tear-filled eyes, still not truly believing he'd exposed my secret, but knowing that he wouldn't, he couldn't, go any further.

And then he'd shoved me hard overboard.

My mouth was open from shock as I hit the waves, and water had rushed in and down my throat, so that I coughed and flailed in panic. It was like reliving the time I'd nearly drowned as a child, like being in my own nightmares. I couldn't call out, couldn't scream – there was no air for it – and for those terrifying minutes there was only gasping, then choking, light then dark, as I emerged then submerged, my arms and legs casting desperately around for something solid, something safe, while the crew above mocked and taunted me for sport.

It was Grace who saved me, her strong arms holding me above the water as she swam us back to the rope ladder she'd thrown over before jumping in to help me. As soon as I collapsed back on to the deck, she'd wrapped a blanket round me before turning her wrath on those who had watched and laughed as I'd nearly died.

'You should be ashamed,' she'd said to them as I'd coughed up my lungs at her feet.

They'd muttered under their breath and dispersed, but she'd grabbed Bronn by the arm.

'What the hell were you thinking?' she'd said.

He'd pulled himself free of her grip and shrugged. As if I meant absolutely nothing to him.

And that's when I finally realised I didn't. Not any more. The friend I'd once had would never, ever have done that to me. Clearly that friend was gone. He'd had a choice – me or the Snakes. And he hadn't chosen me.

I lost what little hope I had of gaining the crew's respect that day, learned a whole new meaning to the word 'humiliation', and I've never truly recovered from Bronn's betrayal.

But now, with our bodies touching, I am reminded of the boy who meant everything to me, and even now it's simply too painful for me to revisit those memories.

'I think I can find my own way from here,' I say and though I hope to sound indifferent, to my dismay my voice is unnaturally high, catching slightly in my throat. Trying to cover it by giving him a curt nod of thanks, I pull away and carry on, walking a little faster and certainly more flustered than before. Frankly I'm relieved when I reach my father's room, though I should be nothing but afraid.

He's sitting by the ornate fireplace, which is purely decorative – I've never once seen it lit – reading a book. Talon sits on his shoulder and squawks at my arrival. Displeasure is written all over Father's face as he takes in my bruised nose, making me feel an unexpected, and highly misguided, sense of triumph. My behaviour has caught him off guard; though it was far from intentional, my disregard for his rules was an unlikely development. But I must be careful. I'm on dangerous ground. So I wait, braced for the castigation that surely is coming.

Instead he gestures to the table where bread and fruit are already laid out. 'Come, sit with me.'

I do as I'm told, still trying to gauge what mood my father's in before I speak.

'I always wanted a son,' he says, and it's like a punch to my gut. 'Did you know that?'

'No.' I fight to keep my voice steady. I'm lying. I've always known deep down. Of course I have. But to hear him say it? It hurts more than I expected.

'Instead I have you.' He looks at me with disappointment. I wonder if he's expecting an apology that I was born the wrong sex. He's not going to get one. 'I would have known what to do with a boy. But you?'

He reaches forward and takes an apple, rubbing it on his sleeve.

'Perhaps I was wrong to raise you the way I would have a son. But I only know one way to make the Viper. The way my father raised me. The way his father raised him. Maybe you think I've been too heavy-handed, but the thing is, Marianne, this is how I was made. Everything I've done to you was done to me.'

I've never heard him speak of his father. Ever. Rumours of his brutality are all I have of my grandfather.

'Why then,' he says, holding the apple up, inspecting its shine, 'do I not see myself in you?'

We don't look the same my father and I, my mother's genes proving stronger. He is tall, I am short. He is white, I am brown. But I know that's not what he means.

And still I don't speak, not trusting myself to say the right thing.

'You're angry with me,' he says.

His reflective mood, his change in direction, his sudden insight – everything about this conversation is disconcerting.

'You're angry because I arranged the marriage to Torin. Yet I was under the impression you had no desire to succeed me as captain of this ship. Was I mistaken?' He slices into the apple with his pocketknife and offers me a piece. When I refuse he gives it to Talon who swallows it whole.

I'm going to have to break my silence, persuade him that he has succeeded in raising a daughter who's as strong as a son.

'You're right that I have no wish to marry a stranger,' I say, choosing my words carefully. 'But you're wrong to think I don't wish to succeed you.' The role of the Viper has always passed from generation to generation, and can only be broken by one who defeats the captain in battle. Our generational line hasn't been conquered for over two hundred years, and while I can't ever imagine commanding my own reign of terror, I don't want to be the weak link, don't want to be the one to let the Isles down.

'Having you in the palace could prove most advantageous. You'll be privy to all manner of conversations.'

I raise an eyebrow. 'You want me to be your spy?'

'Marianne, I want you to be useful. This would be your first assignment as an official member of the crew, and I thought it would please you – you have, after all, always made it clear how much you wish to spend time on land. Your constant pestering to accompany us on shore has not gone unnoticed. This way we all get what we want.'

'I thought we followed the King's orders, not spied on him,' I say, more than a little hesitantly.

It's the wrong thing to say. He grabs the plate and flings it against the wall, smashing it to pieces. He's furious. 'You are *my* daughter. You do as *I* say.'

I think of the dead man I saw last night, the one I'm now certain was from the King's Fleet, and wish beyond anything my father would just be honest with me. 'Is there something you want to tell me about the King? You can trust me, you know.'

He regards me with such obvious contempt I feel my heart break a little, even as it pounds in my chest. 'And yet you fail every test I give you. You claim you wish to succeed me but you live in a dream, girl. You think the Viper can have hands clean from blood? I see only weakness in you, an inability to do what is necessary.'

He pauses from his brutal honesty to take another mouthful of apple. The juice drips from his lip on to his chin, hanging for a moment before he wipes it roughly away on his sleeve. I remain silent, though the voice in my head shouts a thousand defences to the charges he fires at me.

'Marry the Prince. Report to me. Prove you have some worth and then we'll talk about trust.' He leans forward and points his knife at me. 'And as for that . . .' He flicks the blade in the direction of my nose. 'You are to remain in your cabin for a week. Understand? And if you ever dare disobey my rules again and jeopardise one of my missions with your presence, I will not be so forgiving.'

With that he stands up and I've been dismissed. I leave, my ears burning with fury, the depth of my father's disappointment in me never more apparent. Perhaps he was trying to shock me into submission, or frighten my loyalty to the surface, but it's had the opposite effect. For so long I've sought his approval, been so desperate for him to treat me like his second, that despite every bone in my body screaming against what he is, I've still felt I should strive to become the woman he wanted me to be. But not any more. I'm done. I'm not the only one who's a disappointment.

My father may think I'm useless, but I know something's going on. If he's not going to tell me what he's up to, then I'll find out myself.

There was a time, long ago, when I moved unseen from corridor to corridor, hiding in narrow hidden passageways. I don't know who made them, these tight spaces between walls, but whether it was my father or a captain long before him, they were clearly meant for spying.

My favourite thing to do was creep out at night, and slide into the gap that led to a peephole that overlooked the mess hall. Though I had no interest in the crew's boastful conversations about fighting and treasure, sometimes, on particularly wonderful nights, they would share stories – of myths and fables, of where they came from and how they came to be here – and it was this that lured me back time and again.

As I grew older, and the space became increasingly cramped, I stopped going, but now I think it's time to revisit my secret hiding place. No one is openly going to tell me the things I want to know, but I suspect eavesdropping when their tongues are loosened by rum may prove to be illuminating.

Though it's a risk to leave my cabin before my father has lifted his punishment, I don't plan to get caught. There's no one around as I slip out from my room and tiptoe towards the place where, if you know the right spot to push, the panel springs out, and I slide into the darkness as I replace the wood.

It really is squashed in here, far more than I remember, and it's quite an effort to slither along, but I manage to reach the peephole with only a few scrapes of my knuckles, and the occasional snag of my dress. And then I watch.

The mess hall is full, the crew making the most of the time after dinner to unwind, their food long since finished and the rum flowing freely. At first glance they are indistinguishable, a sea of black cloth, but if you look beyond the uniform, differences abound. There are men and women from every one of the six Eastern Isles, though with our history and heritages so entwined, it's hard to be sure where anyone's from simply by the colour of their skin. Each one of them is from anywhere, everywhere, nowhere. This motley crew have nothing in common – except the ability to kill.

They're loud and unruly, and it's hard to pinpoint any one conversation. After about half an hour I'm considering abandoning this pursuit when a voice shouts over the rest.

'Hey, Nestor!' It's a crewman named Briggs, and he has a young woman in a headlock. 'Lynx here's never heard of a keelhauling.'

Lynx's humiliation is obvious even from where I'm concealed, her skin flushed with colour that creeps right up to the top of her smooth, naturally hairless head as she tries and fails to free herself from Briggs's grip. The room falls quiet, bristling with anticipation. They sense a fight is imminent.

But Nestor is one of the older members of the crew and he hasn't quite the appetite for drama. He wants a more peaceful night and gestures for Briggs to let her go. Reluctantly Briggs complies, though he holds her by the arm.

Nestor regards Lynx. 'Call yourself a Snake, and yet you don't know about keelhauling?'

Lynx shifts uncomfortably. 'So what?'

A few of the crew laugh. Nestor does not.

'So what? It's the worst punishment a captain can bestow on a treacherous soul, and if you don't fear it, you should.'

'Imagine a rope passed under the ship from port to starboard,' Briggs says, tugging Lynx's arms behind her back. 'Then imagine being tied to one end of said rope.'

'Your feet are weighted,' Nestor continues, and another crewmember leaps up to sit on Lynx's own feet. 'And then you're thrown overboard.'

Briggs yanks Lynx backwards so she falls heavily to the floor.

'All the crew, your friends, your team, then pull on the other end of the rope, dragging you under and along, scraping your flimsy body against the keel of the ship, your flesh torn to ribbons by barnacles and any skull crabs lurking there.'

'You have no air.' Briggs demonstrates by smothering Lynx. 'The water fills your lungs as you try to scream, and you wonder if you'll live to see the other side.'

Nestor gets to his feet now and strolls to stand over Lynx's body, her eyes wide and pleading as she struggles in vain to breathe through Briggs's clenched fingers. 'Some are hoisted up so shredded they wish they'd drowned in the depths. But here's the thing. The captain don't really want you dead. The crew pull you through fast. Because it's a torture, not an execution. A punishment, not an end. And if you've been really, truly naughty?' He pauses for dramatic effect. 'Then round you go again for a second trip.'

Finally Briggs releases Lynx and she gasps for air, scrambling to get away from them while several of the crew roar with laughter.

I want to smash through the wall and punch that smug expression off their faces, Lynx's public humiliation stirring up painful memories of the one I'd endured. Instead I glance around for Grace, certain she'll step in, only to see her and Bronn lurking at a table in a dark corner. They are entirely uninterested in what's just occurred and while I expect nothing more from Bronn, I'm angry with Grace. How could she just let that happen? Why didn't she come to Lynx's aid the way she did to mine?

I've seen enough. I'm not going to learn anything useful here tonight. I've not heard the merest whisper about the King's Fleet, or a single nugget of information to arm myself with, and so I start my slow shuffle back towards my exit.

Once I'm successfully free of the secret passageway I pause. I should return immediately to my room, but I just can't face it. I'm also starving as I've been on basic rations during my isolation. There's virtually no one about, and I make my decision, heading to deck – after detouring through the galley to sneakily grab a sea biscuit. It's far calmer than the night of the fighting, with only a skeleton crew working, so no one bothers me as I find a quiet alcove to huddle in, nestled between the stairs to the quarterdeck and the hull. It's much more uncomfortable sitting here than in my room, but I find the fresh air the closest place to an escape from the evil that oozes from every corner of this ship.

Resting my head back against the side of the *Maiden*, I gaze up at the night sky and watch as a flock of moonbirds flitter past. Small and silver, they look like stardust falling to earth, and despite everything I smile. There is beauty in this world, even if I can't reach it.

And then, as if just by looking I've somehow infected the moment, one of the dainty bodies drops to the deck with a thud.

I scramble over to lift the bird into my hands, and look around to see if anyone else has noticed. Confident they haven't, I smuggle the bird back to where I was settled and open my hands.

It's not dead, but it's heading that way, its wing broken, its eyes turning glassy. Its little chest rises and falls rapidly, shock its most imminent threat.

I fold my hands back round it, gently, protectively, and close my eyes. It's ludicrous to feel responsible, but somehow I do. Not just about the bird. About Lynx. About everything.

Live.

I will the bird to recover, thinking maybe if it can survive such a fall, I can survive what lies ahead for me. Stupid really.

The sound of voices approaching brings me back to my surroundings, and I shove my hand into my pocket, the bird safely concealed just as two crewmembers stumble up to deck, drunk and loud.

It's Briggs and his on-off lover Choke, a woman named after her passion for crushing windpipes. I wish she'd just go ahead and crush Briggs's.

I hope they won't notice me, but I'm all out of luck as Briggs spots me and nudges Choke.

'Look who it is,' he says, his words slurring together. 'The runt.'

Choke isn't as drunk as Briggs and says nothing, though she grins at me with deadly intent.

Briggs comes over to where I'm sitting and I get to my feet, hand still securely in pocket to hold the bird safe.

'Isn't it past your bedtime?'

There's no point in engaging with him; my only desire at this point is to slip away without causing a scene.

'Yes, you're right,' I say. 'If you'll excuse me . . .'

He presses his fingers to my chest and pushes me back. 'Hey, I'm not done talking to you.' His eyes fall on the nibbled sea biscuit in my exposed hand and light up. 'Been stealing from the rations, have you?'

I shrug, inwardly bristling at the accusation. 'Missed dinner.'

'I'm hungry.' He turns to Choke. 'You hungry?'

She says nothing, just watches with dangerous anticipation.

'Hand it over,' Briggs says.

It's only a stupid scrap of food, but I refuse to be bullied by this poor excuse for a human.

'No.'

His eyes narrow and he turns to Choke with a mirthless laugh. 'Hear that? Runt's grown herself a little pair of balls.'

Oh, please. Only a man would think that was a compliment. One swift kick to his would shut him up and it takes all my efforts not to do so.

Briggs smiles at me, before reaching to snatch the food from my hand. I could retaliate, stop him from taking it, but I fear any movement could risk hurting the bird precariously resting in my pocket.

So I don't react at all.

He studies the sea biscuit as if he finds it repulsive. He holds it up for Choke to see. 'Not sure about you, but I don't want Runt's leftovers. Cowardice might be catching.'

And he casually tosses it into the ocean.

Such a wasteful act is, of course, a great source of amusement to him, but to my relief he's done playing with me, and he rejoins Choke, laughing so hard he starts to cough. I take the opportunity and practically run back to my cabin.

Once I'm alone, I carefully lift the moonbird from my pocket and place it on top of my trunk to examine it. And I smile. The wing I thought was broken appears to be perfectly all right, just a little dishevelled, and the veil of death that was previously descending has now lifted. I was mistaken about how gravely hurt it was, and sigh with relief. Maybe there's hope for both of us still.

The door to my room bursts open. There's no time to hide the bird as my father strides in, and it's obvious he's not here to tuck me in for the night.

I freeze, unable to move.

'You think you can flout my rules?' Father growls as he steps closer. 'You think you can leave your cabin without me finding out? That I wouldn't know you were spying on my crew?'

I have no idea how he knows – there wasn't time for Briggs to tell him – but my protests shrivel away to nothing before they can leave my lips.

'I thought you'd learned your lesson for disobedience with this.' And he presses his thumb hard into my nose. Pain blooms through my head and I think I might be sick. 'But apparently you think you're beyond reproach. Allow me to relieve you of such misconceptions.'

He grabs the moonbird with one hand, and plants the other on my face, palm splayed, holding me back.

'Consider this bird represents you and see what happens when I am displeased.'

And he crushes the fragile body in his brutal grip.

I close my eyes and fight back the sob rising in my throat. His hand still over my face, he pushes me backwards until I hit the wall.

'You will remember who I am, and you will never seek to disobey me again, do you understand?'

His spit splatters on to my skin and I nod frantically.

'Who am I?' he shouts, his mouth practically touching mine.

'My father.'

'Who am I?' he roars even louder.

'My captain.'

'Who am I?'

74

'The Viper.'

'And I will be obeyed.' Then with one sharp thrust he smashes my head hard into the wall before he strides back out, leaving me alone once more.

I slide down, my legs unable to support me a moment longer, and stare at the little body lying on my floor.

The noose strangles me like never before, but despite being shaken to my very core I feel a spark of determination. He wants to silence me, to stop me meddling.

Which means there's something to find.

6

We make port at the Sixth Isle not three weeks later. It's my father's favourite island and we come here frequently, in part because it offers many secluded bays where we can careen the *Maiden*, turning her on her side when she requires repairs, or cleaning the hull below the waterline of barnacles and weed.

Known to most as the Rock Island, the majority of the Eastern Isles' wealth comes from the crystal mining that takes place deep beneath its surface and it's this bounty that truly draws my father here. As he collects the crystal in the name of the King, no one dares challenge him, but I am no longer convinced the King receives most of what we take.

The island is permanently shrouded in darkness and today is no exception. A low wall of cloud greets us as we arrive, having drifted over from the neighbouring Fifth Isle, or Mist Island. The mist makes navigation challenging – indeed for most it would be impossible. But the *Maiden* knows these waters almost as well as my father, and we pass the lethal rocks that surround the island untroubled.

The crew row to shore in small boats. Usually when they disembark here I'm not remotely jealous to be left behind. The surface of the island is barren, every inch unyielding stone so jagged that if one were foolish enough to go barefoot, one's skin would be cut to shreds.

Today, however, I will have to endure the terrain, because, despite my father's best efforts to subdue me, I need answers. In the past three weeks, my every attempt to uncover clues has been frustratingly futile. Secrets are guarded too closely on the ship. I'm hoping the crew's defences might be lowered away from the *Maiden*. Away from me. I strip to my undergarments to make swimming easier but wear my boots for protection. I hate how clumsy I feel in them compared to having bare feet, but the last thing I need right now is sliced soles. If I need to, I want to be able to run.

Only a few shipmates remain behind, and I'm not in the slightest bit concerned about slipping past them. Not one of the crew left has grown up on the *Maiden*, so none of them knows her secrets the way I do, and I glide through the shadows unseen to climb down her side.

And then, just above the water, I hesitate. I'm going to have to overcome all my fears, lower myself into the ice-cold ocean and swim to the island, if I want to find answers. Though the still shallows don't frighten me the way the ocean depths do, I'm still not sure I can do it, my heart beating far too fast as I stare at my reflection.

Panic settles in, my anxiety spiking, and I don't think I can do this. I won't make it. I should go back to my cabin now and give up, but even as I think it I can hear echoes of the crew's hollow laughter taunting me.

There's only one way to silence them, and I take the plunge.

The water's so cold I forget to breathe, my body tense, and for a moment I think this might be the end. It's sheer stubbornness that pulls my mind into focus and makes me calm down. I want answers. I'm going to get them, no matter what. And with more determination than I've ever had, I pull my arms through the water, my legs propelling me from behind, just like Grace once told me to do.

I'm breathless by the time I reach the island, but exhilarated. I did it. But there isn't time to dwell on my achievement. The crew already have a good head start, so I need to get moving if I'm to catch up with them.

Pulling myself on to the rock is made bearable by the leather strapping I've wrapped round my hands, and only my fingers are cut, my blood eager to mingle with the salt water still clinging to the skin. It's good to be out of the water, but it's even better to be on the firm ground, even if it's utterly unforgiving. It's been a long time since I was on land, and I've longed for this moment. If only there was more time to savour it.

Sweeping my wet hair from my face, I crouch low to the ground, my knife pressed reassuringly to my hip. I know which direction my father went in, west towards the mine, but I won't follow their road, even if it would be kinder to my feet.

Instead I veer slightly north, taking a less visible route towards the settlement surrounding the mine. I've spent a long time studying maps in case I require the knowledge in my Initiation, and though charts of the ocean have been my main focus, I've taken the opportunity to study the land I love so much too. Every one of the six Eastern Isles is imprinted on my mind, though admittedly the detail on my father's maps can be sketchy at best. But he has this island particularly well recorded due to his infatuation with its crystal, and so it's with some confidence that I choose my path, relishing the opportunity to put my knowledge to use.

What am I hoping to discover today? What answers could I possibly find in this desolate place? Honestly I'm not sure, but something is happening between my father and the King and I'm desperate for clues, no matter how small. Serving His Majesty, fulfilling a duty to defend the realm – it's what makes my father and his crew honourable. It may be a romantic notion, but it's one that's helped me accept the savagery required of my family. But now we're spying on the King? And killing his Fleet? It makes no sense.

The cloud is low on the land, so visibility isn't great, but it offers me some cover should unfriendly eyes stray my way. It's also quiet. Too quiet? Usually the drone of mining work can be heard even back on the ship, but today I hear nothing, nor do I feel the vibration of blasting underground. I've been too lost in thought to notice its absence until now. It's possible they've ceased work while my father visits, but the quickening of my heart suggests otherwise.

Something's wrong.

I move faster, barely breathing for fear of being discovered, and crawl up to my intended vantage point: the top of the cliff that surrounds the settlement. From here I have a perfect view of the mine, while the rocks provide excellent cover. I lie low, ignoring the sharp points of stone piercing my body, knowing my father would do far worse should I be discovered. And then I watch.

The elite crew of the *Maiden* have already arrived at the settlement, and judging by their expressions they were not expecting the silence that greets them either. My father points at a few of them and they fan out, cutlasses drawn, pistols raised. They are alert, anticipating trouble, when a figure emerges from one of the stone huts, his arms raised.

My father strides towards him, saying something I can't hear from this distance. The man shakes his head and my father pushes him hard so that he falls on to the rock. I wince in reflex, and watch as my father grabs him by the neck and drags him to his feet. I can see now that the man is old, and most likely someone of importance here.

'Tell me why the mine is down!' Father bellows the question so loudly it reaches my ears perfectly.

'Please, don't hurt him.' The voice that now carries is a woman's and she is striding out from another hut with a bravery I admire. 'There was an accident. If you let him go, I'll tell you what happened.'

To my surprise Father does as she asks and releases the old man. The woman runs over to him and wraps her arms protectively round his shoulders, shielding him from my father. I realise I'm holding my breath. I don't trust my father for a moment. My eyes scan the crew until I locate Grace and Bronn. They are both motionless, poised to pounce at a single command. I've never seen them off the ship like this, standing with my father as he terrorises unarmed civilians, and I think I might be sick.

I have to strain to hear the conversation between my father and the woman now that they're no longer shouting, and though I miss most of what's said, I pick up the gist. There has been great suffering here. Long winters and poor conditions had already taken a toll on these people before the accident happened at the mine just weeks ago. Hundreds of lives were lost and those who remain – mostly women, children and elderly – have been left with next to nothing. Their dwindling supply of crystal will be gone by the end of the month.

Though the King had been sent word no aid has come, until now.

My heart sinks. She thinks my father is here to help them and I feel pure fear for her.

Other people are daring to appear from their homes now too. What are they doing? Do they think this is *safe*? My heart beats so loudly it's deafening. They're all in danger. No, no, no. Don't bring your children out. Get back inside. *Hurry*.

My father shoots first. Lazily he lifts his pistol, the bullet passing straight through the old man's head. The woman springs back in horror and starts to scream. Then all I can hear is a murderous chorus. Screams. Crying. Pleading. Begging. My father doesn't even need to issue an order; his crew quick to take his lead.

The villagers are slaughtered in less time than it takes for my father to plunder their remaining supply of crystal – all that they had left to trade for food. They won't need either now.

My mind is a tempest of horrors, my thoughts tossed around in nightmarish fragments, but finally one thought pushes through to make itself heard. *Run.*

I have only minutes – the time it'll take the crew to gather up anything of value – to return to the ship and make sure my presence here goes undiscovered. Scrambling to my feet, I stumble and slide as I race back towards the shore.

They killed them. They killed all of them. Defenceless, unarmed innocents. Children . . .

I shake my head. I can't think about that now. I have to hurry, but I trip over myself as urgency propels me faster than my body can go. Tears are clouding my vision and I wipe them furiously away as I try to keep to my path. Finally the *Maiden* comes into view and I dive recklessly into the sea. My mind screams with panic at being in the water but I press on, knowing some things are more terrifying than the ocean, clambering up the side of the ship and collapsing on to deck before managing to hurry back to my cabin unnoticed.

Only when I've changed my wet undergarments for my dress, and rubbed my hair as dry as possible do I allow myself a moment to breathe and it's then that a sob escapes my lips. I press my hand to my mouth hard, silencing the sound, panic rising like sickness up my throat.

They killed them all. Even the children.

I knew my father was a ruthless man, but I thought he'd limit his cruelty to depriving them of their crystal. To slaughter an entire settlement? That was beyond what I'd thought him capable of. Finally I understand what a fool I've been.

I believed that the Viper existed to protect. Lethal? Yes. Morally questionable? Most definitely. But *always* to defend the innocent. It is this fundamental core value that I have clung to.

Now I see that we have become nothing more than common thieves and murderers. Brutal killers who take whatever we please, helping no one but ourselves. I cannot become one of them. I won't.

I hear the crew coming aboard the ship. My presence will be required to greet the returning party and I try to arrange my face into a neutral expression, then check my hair. It's still a little wet, but hopefully won't raise too many suspicions. No one would believe I'd willingly go near water anyway. It'll be much harder to keep my anger and contempt masked.

As I make my way up to deck, a jolt of movement beneath tells me we've already weighed anchor, my father apparently not keen on staying here any longer. That makes two of us – if I never return to this awful place again, that would be fine with me.

When I reach the open air I see most of the crew are splattered with blood. My father is striding in my direction, deep in conversation with Cleeve and Bronn. Grace walks slightly behind them.

'Welcome home, Captain,' I say as is my duty. 'Did you have a successful journey?' *You murderous bastard.*

He doesn't answer – in fact, I think he's going to walk straight past me – but then he pauses as he takes in my appearance, his eye lingering on my damp hair. He says nothing, just carries on, but the slight smirk he gives me as he sweeps past nearly destroys me. In that moment I understand I've been played for a fool. My father knew I'd disobey him, knew I would follow them to the settlement. Which means that everything that just happened was intended for me. He wanted me to see the slaughter, wanted me to see that there was no limit to his cruelty. And he wanted to drive home to me the reach of his power, that he's as fearful on land as he is at sea.

Grace avoids me altogether and I understand that she too was part of Father's plan. A warning that even those who are important to me ultimately belong to him. To open my eyes to what even my closest friend is truly capable of. A painful reminder that her loyalty lies with him, and not with me. It hurts to be forced to admit that she belongs to a world I do not, and that I must leave her behind. But I'll have to come to terms with it. Because the next time I get off this boat I don't intend to come back.

I need to escape, but I have to wait for the right moment – and in the meantime I can't arouse further suspicion. The easiest way to do this is to continue preparing for my Initiation, which I assume my father means to happen before he marries me off. As far as I know there's still no date set for the wedding, not that anyone would necessarily tell me if there was. Channelling my energy into my training gives me purpose through the long hours at sea, and as my body strengthens so does my mind. Every ability I perfect will be vital to my eventual survival away from the *Maiden* and that knowledge drives me hard.

Though I would be happiest focusing purely on combat, that would mean spending a lot of time with Grace, and since she returned from the Sixth Isle I've been doing my best to stay away from her. Fortunately Initiation requires other areas of study, and after one particularly gruelling session climbing up and down the rigging, my skirt constantly tripping me up, my hair flying in my face, I head to the cargo hold in search of our cooper. He's a master at repairing the essential wooden barrels that contain everything from food and water to treasure, and it's a craft I need to work on. We call him Cooper – though I honestly don't know if this is coincidentally his name or if it's just the nickname he earned from his talent. Either way, he's good with his hands, which are as deadly as they are skilled.

It's gloomy down in the hold, and it takes a while for my eyes to adjust, but it's soon apparent Cooper isn't here. I'm about to leave when a noise stops me. It sounds like a dog whimpering, but there are none on board. Something's not right, and I quickly scan Cooper's tools for his broadaxe, pulling it out of the barrel it's resting in. It feels reassuringly heavy in my hand as I head towards the sound.

Toby is on the floor. He's been beaten, his right eye already swollen shut and a steady trickle of blood coming from his nose. Cleeve is bent over him, his arm raised to land another blow.

The broadaxe has left my hand before I even think of the consequences, pinning Cleeve's arm to the wall by his sleeve. He stares at the blade, which is alarmingly close to his flesh, and yanks it free, spinning round to face me, his expression nothing short of murderous.

'Leave him alone or I'll make you regret it.' And despite it being unlikely I can carry out the threat, I wholeheartedly mean it.

'You bitch,' he says, his voice a growl. 'You dare interfere in my business?'

'It is my business what happens on this ship. One day it'll be mine.' A stupid thing to say when I plan to escape, but it spills out before I have a chance to stop it.

Cleeve's hand hovers in the air, and I can tell he's weighing up the merits of sending the axe right back at me. There's nothing I can do but stand my ground.

Instead he laughs, which in the circumstances is nothing short of sinister. 'Will it indeed?' he says with undisguised contempt. 'One lucky throw doesn't make you fit to captain this crew.'

I'm not insulted by the slight. It's a relief to know Cleeve credits my skills to luck – the last thing I need is my father finding out I've been hiding talents he'd make vicious use of. 'I can try again if you like.'

For a moment I think I've gone too far and that Cleeve will bury the broadaxe in my chest, but he seems to think better of it and lowers his arm. He adopts an air of casual indifference towards the pair of us but glares at me as he walks past. So much for not drawing attention to myself.

When he's gone I kneel down beside Toby and use my skirt to wipe the blood from his face. 'Are you all right?' He nods and I gently take his chin in my hand to inspect his eye. 'Come on, let's get you some salve for that.'

He shakes his head, though, and in a flash is on his feet and running back to the ladder. His speed reassures me that he's suffered no lasting damage, and I decide it would be wise to join him higher up the ship. I don't want to be discovered by a returning Cleeve bent on revenge. Because I'm certain he won't forget this.

I'm not sure what I was expecting on my birthday, but being awoken by Grace bursting through my door before the sun has even risen wasn't it.

'Get up,' she says, pulling back my blanket. 'Meet me on deck. Bring your cloak.'

Blinking sleep away, I watch her hurry out of the room. We've barely spoken since the Rock Island massacre, and I wonder what's made her seek me out.

Grace is waiting for me at the bow when I emerge on to the deck, and she must hear me coming because as I approach she points to the horizon and says, 'Look.'

I squint, and in the distance I can make out the distinct shape of land, a shadow against the rising sun, which sends goosebumps up my arm. 'Is that the Third Isle?'

Of all the six Eastern islands this is the one I've most wanted to explore, something Grace knows. It's more than I dare hope for that we'll land there today.

'We're going over,' Grace says.

'We?'

'You and me,' she says. 'You're mine for the day.'

Adrenaline causes my heart to flutter. This is it. My chance to escape. All I need is a moment alone. One moment and I can be free.

'Don't get too excited. We're going to be training. Taking the opportunity for some target practice.' She's talking about firing pistols – it's not easy to shoot on board, too much potential for disaster – but she's misunderstood why my eyes have lit up. 'I have to gather a few things, but stay here. I'll be back in a minute.'

I stand with my face to the wind, breathing in the salt air as the island comes into closer view, waiting for the moment when I can catch a glimpse of the distinctive shoreline. Like all the islands, the Third Isle is often referred to by another name that reflects its unique landscape, and I confess its name is one of the things that's always intrigued me most about it. The Black Island. I've heard stories about its forests, where the nightheart trees are thin and tall with trunks that glisten like they've been dipped in tar, their leaves charcoal that turns to dust in your grasp. The forest floor is said to be ash and if there is life to be found, it's concealed in dark camouflage. Today I'll finally find out for myself.

I won't get a better opportunity than this to flee. I try to imagine what I'll have to do. Somehow I'll need to lose Grace, and that will be difficult. For a brief moment I remember I'll be holding a pistol but the mere thought of hurting Grace is too awful, so I decide to play that one by ear. Assuming I do manage to slip away from her, I'll then have to hide. But it's an island, and they'll know I'm there somewhere – not to mention I'm at a distinct disadvantage having never been there before. Eventually they'll find me and then what?

The truth weighs me down like an anchor.

This boat is a prison. I am my father's captive. He will make me a killer or he will have me killed. And I have always known this.

The stark reality of it hits me now like it never has before.

I feel a shift in the air and I'm expecting Grace to have returned, but it's Bronn who comes to stand beside me. He's the last person I want to see right now, the last person I want to witness the tears swimming in my eyes.

I want to yell and rage, vent every last scrap of my misery at him, but as I build internally to an outburst, I catch sight of his wrist. Tucked behind the leather band he wears, a scrappy piece of rope, knotted in several places, is straying from its hiding place, and though it's filthy and frayed, I recognise it as one I made him many years ago. I can't believe he still has it, let alone wears it, and my anger falls flat. I'm so tired of being mad at him all the time.

He seems oblivious to my conflict; instead he passes me something wrapped in cloth. 'This is for you.'

'What for?' It's hard to keep my voice steady.

'You didn't think I'd forgotten what day it was, did you?'

When I finally dare to look up at him, I see my own weariness reflected back. Our war with each other has taken its toll. I turn my attention to the gift. It's heavy, and I fold back the cloth to reveal a dagger, the handle bejewelled with black emeralds. It's exquisite.

'Th-thank you,' I stammer, lost for words. 'It's . . .'

'It's nothing,' he says. 'But, you know, it might come in handy one day.'

And with a casual shrug he leaves as if he'd gifted me nothing more than a bit of old loot, which, on reflection, it probably is. I'm tempted to fling it into the sea. Instead I shove it into my belt. For once Bronn's right. Never know when it might be useful.

By the time the anchor drops and the men lower a small boat into the water, Grace has returned with a bag of weapons and supplies. She tosses the rope ladder over the side of the ship and gestures to me. 'After you.'

Not needing to be asked twice, I hurl myself over and downwards, struggling to keep from stepping on my dress.

Grace takes the oars and with elegant strokes sweeps us towards land. As the *Maiden* grows smaller and the land looms larger, I can breathe more easily.

In no mood for conversation, I'm silent as we glide through the water, the sense of defeat I'm experiencing threatening to overwhelm me, the prospect of escape slipping fast away like a dream upon waking. I'm so distracted I don't realise at first that we're no longer travelling straight, instead Grace is taking us round the island towards a previously hidden cove. I raise an eyebrow at her in question.

'Just being cautious,' is all she says.

I lean over the side of the boat, and allow the tips of my fingers to skim through the clear water. Though I look hard there's no sign of life beneath us, no fish or weed, and at first this surprises me, until the water grows murkier and the seabed darker so that I imagine my hand is in oil. Looking up, I see the shoreline is as black as the forests found here. Grace smiles. 'Beautiful, isn't it?'

She jumps out, the water reaching her waist, and drags the boat on to the beach. Mesmerised, I climb out and kneel to examine the sand, which looks like powdered coal, then rub it between my fingers where it leaves a smudge behind. Turning to show Grace, I see she's hauling the boat right up towards the dunes. 'What are you doing?'

She shrugs. 'Just don't want anyone to know we're here.' And she retraces her tracks, kicking sand back over the boat's plough lines.

I frown, suddenly registering that Grace has been quiet too, even for her, and my senses prickle. 'Anyone in particular?'

'No.' But she smiles a bit too brightly. 'Just old habits and all that.'

I'm about to push her further when she offers me a small box.

'Here, you may as well have your gift now.'

Trying to disguise my surprise that she's got me anything, I take it from her and open the lid to reveal a compass. Set in gold, the compass face is surrounded by a circle of dainty cowrie shells that alternate with tiny pink scallops, both as fragile as they are beautiful. In the lid of the box is an exquisite painting depicting the same image of the shells, only with a larger scallop shell in the centre, and the letter V. For Viper. It's like nothing I've ever seen before and tears spring to my eyes. 'Grace, thank you. It's perfect.'

'I've been holding on to that for a long time, waiting for the right moment to give it to you.' Her smile has an unexpected hint of sadness in it.

'I love it.' And for just the smallest moment I see my friend before me, rather than the killer I know she is, and realise how much I've missed her.

'Good. Right, come on. You wanted to see the forest I believe.'

We don't have to walk far before all I can see ahead of us is dense woodland towering ominously like a wall of darkness. When we reach its outskirts, I worry that I'll be as good as blind in there, but Grace walks in with such confidence I'm willing to follow.

Within minutes my eyes adjust to the gloom. All the stories are true. The trees are so narrow it would be easy to mistake them as fragile, and they shine as if wet, but when I brush my fingers along the trunks they're sturdy and dry to the touch. The leaves are sparse on the lower branches, only for the foliage to form black clouds that block out all light on the upper boughs. The ground of powdered ash offers a soft bed to fallen leaves and twigs, and scattered around are tiny black flowers, creating a soft floral carpet. I've never seen them before; Milligan doesn't use them at all. I wish I knew what they were and if they had any medicinal properties. It's exactly as I imagined it would be, yet somehow far more beautiful. And quiet. So quiet that every step echoes like a thousand tiny explosions beneath my feet. There is an unnatural absence of birdsong, and if any creatures call this place home, they are hidden from sight and sound. Yet the stillness causes me no fear, and despite my exertion my breathing feels a little easier, my mind a little lighter.

When we have walked for a half hour or so Grace stops, shrugging her bag from her shoulders. 'OK, this'll do. Up for a bit of sparring?'

'If you're in the mood to lose.'

She smiles. 'You're on. But you'll have to find me first.'

And she sidesteps, disappearing behind a tree, her Snake blacks an ideal camouflage in these surroundings.

My adrenaline starts to pump, the perfect balance of fear and exhilaration, and I cautiously set after her. I tread lightly, not wanting to alert Grace to my presence, but moments later her arm swings round a tree and catches me right in the stomach. Winded, I stumble backwards, though still manage to pivot in time to avoid her next attempt. She tries again, kicking her leg high, but this time I'm expecting it and stop her foot with my hands, pushing her away. Now Grace is the one off balance and I capitalise on her momentary weakness, my arms landing strike after strike on to hers, while she does her best to fend me off.

The exchange is just what I needed. Both of us are glad to be in the open air, free to stretch our limbs and minds, eager for the challenge and hungry for the win. Soon the sweat drips down my back as I try to find a way to break through Grace's defences.

'Come on,' she goads me. 'Getting older's made you slow.'

'Just don't want you to feel bad.'

'I can handle anything you throw at me.'

'You asked for it.'

Jumping up, I grab the branch above me, swinging towards her so she only just has time to duck out of the way. I land behind her, and wait as she springs to her feet. She comes at me fast, and I have to parry an endless stream of blows, our arms moving with increasing speed until I do the only thing I can to end it: twist my feet round hers, my dress tying us in knots. It sends us both hurtling to the floor, where we look at each other and burst out laughing.

'Not bad,' Grace says, standing up. 'Not bad at all.'

'Thanks. What next?'

She hands me a pistol. 'See that tree?' She points to a slightly deformed trunk with protruding knots. 'Hit it.'

'With pleasure.' It's been a while since I fired one, but my aim is sharp and soon the air is dense with gunpowder. When my forefinger is cramping from pulling the trigger, I pause.

'Good,' Grace says. 'I'm impressed.'

She also sounds relieved.

'What's wrong?'

'Nothing.' She rubs the back of her neck. 'I'm just pleased to see you doing well.' She meets my eyes and I know she's not telling me everything. 'But there's always room for improvement. Keep going.'

We train until the hour is late, the sun just beginning to drop and the gloom increasing. When we can barely see any more Grace says, 'Come on, time to go.' But I notice she sets off in a different direction to the one we came in.

Assuming she has good reason, and more than happy to delay returning to the *Maiden*, I follow her. My dress is covered in gunpowder and I smell like battle. When we emerge from the forest the relative light hurts my eyes. We're near the sea, but not at the cove where our boat awaits. Large slabs of dark rock mingle with weeds dusted in charcoal sand and, as we walk over them, I imagine how filthy my feet must be. Ahead of us is a dilapidated building, and Grace seems to be taking me there. She has remained silent for too long and nerves flutter in my stomach as we approach the structure.

Just before we reach the door she turns to me. 'Whatever happens, I'm with you.' And without waiting for a reply she goes in.

The atmosphere noticeably changes when I step into the building. Derelict and abandoned, I suspect we are the first people to stand within its four walls for many years – apart from those waiting for us. All the *Maiden*'s core crew are already here positioned in a semicircle. They're staring at me – even Bronn, whose jaw is clenched. My father waits in the middle of the room. Someone kneels before him, his hands tied behind his back and a sack over his head. I can smell his fear instantly. Beside me I feel every muscle in Grace's body tense, and know something terrible is about to happen.

'My child,' my father begins, and a chill spreads across me in anticipation of what is to come. 'Today is a momentous day. Not only do we honour your birth, but the time has come for your Initiation to take place.'

My Initiation. I hadn't imagined it would take place today; in truth, I had struggled to imagine it ever taking place. For so long I've dreaded this moment, but now there is nothing to do but confront it.

'What must I do?' I try to speak formally, fittingly for the occasion but, honestly, it's an effort to speak at all.

My father walks towards me and takes my hand in his for a moment, before he places a pistol, his pistol, into my palm. Then he takes a step back as I fight to keep my breathing steady.

'Kill him.' He gestures towards the captive kneeling on the floor.

Bile rises in my throat. 'What is his crime?'

My father shrugs. 'None.'

Oh no, please no. Surely there is more to my Initiation than a cold-blooded execution? There has to be.

I stare at my father, who evenly returns my gaze. Panic spreading, I glance at Grace, whose face is set like stone, though her eyes betray her concern. The tension in the room is palpable and I wonder whether anyone other than my father is actually breathing.

'You want me to kill him? An unarmed man? An innocent man?' For the first time my voice reveals a hint of disgust at my father's orders and instantly displeasure flashes across his face.

'Yes.'

The room begins to spin, and I close my eyes, trying to stop myself from falling. This is it, the moment I have been led towards my whole life. It is time to pass my father's test and take my place at his side – there is no escape, no other choice. It is this, or death.

And with absolute clarity I know I can't do it, that I won't do it. My arm remains close to my side, the pistol pointing firmly at the floor. I refuse to become his monster.

When my eyes meet my father's his disbelief is obvious. 'Kill him!'

I shake my head, and though I know what my mutiny means, it's such a relief to finally make my stand. 'No.'

With one step my father is in front of me and the crack of his fist meeting my jaw sends me staggering backwards so quickly I drop to the floor, the pistol falling from my grasp. Towering over me he shouts again, ordering me to be an executioner, threatening to hurt me until I obey, even as he rains blows down on me. Knowing it was coming doesn't stop me cowering away from him, nor does it make the pain any less real. I can do nothing but endure my beating, protecting my face as best I can with my arms, wondering how long it will last, knowing it might never end.

A shot pierces the air. My father freezes as all eyes move to the prisoner's body slumped on the floor and then to Bronn who stands over it, his pistol still smoking. While the room remains frozen with shock, Bronn meets my astonished gaze. Seeing the warning there in his eyes, I do what I should have done long ago. Run.

I hurtle back towards the forest, my mind astonishingly sharp despite my beating, knowing my survival depends on it. Though night is falling fast I plunge into the trees, retracing the path I took with Grace. Branches reach out to snatch at my face, but I pay them no attention. The real danger is the one behind me.

By the time the trees begin to thin and I can hear the reassuring lap of water against the shore, the stars are all that illuminate the ground. There are twigs and leaves lodged in my hair's wild tangles, and my face is well and truly scratched.

Ignoring my wheezing breath and the panic that's threatening to consume me, I race to where Grace hid the boat, and push it frantically down the shore and into the water. I scramble in, willing my damn legs to stop trembling, and start to row.

I'm shaking all over and I have no idea if that's because I'm freezing or terrified. I suspect both. Because there's no way back now.

I challenged my father. In front of all his men. At my Initiation.

He will not forget this, nor will he forgive. And what about Bronn? What was he thinking shooting the prisoner? My father will be furious with him. What will he do? How will he make Bronn suffer? Why, after all this time, would Bronn risk so much to help me? Or was it prearranged that should I fail, then Bronn would finish the job to illustrate my weakness? Was Bronn in on it all along?

Every second the throb in my jaw reminds me of my father's fists, my eye already swelling from its battering, and I wish I had some second-salve with me. Instead I'm alone, carrying only two daggers and Grace's compass, bobbing about on an ocean I fear, wondering how much of a head start I have. If Grace tells them where we landed, they could run on to the shore and spy me any minute. But even if she doesn't, the *Maiden* will catch up with me soon enough, unless I manage to find someplace to hide.

So I press on. Every stroke of the oars shoots pain through my body, but there is no time for discomfort. My best chance is to travel further round the island, putting as much distance as possible between myself and where the *Maiden* is anchored. I can stay closer to shore than she can and if the moon stays hidden behind cloud, I might just manage to remain invisible. If I make it through the night, then I'll worry about tomorrow.

Though my survival should be the only thing on my mind, I can't stop thinking about my Initiation. The simplicity of it confuses me. It was supposed to be a series of tests. I'd spent years preparing so I could show my skill in combat, reel off history and lore, prove I could contribute as a member of crew. If he just wanted me to kill in cold blood, what had been the point in all that study?

Oh.

That *was* the point.

Initiations are all individual, and killing is the one thing I have consistently shied away from, the one thing I needed to prove I could do. When it came to taking a life I was untested. No, more than that. I was unwilling. And you can't be an assassin if you won't kill.

Not that it matters any more.

I stare up at the sky. The stars are as many and as scattered as the freckles on my face, and I remember Bronn telling me if I were lost they would guide me home. They tell me nothing. I have no home – the price of freedom it would seem – just a little boat that carries me slowly away from the only life I've known.

The night is long, with no breath of wind to keep me company; only the ripples I make disturb the tranquillity. By dawn I've reached the other side of the island and there is still no sign that I'm being followed. Perhaps no one is coming for me after all. Maybe my father has better things to do than track down his rebellious child. Does failing Initiation mean I'm no longer considered an asset worth recovering?

I can't hide in the coves of the Third Isle for ever, and the absence of any pursuit gives me the courage to head out into open water – a dangerous but necessary part of the plan I've cobbled together overnight.

I've had no sleep, and the lack of food and water is causing unwelcome dizziness. Even just after daybreak the sun is already fiercely hot, and beads of sweat trickle down my forehead to hang like diamonds from my lashes. I'm seriously thirsty, and I am sorely tempted to drink from the sea, though I know it'll only make me sick. Blisters have formed on both my hands, the chafe of wood taking a layer of skin off with every stroke, and my lips aren't faring much better, cracking with dehydration.

Several hours later, I allow myself a brief pause. I dip one hand at a time into the sea, letting the salt burn then soothe my broken skin, before thinking better of it. There are all manner of creatures lurking beneath who would consider my bloody fingers a tasty treat, and I'm cursing my lapse of judgement when I catch sight of a boat on the horizon.

My initial reaction is panic, but after a second I scold myself for being childish. The boat approaching is a relatively small brig with only one sail raised and is clearly not the *Maiden*. It's probably traders, which means they're more than likely to have food aboard. That's enough to make up my mind. I'm as good as dead if I remain drifting in this heat, so I'm going to have to get on that boat.

I stand up, ignoring the rocking my unsteadiness causes, and begin to wave for attention. It only takes a moment for the boat to change direction and move swiftly towards me. The daggers at my side give me some reassurance, but I'm nowhere near calm. I close my eyes and focus. If they're not friendly, if they won't allow me to hitch a ride, then I'm going to have to commandeer their vessel.

I realise which it's going to be as soon as the brig pulls alongside my little boat. There are three men aboard, all ageing badly, their skin weathered and loose on bony frames. Life has no doubt been hard on them, but the moment they see me all of them light up in the same way Cleeve used to when his eyes lingered too long on my chest.

Nothing's ever easy.

With their intentions obvious I know what I have to do, though the prospect gives me no pleasure.

'Morning, young lady,' the one with a beard says. 'You in need of assistance?'

'I am,' I say, and I can see the men think I'm easy prey. 'I don't suppose you're headed towards the Fourth, are you?'

'Can't say as we are,' Beardy replies with an unpleasant leer. 'But we might be persuadable.'

'Thank you,' I say as Beardy tosses over a towline, which I quickly fix to my boat.

One of the other men, who has all of his top front teeth missing, offers me his hand, and though I could easily climb aboard myself, I want them to believe I'm helpless and let him pull me up on to their deck. His gummy grin turns my stomach a little, but then my eyes fall upon the crates of produce they're transporting. Food.

'It's a good thing we found you,' Beardy says. 'These waters aren't a safe place to be alone.'

'Especially for a pretty little thing like you,' Toothless agrees. I am in no doubt I was safer alone than with them.

'Well, I'm in your debt,' I say, and don't flinch when the third man, the one with a patch over his right eye, reaches to stroke my face.

'We're making for the Second Isle,' Beardy says. 'So if you're wanting us to detour all the way back to the Fourth . . .' He lets the thought linger.

'That would be very kind.'

Beardy's eyes narrow. 'Then we'll be wanting to see some of that persuasion we talked about.'

'What do you mean?' I say with what I hope is enough innocence to convince these despicable creatures that I am no threat, that they should step closer. I'm surprised at how completely my disgust outweighs any kind of fear at this point.

'No need to be coy,' Toothless says as he lunges to grab hold of my right arm. Patchy clutches my left, while Beardy pulls a dagger from his boot and waves it through the air, a threat dancing before me.

'Now don't struggle,' Beardy says, raising the blade. 'I don't want to mark such a lovely face.'

I steady my nerve, waiting, and the moment he's close enough, I strike. Using the two men's hold, I push my legs off the ground and kick Beardy hard under his jaw. He stumbles backwards, dropping the knife.

The other men loosen their grip in surprise and I easily break free of them, my left hand jabbing Patchy in the throat while my right simultaneously snatches Toothless's wrist. With one twist I bend his arm up behind his back. The snap, along with his scream, tells me it's broken, and he drops to the deck. A quick knee to the groin sends Patchy down to join him and then I pull out my knives as I stride over to Beardy, knocking his blade out of the way with my foot.

'Think you all need to learn some manners,' I say as they stare at me in confusion, nursing their injuries. 'Now get up and sit over there.'

The men are cowards, so stunned to have been attacked by a woman that they don't retaliate further and instead willingly sit in a huddle by the stern. I wrap some rope round them, my heart aching a little as I tie a triple knot Bronn devised himself. He told me if I were ever in need of something really secure, this was the one to use. I wonder what that old Bronn, the one who was my closest friend, would say if he could see me now?

Toothless's cries grow louder, presumably from the rope pressing hard on his fracture, so I oblige him with a fist in his face, knocking him out cold. I tear Patchy's shirt and fashion gags and blindfolds for them all, and once I'm certain they can't disturb me I waste no time in plundering their crates, which I discover are full of mangwyan fruits. The tough skins preserve their juicy flesh for long periods of time, making them ideal food for sailors, and I eat until I'm fit to burst, revelling in what I just accomplished. The thrill of the fight has given me as much cause to smile as the gentle breeze blowing me towards my destination.

Grace's birthday gift couldn't have come at a better time. My studying of charts has paid off and I know exactly how far south-east I need to travel to reach the Fourth Isle. With a good wind in my sails I should be there in two days – so long as I don't have any more undesirable encounters. It's possible my father could be bound for the same place, but my gut tells me he'll head for the Second Isle, given its closer proximity to the Third. His opinion of me is so low I'm certain he'll expect me to take the easier route.

My instincts serve me well and I sail undisturbed all the way to the Fourth Isle. By the time I arrive in the shallows I've fully raided the traders' supplies and am well fed. Though I've not felt safe enough to fall into anything more than a light doze, I'm partially rested and ready to leave the ship. My prisoners remain tied up, though I've watered them, which is possibly more than they deserve, but I've just run away from the *Maiden* to avoid killing people. I'm not going to start now.

We see no other ships, which is strange. Unless I'm mistaken, I'm travelling in what should be busy trading channels, and though I'm grateful to pass unnoticed, the emptiness of these popular passages is troubling.

I help myself to one of the men's satchels, removing the tatty papers inside and replacing them with food and coins, pausing only briefly to consider my bandit-like behaviour. I shrug off any guilt with the certainty that had they behaved in a more gentlemanly manner I would never have considered stealing from them. As it is I'm more concerned about my own survival than theirs, and make sure my flask is full with water from the barrel.

When I climb down into my little boat, ready to row to shore, the men hear me leaving and start to raise their objections through muffled screams. I ignore them – someone's sure to come to their aid sooner or later (hopefully much later, when the wind has carried them far away) – and focus on getting to dry land.

Though it is the smallest, the Fourth Isle is, in my admittedly limited opinion, the most intriguing of all the Eastern Isles. The Floral Island. In my studies I've learned about the peaceful meadowlands where flowers of all colours grow in abundance, and the people are famously as tranquil as their surroundings. I've read that on the higher ground there grows a plant known as day's end. At sunset the wind whistles through its russet spires like melancholy music. The blossom woods are said to flower all year round, the black petals of the ashblossom a startling contrast to the luminous orange of the sunblossom, both gently complemented by the pale pinks, mauves and whites of the sweetblossom. As older petals fall to make way for new ones, the ground becomes a vibrant tapestry laced with the sweetest perfume. And most intriguing to me are the fields full of inkbells, a flower that shifts from pale green through to darkest blue depending on the light, and which ripples in the breeze like the ocean, so that at a first glance many have mistaken it for actual water.

My father only landed here once to resupply and never bothered again. There is no vast wealth to be excavated, just rolling hills and breathtaking beauty. It wouldn't occur to Father to seek shelter somewhere with such simple settlements and lack of resources, and I can only hope his prejudice will outweigh any suspicion that I might be drawn to such a place. If so, I might just be able to disappear, away from his vengeful eye, and start a new life free from bloodshed and violence.

Following Grace's example, I drag the boat far up the beach, concealing it behind the high sandbanks, and then retrace my steps to smooth over the drag lines. A warm breeze caresses my hair and I pause, leaning my head into its touch. The strangest urge grips me: to launch the boat back on to the water and head west. Somewhere my father would never go looking for me. So strong is the impulse that I'm halfway back to the boat before I come to my senses. Mounting an expedition into dangerous and forbidden waters is a bad idea at the best of times – right now it would be certain death. So I silence the voice whispering into my ear and I set off, heading as far inland as I can manage.

I reach the first settlement without seeing another living soul. Not even a mangy dog scavenges on the streets, and my skin prickles with unease. The settlement seems as abandoned as the road that led me here, the skeletons of cobbled buildings bound together by ivy. And yet I can sense I'm being watched. Somewhere in the shadows, behind closed doors, my presence is being monitored. I realise too late how exposed I am. If my father comes looking for me, he has but to ask these people and they will point him my way.

Suddenly someone grabs my wrist from behind. Both the shock and the force with which they pull me round pushes the air from my lungs, and I fear the worst, but find myself face to face with only an old woman, her hair wilder than a storm, her skin plagued with boils, and her breath so foetid it could skin a cat.

'You'll be looking for me, miss,' she says, and my eyes water at her stench.

'No, thank you,' I say, trying to pull away, but her grip is tight.

'Old Tatty's been waiting for you. Potions, is it not? Remedies you're after? I've got them all.' And she licks her lips as if in some sort of invitation.

Years of hiding my emotions pay off. I remain impassive despite wondering how she could possibly know of my interest in healing.

'I'm not looking to buy anything.'

Old Tatty reaches up a gnarled hand and touches my cheek.

'There's more than a touch of magic about you,' she says. 'Snake.'

My blood turns to ice as she laughs at my paling skin. Fear is pounding in my ears, and I pull myself free from her grasp. How could she know that? Nothing about my appearance ties me to the Viper. Walking quickly away from her, I block the sound of her laughter from my ears, wanting to put as much distance between us as possible. I have the strangest feeling that in her presence my secrets are no longer my own and protectively hold them close to my chest. If I am to survive, they must stay buried deep within me. Even to my grave.

As soon as I'm past the settlement I veer off the path and take a slightly more scenic track towards the centre of the island. Once I'm safely in the middle of nowhere I'm happier, but I can't help but wonder why this place is so lifeless. What has made everyone so afraid that they hide in their homes during daylight? In such a magical landscape it's hard to imagine anyone being anything but calm. The air is fresh, the sun warm, and though fear is a constant echo in my mind I wonder if this is what freedom might taste like in a world where the Viper didn't exist.

The Floral Island has only a small population, so I manage to avoid meeting anyone else for the remainder of the day, and though the quiet is ominous I can't help feeling grateful for it. I'd as soon forget about the encounter I've already had. But I am discovering the island isn't quite as lacking in resources as my father believes. He doesn't value plants or flowers in the slightest, so he wouldn't have taken the time to notice, but among the fields of colour I've seen the pale pink of the duskal plant, the seeds of which can be used to treat a cough; the small white moonflower, which powdered down can be used to create a burn remedy; and the tall distinctive catkins of silverbud, which has many uses, including being a potent sedative when added to a tonic of eldercress and mistlewort. I feel certain the island is brimming with ingredients that are sold to healers all over the East, and if that's not a vital resource, I don't know what is.

When night falls I find a sheltered corner of a meadow to lie low in, taking the opportunity to eat some of the food I've brought with me, but even in this beautiful place with my knife in my hand I allow myself very little sleep.

I'm back on the road again before the birds are awake, every step away from the sea feeling like a small victory. I slowly allow myself to believe that I've done it; I've escaped my father's clutches.

It's only when I stroll through a field awash with lilac wildweed that my skin prickles at some unseen danger, the birds falling quiet, the air growing still. And that's when I hear the cocking of a pistol I'm certain is aimed straight at my head.

Instinctively I raise my hands in surrender. If the pistol belongs to one of my father's men, it won't matter; I'm already dead. But if not, then I don't want to give the person cause to shoot.

Nothing happens.

Sensing the attacker's hesitation, I begin to lower my arms.

'Keep them up!' an unfamiliar male voice booms across the field from my right, and I turn ever so slowly in its direction.

'I'm unarmed,' I say, hoping he can't see my knives from his distance. 'Lower your weapon. I mean no harm.'

'Who are you? What do you want?' The man is still uncertain about me, but I can sense the immediate threat has gone.

'My name is Marianne. I'm just passing through, looking for somewhere to shelter.' Instantly I regret my honesty. I should have used another name.

Another pause. 'Are you alone?'

'Yes.'

Finally my would-be assassin emerges from the hedge. He's a middle-aged man who has a kind face that's currently etched with fear, and nervous eyes that dart around, checking for trouble.

'You're a long way from anywhere. What brings you out this far?'

I smile. 'Trying to get a long way from anywhere.'

'Running away, huh?' He weighs me up now that he's come close enough, taking in my bruised face, and raises an eyebrow when his eyes rest on my daggers. 'Unarmed?'

I shrug sheepishly. 'Just something to skin a rabbit with.'

He brushes faded hair off his forehead as he works out what to do with me, then reaches a decision. 'Why don't you come on home with me? My wife will be happy to feed you, and you can tell us where it is you've travelled from.'

I stare back, wondering if he can be trusted. The people here are supposed to be peaceful, but my experience with Old Tatty was hardly testament to that fact, and I certainly didn't plan to stop moving for another day or two at the very least. The eerie absence of people warns me that I shouldn't lower my guard. And yet a safe place to rest is appealing, not to mention some companionship. If he turns out to be trouble, then I'm more than capable of taking care of myself.

'Thank you. If you're sure it wouldn't be an imposition?'

'No more than you trespassing on my land.' But he says it with a twinkle in his eye and instantly I warm to him. 'The name's Joren.'

I shake his outstretched hand. 'Pleasure to meet you.'

He gestures towards a line of trees and I start to walk with him. 'I'm sorry I crossed your property,' I say. 'I didn't realise anyone lived out this far.'

'You're not from the Fourth, are you?'

I don't deny it. What would be the point? 'Is it that obvious?'

'You wouldn't be out wandering alone if you were,' he says sadly, which only confirms my feeling that something's not right. What has happened to this place?

Though it's tempting to ask, I suspect Joren is the kind of man who won't reveal too much to an outsider and so I don't push the conversation as we amble out of the field and into the adjoining woodland.

'It's just through here,' Joren says and then I see it. Nestled in the heart of nature, a babbling stream running past, is the prettiest cottage I've ever seen.

He leads me in, the smell of fresh bread causing my stomach to dance with excitement.

'Clara? We have a visitor!'

Joren gives me a reassuring smile as his wife hurries in, her face not able to disguise her displeasure.

'Joren?' Her voice wavers with uncertainty.

'Found her out on the top field. Damn near shot her too.'

'I'm sorry to intrude, ma'am,' I say, hoping to assuage her misgivings. 'I'm Marianne.'

'You one of those bandits?' Clara thrusts her hands on her hips and it's clear she's angry. 'Come to steal what little we have?'

'No! Wait, there are bandits here?' Like my father, the bandits don't usually tend to bother with the Fourth. What is there to take other than a nice bunch of flowers?

Clara and Joren exchange looks.

'Perhaps we should start on supper,' Joren says. 'Talking's always better on a full belly.'

It takes Clara a moment longer to agree, her eyes lingering on the burn on my wrist, but eventually she nods. 'Take a seat,' she says to me, still slightly scowly. 'Tomas! Dinner's ready!'

Joren shows me through to the kitchen and as I'm about to sit at their chunky wooden table a small body brushes past mine. I look down to see a pair of big brown eyes staring up at me from behind a curtain of hair that's as red as his mother's. From his height I'd guess he's seen no more than seven winters.

'Who are you?' The question has no malice, only a child's curiosity.

I give the boy a smile. 'I'm Marianne. Are you Tomas?'

His eyes widen, as though I'm magical. 'You know my name?'

'Good grief, the girl heard me call for you,' Clara says, affectionately pushing her son round to his seat and out of my way. 'Nothing more exciting than that.'

But common sense doesn't matter to Tomas. I can tell I've made a little friend for life.

The meal is more delicious than anything I've ever had before, though it's modest in quantity. Accompanying the fresh bread are vegetables pulled straight from the ground, roasted until sweet and crisp, along with a bowl of mashed potatoes. Hunger I hadn't realised I had roars to take over, but manners slow me down, forcing me to take small portions and even smaller mouthfuls. Clara's eagle eye never leaves me, and I sense that both she and Joren have many questions for me, but they're waiting for their son to leave the table.

When the plates are empty and the table cleared, Joren suggests Tomas goes outside to play.

'Can Marianne come with me?'

Joren kisses the top of his son's head. 'Maybe later. Your mother and I want to talk with her first.'

Tomas turns and gives me a sympathetic look. 'Don't worry, I get into trouble all the time, but they still love me.'

I laugh, strangely comforted by the boy.

Once he's gone, Joren leans back in his chair to consider me, while his wife places a mug of ale in front of him.

'So, Marianne, we've already established you're not from this island, so where is it you have come from?'

Clara makes a pretence of ignoring us, busying herself at the sink, while clearly listening to every word.

I pause before answering, trying to decide the safest response. Both for me and for them. 'You've been so kind to me and I don't want to lie to you. I can't tell you where I've come from. Trust me, you don't want to know.'

Joren frowns, so I continue.

'But I can promise you I have no dishonourable intentions. I simply need to start over. I'm after a quiet life.'

'Then you shouldn't have come here,' Clara says, before remembering she wasn't supposed to be listening.

'Why don't you join us?' Joren says to his wife with a smile. She puts down the dishes and takes a seat opposite me.

'Why not?' I ask Clara, wondering if there's a reason she doesn't want me here. 'I always understood this to be a peaceful island.'

'No such thing any more,' Clara says shortly.

I look to Joren, hoping for more of an explanation. He takes a large gulp of ale. 'You've come from a ship, am I right? A sea-girl? Trader, perhaps?'

I nod. That's as close to the truth as I want him to get.

He watches me closely. 'You catch many rabbits at sea?'

My mouth gapes open, caught in my earlier lie, but then I see Joren's smiling at me and exhale. He's not angry; he just wants me to know I haven't fooled him. I give an apologetic tilt of my head, which he acknowledges, and then the moment is swept away.

'Makes sense,' he says, continuing with the matter at hand. 'I suppose you wouldn't know what's been happening in that case. Poverty and hunger are growing, not just here, but on every one of the six islands. All these accidents on the Rock Island mean the mining has virtually come to a halt. Without the crystals they can't trade with the other islands; the moneylenders have panicked and closed the vaults on the First, and the knock-on effect is feeding its way down through the Isles' economy. Bandits are running wild, unchecked, and fear of them has sent people even further inland where there are still fewer resources. And all the while the King does nothing.'

I think about the delicious meal we just ate. 'But you're safe here?'

Joren sighs. 'We've fared better than most, mainly because we grow our own produce and are away from prying eyes. But in time we'll be discovered and all that we have left will be taken from us. Even if we manage to survive that, I'm a flower farmer. If the traders won't come any more to take flowers to the First, eventually my coins will run out.'

'And the King hasn't sent his Fleet?' An image of a dead man on the *Maiden*'s deck flashes unbidden into my mind.

'He's sent no one.' Clara's eyes are dark with sadness. 'I've already lost one son to bandits; I won't lose another.' And she stands up, turning her face away from me.

'I'm sorry,' I say. 'I had no idea things were so bad.'

'You've been at sea,' Joren says, reaching his hand out to comfort his wife. 'Have you seen anything? Are the King's Fleet aiding other islands before ours?'

I don't even have to answer for him to know I've seen nothing that'll make him feel better.

'He's probably recalled them all to the First,' Clara says bitterly. 'Protecting his own skin.'

Joren nods. 'I've heard rumours that those who can are fleeing to the First for safety.'

I fall silent, thinking of Torin. Did he know the Isles were suffering so greatly? My father has certainly kept me blissfully unaware of the islands' plight. But now the incident at the mine on the Sixth makes so much more sense and I'm furious with myself. I've been so preoccupied with my own situation that I've completely failed to notice what's been going on around me.

'Is there anything I can do to help?' Hollow, useless words, but they're all I have.

'Think you could help me plough a field?' Clara gives her husband a horrified glance as he asks the question. 'Could do with an extra pair of hands getting next year's harvest planted.'

A nagging voice in the back of my head tells me to get up now, leave this place and never come back.

'As I see it, you've got nowhere to go, and it's not safe out there. We can offer you a bed and food in exchange for work.' Joren ignores his wife's falling face, and urges me to accept his offer. 'Just until you figure out what to do next.'

I silence the voice now screaming at me to go, and smile. 'Thank you, you're very kind.'

Joren is delighted, Clara less so, and I continue to ignore my instinct that I've not run far enough. I can run again another day.

The sun rises differently on land than at sea. When I lived on the *Maiden* dawn would break in a fiery blaze burning across the water, turning all the world around us to blood. Here, though, the ground swallows up the sun's intensity, leaving only a soft glow to coax us into the day ahead.

Every morning it takes my breath away. I'm nearly always in the same place, walking with Joren down to the meadows when it happens – the light suddenly spills over the horizon, flooding the fields with an amber hue, each flower reaching up to the warmth of its splendour.

I stop to drink in the beauty, and Joren walks on, chuckling to himself at my childish wonder. To start with, Tomas would join me and slip his little hand in mine, and we'd watch the world come alive together, but even he's grown bored of the sight now and tugs me along to catch up with his father.

'Come on, dreamer,' Joren says without fail. 'There's work to do.'

And I follow on, eager for the opportunity to spend any time here with these people.

Joren works me hard, but he's good company and I'm finding it unexpectedly fulfilling tilling the land, hoeing stubborn earth until it surrenders its secrets and allows us to plant all manner of seeds, so that by early spring this field will be awash with colour. And I no longer have any intention of leaving. To start with I convinced myself I would just stay for a few days, that I'd go eventually. Now I'm done pretending. I love it here. If nothing else, I have to stay and see the fruits of my labour.

Joren tells me how he believes the last remnants of the old magic dwell in the Isle's earth, and credits this for his stunning crops. When I push him to tell me more he says, 'Would be a fool to deny it. It's in the roots of the trees, the colours of the flowers. Nature is magic, Marianne, even the alchemists would have nothing without it.' He stoops to run the soil through his fingers, and presses a warm clump of it into my hand. 'People say the old magic is lost, but I say they just aren't looking hard enough.'

I can almost feel the buzz of magic as the earth rests against my skin, hear the air crackle with unspoken secrets waiting to be discovered. I'm ready to start looking.

Tomas – adorable, wonderful Tomas – helps us while we work, entertaining me with stories of creatures he's discovered, animals he's rescued. He has a healer's heart, always wanting to mend broken legs or cure disease, but his parents are less than happy about his affinity. They tend to want to eat what Tomas brings home to nurse.

The relationship between Joren and Tomas has taken some getting used to. One morning, when the sun was fierce and our labour intense, Joren had asked Tomas to fetch us some water. Ever obedient, Tomas had run home before returning dutifully with a full pitcher, but as he raced towards his father, eager to complete his mission, he'd tripped, falling forward and emptying the pitcher's contents over the earth.

My heart had leapt to my mouth, fearful of the repercussions. Would Joren take his strap to little Tomas? Or would the punishment be worse? I knew what my own father's reaction would be towards such careless behaviour.

Joren had sprung to his feet, but not in anger. In seconds, he'd been by his son's side, helping him up, brushing the dirt from his knees.

'Are you hurt? Went down hard enough to break the ground.' His voice was tender, but light. Concern concealed behind humour.

Tomas had smiled. 'I'm OK. Sorry about the water.'

Joren had thrown his arm round his son's shoulder and squeezed him tightly while I had stood frozen at the sight of them laughing.

My father would have forced me on to my hands and knees to drink the spilled water from the ground like a dog.

I've only ever known one family. It had never occurred to me there was another way of being, and the open

127

affection between Joren and Tomas continues to astound me. What's more, Joren has extended the same kindness to me: when I make mistakes I'm not punished, I'm educated; when I fail, I'm picked up and encouraged on. He's folding me firmly into his family so that I'm beginning to believe I'm part of it.

Even Clara is slowly warming to me. I know she'd never admit to it, but she can't disguise the fondness in her eyes when she talks to me, or more often scolds me, and I wonder what my life would have been like if she'd been my mother.

There is so much joy and love in this small corner of the world.

And still the voice tells me to run.

I ignore it. After all, I'm useful to Joren. And if bandits find their way here, I can defend my new family better than they could possibly imagine. I'm going to stay. I want to stay. I'm happy here.

Why would I ever leave?

The only rest I get is when Joren travels to the nearest settlement every week to deliver crops to the tradesmen. When I first arrived he offered to take me too, but I was reluctant to risk being seen by unfriendly eyes, and since then he's not asked again.

Of course, it's only rest from working the land. Clara always has chores for me to do – today we're baking bread – and we work together in a respectful, easy silence. I think she likes having some female companionship and passes her wisdom to me as though I was her daughter. Her exterior may be all prickles, but beneath it is such wit and warmth, and teasing a rare smile from her is worth a thousand treasures.

Sometimes, though, the silence allows too many unwanted thoughts to creep in. Thoughts of the life I ran from. It's been nearly six months. Does Grace ever think of me? Does Bronn? I don't want to think of them, or of my father's failure to protect the islands from bandits. I want to pretend there aren't horrors waiting out there for me, want to forget the prince I was supposed to marry, the sham of an alliance we were supposed to make. I wonder what my father will tell the King about me . . . no. No, I don't want to wonder, or imagine; I want to forget, and I pound the dough, kneading it with the full force of my denial.

When the lunch is made and Tomas has been called for several times, Clara turns to me with a sigh. 'Go and fetch him, would you? No doubt he's down in the meadow finding some rodent to rescue.'

I laugh, because that sounds just like Tomas, and with a promise to be back soon I wander out into the heady midday air.

The meadow smells sweeter than honey and I inhale its intoxicating perfume as I stroll over to where Tomas is sitting among the blooms.

I kneel down beside him. 'You're wanted.'

He turns his beautiful face to me and beams. 'Look.' And he holds up a small piece of wood.

Carved into it is a profile. A very familiar one. Mine. 'Do you like it?'

I slowly take it from him, unable to believe what I'm looking at. 'You did this?'

Tomas nods enthusiastically. 'It's you.'

'I can tell. It's amazing. I didn't know you could do this.'

He shrugs. 'I can teach you if you want. But you'll have to use a knife and Mama says they're dangerous because they're sharp.'

I look at the small blade in his hand, half blunt with age, and can't help but smile. 'I'll try. But you'll have to show me another time; right now your mother wants you to come and eat.'

I'm about to stand up when I catch sight of it and freeze. Across the meadow, using the height of the flowers for cover, a she-wolf is prowling towards us, her intent clear. We're lunch.

'Give me your knife,' I whisper, gesturing to Tomas to keep as still as possible.

He's seen our hunter too, and I can sense his fear as he presses the weapon into my hand.

'Be careful,' he says, curling his fingers into the folds of my skirt as I position myself in front of him.

The shot's not a difficult one; I've hit far smaller targets much further away. But if this dull blade doesn't do its part, we're going to be in trouble.

The knife feels comforting in my grip, like my body has been incomplete without it. Tending the earth is satisfying, but this feels *right*. The realisation shakes me slightly, but there isn't time to dwell on it. I quickly take aim and throw fast. The knife buries itself firmly into the animal's chest before she drops to the ground with a yelp. Exhaling with relief, I turn to Tomas, who's staring at me with a whole new degree of awe.

'Wait here. I'm going to check she's dead.'

I move cautiously through the crops, until I reach the she-wolf's body. She's emaciated, which makes sense; she'd have to be starving to target humans. I stretch out to retrieve the knife but hesitate as I do so. I'm not certain she's dead.

She must be, because my aim was direct to her heart, but there's still something there. The barely discernable hum of life buzzes around her body. I've sensed this before, in birds, in people – the last whispers of life that cling to a body once they've died. It always takes a moment before that goes, but this is stronger than I've ever felt before. It feels like, if I just knew how, I could reach out for that life and tug it back entirely.

'Don't.'

I look up at Tomas in surprise. 'What?'

He's walking towards me, confident that our predator is no threat, and yet he still looks afraid. 'Don't bring it back.'

'You feel it too?' I thought I was the only one ever to notice this strange sensation.

Tomas nods. 'It's like knotted threads that you want to untangle and put neatly back in place.'

I'm astounded. 'Have you tried?'

The look he gives me tells me he has, but unsuccessfully. 'It doesn't always happen. But sometimes when an animal dies it leaves something behind.'

A spark of energy, a remnant of life, even in death.

'Who taught you this? Can Joren feel it too?'

Tomas shakes his head. 'Only me. And now you. It's magic.'

A memory stirs to life, of a silver moonbird, broken, dying. Of how I wrapped my hands round it and willed it to live. How it had recovered before my father's fist crushed through bone and breath. And I wonder.

I stare at his open eyes – full of innocence, free from questions – and almost choke on the rush of affection that rises in me. 'I think you're right.'

To have found someone so like me, from his love of healing to this, brings such a strange reassurance. I no longer feel alone.

A voice shouting our names in frustration reminds me that Clara is waiting for us. 'Come on,' I say, wiping his knife clean on the she-wolf's fur. 'We'd better get home before your mother decides to eat us for lunch.'

As we walk through the field an odd thought occurs to me. 'Tomas, have you ever wanted to go west?'

He shakes his head. 'No, I like it here.'

I nod, squeezing the hand he's wrapped round mine, and turn my head westwards. It's foolish to dream of venturing into such dangerous unknowns. I don't need to go anywhere. I've found everything I need right here.

And yet, when my chores are complete, I sneak back out to the meadow, where the she-wolf's body still lies, a haze of flies hovering over her. It's been a long time since I cut open a bird or a rat, and I need, *need*, to know what that was, that energy that felt so tangible.

This time I use the blade that Bronn gave me, and it cuts through fur and skin without hesitation. Carefully I fold back flesh, exposing the soft mass of organs beneath, and exhale with wonder. It is a beautiful mess. I want to map it out, make charts like my father did of the islands, learn the routes that life flows through to make a body come alive.

The she-wolf is much easier to explore than a tiny bird, and I root around, identifying the stomach, the liver and the kidneys, all remembered from Milligan's teachings. I have to crack the ribcage apart to find the heart, and wonder at how such a small thing can be hurt by so much. A blade, a loss, a word. Would mine still look so whole, or is it covered in scars beneath my chest?

I dig further, because there is no trace yet of the energy, the magic I saw earlier. I know Tomas warned me away from it, but I tasted it, the power. Maybe I shouldn't have wanted to bring the she-wolf back, but I did. I do. And that hunger for knowledge drives me on as I take the animal apart, piece by piece, in my search for answers.

'Marianne?'

I hadn't heard him approaching, and spin round in shock.

Tomas is looking at me in a way he never has before. Like he's afraid of me.

I see the scene through his eyes: the gore, the scattered innards, the bone in my hand, the blood on my skin. And I'm ashamed.

'Tomas,' I say, not knowing quite how my sentence is going to finish. 'I'm sorry.'

I put the bone back down, and wipe my hands on the grass.

'What are you doing?' he says, trying to peer round me as I stand to block the sight.

Deciding it's best not to lie, I say, 'I wanted to learn.' I step towards him, wanting to draw his vision away from what was once the she-wolf.

'About the magic?' His voice is small and he can't bring himself to look me in the eye.

'Yes, about the magic, but also the body. So if anything ever happened to someone I care about, I could heal them.'

Tomas is quiet a moment more. 'Would you heal me? If I got hurt?'

Oh, this boy. 'Of course. You're the first person I'd heal. Because I love you.'

He does look at me then, his warm eyes willing to forgive, and he reaches out to touch the freckles on my face. 'We match, don't we?'

I raise my fingers towards the freckles on his, red where mine are brown, but see the blood stains on my skin and stop short of touching him. 'We do.'

'Because we're family, aren't we?'

Wrapping my arm protectively round him, I plant a kiss on top of his head. 'We are. Now come on, it's getting late.'

I guide him back inside, gently suggesting we don't mention any of this to his parents. I will come back to bury the she-wolf later. I shouldn't have done what I did. Shouldn't have risked getting caught. Shouldn't have exposed Tomas to such a sight.

But all I can think is how disappointed I am that I was interrupted.

I sleep well in the cottage, the bed Clara made up for me soft and warm, the stillness that comes from being away from the sea so calming. Long hours of physical labour followed by good food leave me exhausted, and the security that comes from a sense of belonging lures me into deep sleep, far beyond the reach of dreams.

So when I wake in the middle of the night, in need of a glass of water, it takes a few moments to push past the groggy confusion and for my eyes to adapt to the gloom – just in time to see a glint on the knife poised to plunge into my neck.

All senses suddenly painfully alert, I roll out of the way and fall off the bed. My attacker loses his balance at my unexpected movement, but is quick to jump up, lunging towards me, swinging the blade in the hope of catching me.

But my fear makes me fast. I duck his attacks, which come with frantic speed, and run to where my own knives lie carelessly out of reach. I've grown complacent.

Snatching them up, I'm able to launch an attack of my own, and we dance around the room, twisting and turning to avoid fatal blows. My mind is growing clearer with every second and I don't believe this is any ordinary bandit. He is too light on his feet, too quick, too skilled.

And then the moonlight streams through the window revealing his face, confirming my nightmare.

It's Briggs.

I should have kept running.

Briggs is struggling, though, because he wasn't expecting me to fight back. He will adjust quickly but I have a momentary advantage.

I punch him in the face. Hard. It sends him staggering back, and before he can regain his footing I kick him in the guts, then in the jaw, then the groin. Briggs splutters as he tries to catch his breath, but I'm not stopping. He tries to lunge for me once more, and I swing my knife out, slicing him straight across his face. He howls with pain, but rather than retaliate he turns and flees, leaping out of my window and disappearing into the night. He always was a coward.

Stunned, I wonder if I should follow him. He'll most likely return, this time with others and I don't want any harm to come to . . .

My heart stops.

I run out of my room, straight into the kitchen – where Joren lies in a pool of his own blood. I slip in it as I racc to his side and cry out when I see the open throat, the lifeless eyes where once there was such warmth. I force my grief down, and run to Tomas's room.

I didn't know a heart could scream until mine does, confronted with the sight of the small boy murdered while he slept. As I lift Tomas into my arms the noise that escapes me is feral. My sorrow knows no boundaries. His perfect face is pale, his body forever frozen in boyhood, and I stroke his soft hair, cradling my sweet

Tomas, willing him back to me. My senses desperately search for any thread of life clinging to his body, but he's gone. Utterly gone. There's nothing I can do to bring him back, and the pain of such loss is an unbearable agony.

Above my sobbing, I hear a wounded groan. Gently I lie Tomas back down and follow the noise into Joren and Clara's room.

Clara has been stabbed, several times by the looks of things, and she lies on the floor, cut down even as she was running towards the danger. Running to protect her son. Her breathing rattles as she drowns in her own blood and I hurry to her side, resting her head in my lap, my tears falling freely beside her.

Her eyes meet mine. 'Tomas?'

I shake my head, and a single tear spills down her face. 'He didn't suffer,' I say, hoping to lessen her pain, knowing it's not possible.

Clara raises her hand a little, and moves it to rest on my burnt wrist. She gives me a look, all at once telling me she knows I've kept secrets from her, and forgiving me in the same moment. 'Make them pay.'

I nod, holding her head while life abandons her for ever, and as she finally slips away something inside me snaps. Grief bleeds into rage. Consuming, blinding rage. I get to my feet and run.

It doesn't matter that I'm in my nightdress, that it's

138

dark or that I'm unarmed. Clara's words ring loudly in my ears. 'Make them pay.' And I will. I swear I'll make Briggs pay.

He might have a head start, but I know this island, these fields, and fuelled by hatred I hunt my prey. There is no sense to my thoughts, no skill to my quest, just a fierce instinct to find him, hurt him. He will suffer as they did. As I do.

From his tracks I can tell Briggs is heading towards the coast, but he's taken an indirect route. I know a better one. I can cut him off. He won't see me coming.

The world is silent as I run. I'm aware only of my pounding heart as I sprint through the trees. Darkness has me in its unrelenting grip. Revenge is my mistress and I will be obedient.

I see Briggs now, through the branches, running parallel to me, and in a heartbeat I switch course. I plough into him, the force of the collision knocking us both to the ground. I sense his shock that I'm here, and he tries to throw me off, tries to fight, but I'm hitting him, hitting him, hitting him. I'm blinded by white fury, driven by the agony of loss. He stole their lives, he took my future and I have nothing left but this need for his pain. I hate him. I hate all of them. How could they do this? Why, *why*, would he do this?

A noise penetrates the violent fog clouding my mind. A roar. No, more visceral than that: a shriek, a howl, a wail. Slowly the madness lifts, like waking from a terrible dream. The sound is coming from me.

I'm still hitting Briggs, straddling his body. But he no longer retaliates. He doesn't move at all, his face barely recognisable. I stare at the blood, both his and mine, and hold my hands up in horror. I hadn't known they were capable of inflicting such damage, but there is no doubt they're responsible. I'm shaking now, and I slide off him on to the earth, consumed by shock.

I've killed him.

I am no better than the father I fled; my scream of anguish echoes through the trees.

Clambering to my feet, half numb with grief, I stumble back towards the place I'd called home. I leave Briggs where I've murdered him, unmourned, for the wolves to find. And as I walk I weep for the family I have condemned, and cry until there are no tears left.

I should have run.

When I return to the cottage I pause. All the warmth of this place I once loved is gone, its heart ripped out. I stand there, the night air brushing my blood-soaked nightdress, utterly lost.

I want to lie down, give up, fall asleep and never wake. It would be so, so easy.

But then I think of Joren, my beloved Tomas and Clara, and I know I can't. I won't.

Night gives way to day as I dig their grave. I make just one, wanting to rest them together, in each other's arms for eternity. It is difficult to drag Joren and Clara out of the house and into the pit, and I leave blood trails everywhere. Tomas is light as air, and I stay holding him for a long time before I'm ready to say goodbye. Dearest Tomas. You did not deserve such an end.

I broke my promise to him. Told him I'd heal him if he got hurt. I would do anything to bring him back now.

In my hand I hold the carving he made of me. I look happy. The girl this place made me. Before the she-wolf. Before Briggs. I don't recognise her any more. Reaching down, I place it on Tomas's chest. That Marianne is gone – she lived with them, she died with them.

When they are all settled in their final bed I cover them with the earth Joren loved so much. Now he will become one with the land he treasured. I pick some windflowers and scatter them on top of the grave and then I sit there crying until the sun sets. Light, life and love are all extinguished here – no more magic to be found.

The guilt, the loss, it is all unbearable. I should never have come here, and certainly should not have stayed.

I allowed myself to believe in a fantasy, but now I see the ugly reality. There's no such thing as 'safe' anywhere; no such thing as freedom. Not for me, not for anyone.

It's time to wake up, Marianne.

I sit up all night in the cottage, the cold shard of hatred that has lodged in my heart causing me to shiver, though the night is warm. I have been such a fool. A fool to believe I could escape my father so easily. A fool to believe I could stay here. A fool to believe nothing bad would come of it. And I hate myself for it.

Something has broken inside me. For the first time I truly wanted to hurt someone, wanted to punish them and I did, losing all control, surrendering to the powerful instinct without question. I can still feel it within me – wild, unpredictable – and it terrifies me.

'Make them pay,' Clara said. But she didn't mean for me to lose myself to the darkness. I'll need to be stronger than ever if I'm to keep my promise to her. Because she didn't want revenge just for her family. She was telling me to fight for all of them, for every family who had been savaged like hers. Clara knew I was more than I said, and she trusted me to go to war for the islanders.

And if that means going to war with the crew I once called family, then so be it.

I won't let Clara down again.

Today I buried my innocence with my true family. I know that Briggs won't be the last to come for me. My father will send more. But this time I'll be ready.

And so I wait.

It's when the moon is at its brightest that I hear the softest tread passing over the threshold.

Silently I'm on my feet, the knife in my hand itching to spill blood, and when the intruder enters the room my blade is immediately at their throat.

Only trouble is, theirs is at mine too.

We stand for a moment at an impasse, and my heart sinks when I see who it is. Anyone but her.

'This isn't quite the welcome I hoped for,' she says, but lowers her blade.

I hesitate before lowering mine. 'I never thought you'd be the one sent to kill me.'

And Grace laughs.

It isn't a cruel sound, more a tired one.

'I'm not here to kill you,' she says, striding past me and sitting at the table.

I watch her uncertainly, still clutching my knife. 'Are you alone?'

'Of course.'

'What do you want?'

Her dark eyes glimmer like the ocean's depths. 'I told you at your Initiation that whatever happened I was with you.'

'Really? I don't recall you stopping my father from beating me and I certainly haven't seen you since.'

Grace sighs. 'Well, I wouldn't have been much use to you dead, would I?'

I'm nowhere near believing her. 'What makes you think I'd trust you for a second? Your loyalty lies with my father and I'm far too well acquainted with the pleasure you all take from cold-blooded murder. I want nothing to do with *any* of you.'

'My loyalty has never been to the Viper,' she spits with anger. 'He is a butcher and I've despised having to take orders from him. But some things are more important than what I want.'

I frown. 'Such as?'

Grace doesn't answer, though, to my frustration. Instead she looks at me, confusion spreading over her sharp features. Perhaps she no longer recognises the girl standing before her. I certainly don't. 'Look, if I had wanted to betray you, it would have been easy. I could have given up the location of our boat, but I didn't. I told the Captain we'd landed in a different cove altogether; I wanted you to escape. And I came as soon as I could. I wanted to know the Captain's intentions once you fled.' She pauses, as though what she has to say next will be hard for me to hear. 'You're not safe here. He's sending assassins to every island to bring you back.'

So he doesn't just want me dead then. 'Yeah, thanks, but I got that message when Briggs came for me last night.'

I can tell from her surprise she thought she'd found me first, and then her eyes linger on my bloodied knuckles. 'You killed him?'

I don't want to answer. Saying it out loud will make it too real, and I try to hide my hands in shame. 'He murdered the family I was staying with.'

It's as though pieces click together for Grace, my anger suddenly explained. 'I'm sorry,' she says. 'That I didn't get here sooner.' But she sounds as impressed as she is shocked at what I've done, and it bothers me. I don't want her respect. Not for this.

145

'I'm sorry I ever stayed.'

We're silent for a while, and though I move to sit opposite her at the table, my knife remains firmly in my grip. She still hasn't given me her reasons for remaining a Snake so long. Until she does, I cannot trust her.

'What do you plan to do?' Grace says eventually. When I raise my eyes to meet hers she smiles. 'You won't just give up. I know you too well.'

Oh, really? 'I'm going to the First Isle.'

I don't think Grace could have looked more startled if I'd said I was heading back to the *Maiden*. 'Why?'

Because things cannot be allowed to continue like this. Someone has to help the islanders. If the Viper isn't prepared to protect the people, then his daughter will.

'I need to talk with my fiancé. I think his father needs some help.'

'Then I'm coming with you.'

I suppose I could have refused, could have told Grace to leave me in peace, but I didn't want to. Though I still refuse to trust her, I also can't bear to be alone right now.

The following dawn, I sit by the grave, searching for words to say farewell. There are none. It hurts so much to have to leave them. But I must.

Grace and I walk for two days straight to reach the small fishing port off the western coast. A gold coin crossing palms is all that's needed to secure our passage on a small fishing vessel headed for the First Isle.

The journey takes over a week, with the weather kind and the fishermen anxious to keep out of our way. Though Grace hides her Snake blacks beneath a travelling cloak, she makes sure they see enough to instill fear in them. It's a calculated risk – word of where we are could get back to my father. But it's a risk worth taking for the protection it provides. Only a fool would want to get on the wrong side of a Snake.

Grace is doing her best to regain my trust by telling me what's happened since my Initiation, and I sense an honesty about her I never did before. After such a public defiance, such an obvious failure, my father only had one choice. I have been disowned. He has given orders for any member of his crew to bring me back in whatever condition pleases them, so long as I'm alive. He wants the final punishment to be his alone. I understand. The Viper must have absolute authority, total respect from his crew, and any sign of weakness could be his undoing. Nothing says 'don't cross me' like the public slaughter of your own child.

The thought of the man I once so desperately sought approval from wishing me dead is crushing, but that pain is shoved deep down, stowed away in an inaccessible part of my being. It's there alongside the memories of Tomas and his parents, because if I stop to dwell on all

147

that I've lost, the grief will drive me mad. I must look only forward if I am to survive.

Grace doesn't mention Bronn at all, and I'm too scared to ask about him. Certainly I've done my damnedest to silence the thoughts of him that have crept unbidden to my mind since I fled the Fourth. I'm so afraid that he's dead, punished for his part in my Initiation. But if he's alive, then that means he was working with my father, which brings me no comfort either. So I find it's best to try not to think about him at all.

We have, however, spoken about Torin. It remains to be seen whether word that my father has disowned me has reached Torin and – if it has – whether he still considers me his fiancée. I'm relying on holding some sway with Torin to be allowed to speak to the King. I'm sure they don't let just anyone stroll up to his throne.

I've asked Grace what her opinion of Torin is, whether he can be trusted. She's said only that she barely knows him, but that she doesn't believe there's any love lost between the palace and my father at the moment.

'Because my father's attacking the King's Fleet?' I'd asked, causing Grace to look surprised. 'I'm not completely stupid.'

She'd given me a nod of respect. 'Yes, I doubt that's helping, though the King will only have his suspicions as to who is attacking the Fleet, not proof. The Captain is careful to leave no survivors to report back.'

And yet for all our conversations, she continues to offer no explanation as to why she's remained a member of a crew she now openly admits to despising. So while I'm willing to listen to what she has to say, I'm guarded with my own thoughts. And one evening, when she joins me on deck carrying two flagons of rum and asking more questions, my patience finally runs out.

'You don't get to hear what I've been through,' I snap when Grace pries once more into my time on the Floral Island. The wild fury whips up inside me like a storm before I'm able to rein it back under control.

Grace sighs, drinking deeply from her flagon. She says nothing and I think perhaps she's going to leave me alone, but she stays and eventually breaks the silence. 'Did you know you have a birthmark on the back of your neck?'

It's about the last thing I'm expecting her to say and it throws me off guard. 'Do I?' I touch my neck instinctively, but feel nothing.

'It's hidden by your hair, but I've glimpsed it several times over the years, though I never get used to seeing it.'

I remember the way she'd behaved oddly the day I got engaged, when I suggested putting my hair up, and wonder if that's why. 'Lots of people have birthmarks.'

'True. But only a few bear the mark of the crescent moon.'

'OK, you've lost me,' I say, and, though I laugh, it's a nervous sound.

Grace sighs, and runs her fingers through her hair. I've never seen her looking so uncomfortable. 'You want to know why I've stayed with the Captain all these years?'

I nod, unsure how this is all connected.

'I'm from the Twelfth Isle.'

I stare at her in disbelief. 'You're a *Westerner*?'

She nods proudly. 'I'm a Guardian of the Royal Bloodline.'

She says it like it's something I should have heard of. But I haven't, even though I know my history well. I know all about the war two hundred years ago that ripped the Twelve Isles in half. How after centuries of the kingdoms existing harmoniously alongside each other, the Western King, Gormand the Destroyer, grew jealous of the East's riches, its bountiful mines and thriving trade. Greed corrupted Gormand and he waged war against the East. To defend his Isles and his throne, the Eastern King sent his Viper to the West. The Viper assassinated Gormand, as well as his entire family and anyone with a close allegiance to them.

But instead of this bringing peace, without a ruling family anarchy descended over the Western Isles, plunging them into a lawless chaos. War raged pointlessly as the Eastern King tried to claim the Western throne for himself, with neither side accumulating anything other than losses until the Eastern King retreated. Little has been heard from the Western Isles ever since.

Certainly nothing about guardians of a royal bloodline.

I'm unsure where to start. 'The Western royalty were wiped out.'

Her eyes sparkle with excitement, the relief of finally sharing her secret apparent. 'No. There was a survivor. A servant helped the youngest prince hide, and then took him far away to keep him safe. That servant was my ancestor and my people have striven to protect the bloodline ever since.'

'Your people? Grace, this is crazy.' Where is all this coming from?

'I know how it sounds, but it's the truth. We lost the last known descendant just over twenty years ago when I was still a child. She just disappeared one day and it's been my life's purpose to discover what happened to her. That's why I joined the *Maiden*, to go places I couldn't otherwise, to expand the search.'

A knot is forming in my chest. 'Why are you telling me this? Why now?'

Grace fiddles nervously with a thread on her sleeve, before she takes a deep breath and looks me right in the eye. 'Because I think you're the last of the bloodline. In fact, I'm certain of it.'

My mouth parts but no words come out. Eventually I manage a simple, 'That's insane.'

Grace smiles, a knowing look on her face as if I'm reacting precisely how she expected. 'I joined the *Maiden* when I was sixteen, my training as a Guardian complete. Though my talent was enough to get me on board, your father didn't like me one bit. But I worked hard to gain the crew's respect, knowing how important it was for me to integrate myself. And then I had my Initiation.' She pauses and sighs. 'Adler always has been a perceptive bastard, seeing all our weaknesses. I thought I'd been clever, hidden mine away. But for my final test he gathered his most senior Snakes, including Cleeve, and challenged me to fight them. To keep my place on the ship I had to beat my peers, humiliating them publicly, undoing all my efforts to be accepted. By the time I was done I knew I'd have no friends left, and I was right. But it was worth it. I was a Snake. Now my real work could begin. But do you know what my first mission was? To look after you.'

Now her smile reaches her eyes as she looks warmly at me. 'I was so mad to be stuck with the Captain's brat and I'd almost resolved to leave the ship and continue my search in some other way. But then one day we were practising your fighting. You were dressed ridiculously for such work, and I snapped. I told you to strip down to your undergarments, and to tie your hair out of your face. If we were going to train, we were going to do it properly. That was the day I saw your birthmark for the first time and everything changed. I had been looking for a woman, and somehow I'd stumbled upon her child instead. Because there could be no doubt. Every known member of the Western royalty has borne the mark of the crescent moon.'

I remember that day. I had been desperate to impress her. I was just eleven, and looked up to Grace with almost blind adoration. I was so excited my father had considered me worthy to be tutored by her that I would have stripped naked and cut all my hair off if she'd asked me. It stings to realise training me was a punishment and not an honour. I have to force myself to focus on the most pressing part of her story, the part where I'm supposedly a royal Westerner. 'You do know it's not possible?' I ask as gently as I'm able, because she seems so sincere. 'You know who my father is.'

'But do you know who your mother was?' She has me there and she knows it. 'Who's to say your father didn't unknowingly fall for the Western Princess, the woman lost two decades ago?'

'It's a big assumption,' I say, still not believing it's possible. But a seed of doubt has been planted.

'Perhaps. But what I do know is the last confirmed sighting of her was on the Eighth Isle. Then, somehow, she disappeared. No one really knows what happened, and of course the Guardians never stopped searching, but since then all we've had are rumours, one of which spoke of her being seen with a man and child. That was nearly eighteen years ago. And now here you are bearing the mark.'

'You think that man was my father? It's impossible. There's no way he'd ever cross into Western waters, let alone set foot on the islands.'

Grace doesn't seem bothered by my logic. 'I don't pretend to have all the answers. All I know is you bear the mark. You are descended from Western royalty.'

My scepticism isn't ready to be silenced just yet. 'Don't you think this is all just a bit convenient? You're looking for royalty and there I am, right on the ship you chose?'

She ignores my sarcasm. 'What you call convenience, I call fate.'

I take some deep breaths. 'Suppose you're right, just suppose,' I hasten to add, 'what would you want with me?'

'The Guardians have protected the descendants for centuries in the belief that one day the throne will be reclaimed and peace brought to the Western Isles.' She sees the look of shock on my face and continues quickly. 'But it's become more than that for me. You asked me why I remained a Snake? I stayed for you. I've taught you everything I know, have watched over and protected you. But you're not a child any more. I'm so proud of the woman you've become, Marianne. Whether you want to reclaim your throne or not, my allegiance, my loyalty is to you. Wherever this journey takes us, I will be with you to the end.'

And she reaches for my hand, wrapping it in her own with such affection it almost breaks me.

What do I say to something like this? To something most probably nonsensical, but horribly rooted in enough uncertainty to make me wonder? It's clear she believes it, though, and I realise that's all that matters.

The anger I've been directing at her falls away like a blanket slipping from my shoulders. It was never meant for her in the first place, and I no longer have the energy to keep pushing her away. Especially after such a pledge of devotion. 'And I'm glad you're here.'

'Me too,' she says with a smile brighter than I've seen in a long while. 'But I don't think you should tell anyone about all this. Not until we're certain who we can trust.'

I have no intention of repeating such nonsense to anyone, but don't want to hurt her by saying so. 'The only thing we need to discuss with the King is how we can help him.'

'You think he'll listen?'

'You think he won't?' When Grace answers with a sceptical frown I sigh. 'All I know is the people are in need of protection. The King can't give them that while my father's destroying his Fleet. That's where we come in.'

'That's assuming he wants to help his people.'

Her cynicism reminds me of Clara, her suggestion that the King cares nothing for his subjects, only for himself.

So as we enter the waters surrounding the First Isle, my insides knot. Perhaps Grace is right, perhaps the King won't listen to what I have to say. But still, I have to try.

The ports here are always bustling with life, ships of all sizes and from all islands here for business, and today is no exception – it's heaving.

The First Isle – which for a long time went by no other name until the King insisted we start calling it the 'King's Isle' – is nothing like any of the other five Eastern Isles. For a start it's about four times the size of the others, and is the most industrial and heavily populated. The pulsing heart that keeps the rest alive. Tall chimneys decorate the skyline, pumping smoke of varying colours into the air, signalling that business in the many factories located in this southern peninsula is yet to be affected by the discord elsewhere. Seeing the smoke comes as somewhat of a relief. I'd half expected all industry to have ground to a halt given the state of the other Isles.

The First is the one island my father allowed me to visit and I have twice before been permitted to peruse the markets in this part of the town. Despite my armed escorts, I always felt enchanted not only by the fragrances of spice and flowers that filled the air, but also by the traders themselves who represent the beautiful diversity of the Isles.

A long time ago, it was easy to see which island people belonged to. Those from the Second had an earthy complexion, their skin ruddy from the farming their island is famous for, while the Fourth islanders were as alluring as their flowers. Those that raised livestock on the vast plains of the Fifth were sturdy pale souls, like their beasts, while the inhabitants of the Sixth Isle were as intimidating and as hard as the rocks they mined. The Third islanders always kept a low profile – even now they don't attend the market, preferring to use couriers to bring their goods – but their skin was as dark as the trees they carved. But over many centuries people moved around, fell in love, resettled, so that now it is almost impossible to tell a person's origin simply from the colour of their skin. My father always said such variety made it easier for assassins to move around unnoticed, to blend in and never stand out. But to me it spoke of the love and respect all the islands had for each other, that they were bound together by more than just the ocean.

Years ago, Bronn drew me pictures of the islands, so I could visualise each one's unique terrain. Though all of the islands are self-sufficient to a point, most of the crops are grown on the Second Isle – Fallow Island – and Bronn drew its fields of fertile ground nestled among moorlands. He drew the paths where water had carved its way down and through, pooling in some places, rushing in others. My favourite image was of a still lake of clear water reflecting the full moon so perfectly it looked as though it had fallen to earth.

His pictures of the Black and the Floral Islands were among the reasons why I desperately wanted to visit them, and it seems strange that so much has happened since I used to lie in my hammock imagining what they'd be like. All the horror. All the joy. All the pain. Still, his drawings will always be magical to me: the darkness of the forests, the beauty of the meadows.

The only other island I've not been to is the Fifth, which Bronn depicted in just one sketch: small woollen animals roaming the hard grazing land against the backdrop of a mountain range, camouflaged by mist swirling around them. He said there wasn't much else to see, but I liked to think the island simply guarded its own secrets.

For the First he sketched the settlements: swordsmiths busy making weapons; shipwrights building and repairing vessels at the dockyards; the fishermen hauling their catches to shore. He managed to capture the constant activity of the bustling market with a few deft strokes of charcoal.

The market sells everything the Isles have to offer. If you want to purchase fruit, vegetables or any kind of cereal, the Fallow Island will oblige. If you're after cloth, then visit the traders from Mist Island; their beasts provide soft wool that the islanders often dye using extracts from the flowers from the Fourth. Before the mining disasters, the Sixth Isle sent crystal and other rocks and minerals to the First, both to keep the kingdom's vaults full, and to turn into anything from tools to gunpowder. Most of these wares can be purchased at one or other of the many stalls.

All the islands are brimming with talent, and I'm always astounded at what craftsmen can do with raw materials. Food, perfume, clothing, jewellery, decorations – it all can be found in this gathering of wonders.

But I won't be wandering the market today. Instead I will be seeing the palace for the first time.

The boat we've been travelling on isn't huge, so the fishermen guide it to one of the smaller jetties where the man who throws over the rope smiles at us as we disembark. Grace doesn't return his smile, instead slipping a coin into his hand.

'You didn't see us, understood?' she says, and the man nods in agreement, biting the coin to check its authenticity.

It's good to be back on land again, but it doesn't take long for me to realise how things have changed since my last visit several years ago. Though the streets have always been bustling, now it isn't only traders milling about. There are beggars wherever I look, desperate for a scrap of food. Crowds of travellers arriving off boats from the other five isles are herded together by soldiers, who prevent them from passing beyond the edges of town. There is no fight in these people; they simply look defeated. Confused. Unsure where they should be, where they belong. Instead of music being played in the streets, now children's cries can be heard above the shouts of traders and the barking of dogs. My heart sinks. What is the King doing to help?

Grace and I navigate the narrow streets with ease, Grace knowing exactly where to go, but as we turn a corner it soon becomes apparent getting out of the town isn't going to be simple. Stationed at the road leading towards the country residence of the King are armed palace guards, turning away anyone who doesn't have a legitimate reason to proceed inland.

'Well, we wouldn't want things to be too easy,' Grace says with a smile.

We approach the crowd petitioning to continue their journeys, and wait with some impatience until we reach the soldiers, who raise their spears to block our path.

'No new arrivals to the island may stay,' the soldier closest to us says. 'Return to your vessel and make your way home.'

He's clearly been parroting that sentence for weeks; there is no meaning behind it any more.

'We have business with the King,' I say, causing the soldier to give me a look of disbelief.

'Move on,' he says. 'I haven't got time for this.'

Grace steps forward now, and slowly the soldier takes in what she's wearing. He swallows so deeply I'm concerned he might be sick.

'Do you know who I am?' she says in her most menacing voice. 'Do you know who I work for? Are you sure you want to try to stand in my way?'

It's clear from how quickly the blood drains from his face that the soldier knows exactly what crew Grace belongs to.

'And we'll need transport,' she adds, sensing she has the upper hand.

He doesn't look pleased but clicks his fingers, prompting another guard to bring two horses over and pass us their reins.

'You may proceed.'

Grace glares at the soldier for a moment. 'If you, or any of your little friends think it would be wise to speak of my presence here, I should warn you I have a fondness for removing loose tongues. Understand?'

The soldier nods his head, trembling slightly now. Interesting. I knew the *Maiden*'s crew were feared by the islanders, but by the King's men? Things are far worse than I imagined. The crowd watch in interest, unable to hear exactly what's being said, but loving that the soldiers are rattled.

Once Grace is satisfied her threats have been taken seriously, we mount our horses, though I do so with some trepidation. I've only ridden once before, with much assistance, on a small mule. This beast is far larger and more spirited, and when I squeeze his sides he's quick to spring to a gallop, as eager to escape the town as we are. I have to draw on all my balance not to fall off, my fingers wound in his mane for support.

When we've put sufficient distance between us and the town we allow the horses a rest, bringing them to a walk along the bumpy cobbled road. It's as far inland as I've ever been here. The industrial terrain of the town slowly peters out before merging into woodland and then eventually rolling hills. Cottages dot the landscape and children play in the street, but at the sound of our approach mothers hurry out to take their children inside. The roads are quiet – too quiet – and though Grace doesn't say anything I can sense her unease matches my own. Fear is a plague and it seems even the First Isle is infected.

'Do you think word will get back to my father that we're here?' I ask Grace when the silence becomes too uncomfortable.

Grace nods. 'They'll all be willing to sell us out for a

price. But hopefully by then we'll be long gone. If we keep moving, we'll be fine.'

Well, that's reassuring.

After riding for most of the day we round a corner and the palace comes into view, its pale stone reflecting the sun back at us so that I'm momentarily blinded. When my eyes adjust, my heart sinks at the sight before me. Nestled in its own valley, the vast castle must surely have once looked magical, with a waterfall spilling down the cliffs behind it before running straight into a natural moat. The six island pennants hang from the turrets, alongside the collective Eastern Isles' flag, and the blue and green royal standard. But they are tattered and faded, and the flowers that once filled the valley have withered and died. Though it's far from a ruin, the air of neglect is unmistakable, and perhaps it's not surprising that the King has done nothing to help his people's plight when he seems unable to care for his own home.

Our horses whinny gleefully at the prospect of returning to their stables, but though the drawbridge is down, the portcullis is firmly in place and remains so even as we are greeted by more unfriendly-looking guards, who question us endlessly through the latticed grille before making us wait. Eventually word returns that our request to enter has been granted, and once the portcullis is raised we're permitted into the courtyard where our horses are taken away along with our weapons, before we're led through into an arched passageway.

Courtiers in fine garments move briskly out of our way as we're escorted deeper into the castle, and I notice that while most avoid looking at Grace, presumably terrified by her mere presence, many openly stare at me, not bothering to hide their disdain at my shabby appearance. My dress made me stand out on the *Maiden* and it makes me stand out here. The only place I ever fitted in was with a loving family who made space in their lives for me just as I was. My heart twists tight at the thought.

There is a further wait outside two imposing wooden doors, which are carved with an intricate map of the Eastern Isles, before they open and we are summoned in.

The King sits directly ahead of us, his throne raised on a marble platform separated from the floor by five deep steps. Like his son, he is younger than I expected and far more attractive, his face clean-shaven, his skin luminous from the sun, and only when we stand at the base of his platform can I see the lines around his eyes that betray his age. I struggle to reconcile his image with the one I'd pictured whenever I thought of him and my father concocting their dark schemes.

'Your Majesty,' Grace says and bows deeply. I follow suit.

'Grace,' the King says as if they're old acquaintances. I presume my father must have talked of his crew to such an extent that the King feels a familiarity towards them. 'And, Marianne, welcome. This is an unexpected delight.' Nothing in his tone suggests sincerity. 'Captain Adler gave me no warning to expect your company, so I confess I'm left wondering what I can do for you?'

'Forgive our intrusion,' Grace continues, 'but Marianne was keen to see your son. He extended an open invitation to her when he dined aboard the *Maiden*.'

It's possible I'm imagining it, but I think the King looks relieved.

'Alas, Prince Torin is not currently at court,' the King says, and I have to mask my disappointment. 'A fact I'm sure he will deeply regret when he learns of your visit.'

He nods to his guards, and they move closer, ready to escort us back out of the hall. He certainly seems anxious to be rid of us.

I step forward. 'Actually, Your Majesty, it was you I wished to speak with.'

The King raises his hand slightly and the guards stop moving. He regards me with undisguised suspicion. 'Was it indeed? Has your father made you his messenger now?'

I hesitate, wondering how much to say. Everything I've seen since we arrived – from the chaos at the harbour to the unfriendly welcome here – has made me less certain that I should have come. But at least the King seems oblivious to the fact that I've been disowned. Apparently my father didn't want anyone else to know about that embarrassment.

'No, I've come of my own volition.'

The King's eyes flick from me to Grace as he weighs up the truth of my words. 'I see. Well then, speak.'

The air is thick with mistrust and my hopes are rapidly sinking. 'Your Majesty, it is a private matter. May we talk alone?'

He stares at me for a long time before he nods. 'We will, you and I. But on one condition.' He points at Grace. 'For the duration of your visit she remains behind lock and key. I'm not foolish enough to allow such a skilled assassin freedom in my home. You have my word she will be treated well.'

So he's looked me over and deemed me to be no threat to him. Though part of me is sick to death of people misjudging me like this, right now it's a good thing. I want him to underestimate me. I glance over at Grace, who nods slightly to show her willingness. I doubt a locked door is of too much concern to her anyway.

'Agreed.'

'Good, then let us dine together.'

Grace gives me one last look before she's escorted away. A look that warns me to be careful. As if I need reminding.

I'm shown out of a different doorway to the one I entered from, and am led through to a smaller, more intimate room, the sheer opulence of which astounds me. Material possessions are a rarity on board the *Maiden* – if it has no purpose, it has no place. Quarters are cramped enough.

But here it is the opposite. Furniture is swathed in plush upholstery, crystal hangs from the ceiling, and the walls are decorated with platters of varying sizes, which appear to have been dipped in liquid gold. In the centre is a preposterously long table buried under enormous quantities of food. More extravagant still are the plates piled high with fruit made entirely of glittering jewels. Such wealth flaunted in something entirely pointless is sickening when I know that so many islanders are starving.

The King comes into the room behind me, and gestures for me to sit down. I do so, and as he sits opposite me several servants quickly provide us with wine.

'Please, help yourself to whatever appeals,' the King says, gesturing to the selection of meats and dishes, some of which are so elaborate I can't actually identify them.

I take a small bread roll, but consider it with caution. The King wouldn't be the first host to poison an unwelcome guest. Besides, I don't want to be distracted by cuisine right now, no matter how vocal my stomach has become.

The food must be safe, though, as the King fills his plate with enough to feed a large family before ordering his men to leave. Just like that I find myself alone with the ruler of the Eastern Isles.

He runs his fingers through his pale hair. 'I have to say, you're nothing like I expected.'

I can only imagine the portrayal my father has given of me. A weak but suitable daughter-in-law, inoffensive to look at and of childbearing age. 'Oh, really? Why is that?'

'I suppose I envisaged a younger female version of your father. You are altogether more pleasing.'

Which I think translates as altogether easier to manipulate.

'Your Majesty, there is nothing pleasing about what I have to discuss.' May as well just come out with it. 'My father has turned against you. The islands are no longer under any protection and the people, *your* people, are suffering. Even here there is chaos at your ports. I've come to offer my help.'

The King is silent for a moment, resting his cutlery on his plate and chewing a mouthful of meat. He washes it down with a swig of wine.

'You're here to betray your father?'

'My father no longer deserves the title of Viper. He protects no interests beyond his own.'

The King leans back in his chair and belches loudly. 'And what do you want in return for this information?'

'Nothing. I only want peace for the Isles.'

The King presses his fingers together and gives me a sickly grin. 'Don't we all?' He refills his glass with blood-red wine. 'Sadly, Marianne, you're telling me nothing new. I've long been aware of the unsanctioned killings done in my name, as have I known Adler's been siphoning off far more crystal for himself over the years than he should. For his loyalty I have overlooked such matters.'

He takes a morsel of meat dipped in sweet sauce and pops it into his mouth before sucking his fingers clean. All these years I'd believed the King and the Viper worked together for the good of the islands. The last fragments of that foolish notion are now entirely shattered. Just like my father, the King appears to care for no one but himself.

'But over the past few months my Fleet has suffered substantial losses and I don't think either of us believes the attacks were made by bandits. Of course I know your father plans to overthrow me, why else has he been ridding the waters of all possible opposition? He wants ultimate power over land and sea.'

I stare at him, astonished at his apparent indifference. 'Then what do you plan to do?'

'Your father may have the upper hand on the waves, but on land I have the advantage. With all my troops recalled he'll have one hell of a time taking my throne from me.'

My disappointment in the King is crushing, and it would be so easy to give up right now, but how dare he? How dare he care so little for his people? They are counting on him. Joren, Clara, Tomas – they were counting on him. It's clear I was mistaken to think he needed help. He's abandoned the people and barricaded himself into his palace, protecting his life above all others.

'If you knew all this,' I say, fighting to keep my voice steady, 'then why would you agree to let your son marry me?'

The King drains his goblet dry and immediately refills it. 'As a matter of fact I agreed to no such thing.' He looks at my wrist, the mark of binding there for all to see. 'It would appear your father and my son have made their own arrangements.'

The horror of the binding ceremony returns to me so vividly I wince. I can only presume my father used Torin in the hope our marriage would give him the control he needs on land. And what is Torin's part in all this? Does he wish to overthrow the King too? Is he working with my father? The thought that I endured all that pain for nothing more than some scheme my father and Torin concocted only stokes the anger already burning inside me.

I push my feelings aside. They're irrelevant right now. I'm here for one reason only, and that's to get the King's support. So I swallow my pride and bow my head subserviently.

'My apologies, Your Majesty. I had no idea.'

The King's drunk a lot of wine now; his cheeks are flushed, his eyes bloodshot. 'Though perhaps a union between royalty and Viper could be a good thing . . .'

I frown. 'You support my engagement then?'

He looks dead at me. 'No. Not to my son.' My heart starts to beat faster as the King stands up and walks round the table. When he's standing beside me he offers me his hand, and I can hardly refuse. He pulls me to my feet, and lets his fingers run up my wrist to my binding scar.

'My wife has long been in her grave. Perhaps it's time I took another.'

His grip is surprisingly tight. He's holding me in a way that's controlling rather than seductive, and as he presses himself close to me I'm no longer just angry. I'm also afraid.

'Just think,' he says, lowering his head towards mine, 'a king and his Viper queen. We would be invincible.'

His mouth is on mine before I have time to stop him, and his tongue forces its way in. I can taste how much wine he's consumed.

On instinct I push him away. I stare up at him only to see anger flashing in his eyes, humiliation at my rejection. You don't refuse a king.

'Forgive me,' I say, desperately trying to think how to salvage the situation. I cannot afford to make another powerful enemy.

The King takes a step away, considers me for a moment, and then returns to his seat. I sit back down too, and for a moment we don't move, frozen in time like a portrait.

I may be still, but inside everything's racing. My heart. My thoughts.

He is not a good man and I feel nothing but contempt for him. I wonder how many of the killings he's instructed my father to carry out have actually been to protect himself, rather than for the good of the Isles. He is as much a traitor as my father is. Worse – he's a coward, content to hide away in safety while others suffer. But the depressing reality is he's still my best hope in this murky pool of politics.

'I'm very flattered by your offer,' I say, choosing my words carefully.

'But you decline.' The King is not going to be easily placated.

'It was unexpected, that's all,' I say, hoping to stall him. 'Will you allow me some time to consider?'

Another gulp of wine is consumed before he answers. 'Very well.'

I inwardly sigh with relief. 'In the meantime,' I say, determined to reclaim this discussion, 'you still need my help. My father is out there plotting against you and destroying your Fleet. Soon he will have control of the seas, then the other islands. Then he'll come for you. Unless someone stops him. Let me be that someone.'

The King locks his fingers together, pressing them to his lips. 'How?'

'I need a ship. And the support of your Fleet. The support of your crown.'

His eyes narrow. 'You think *you're* capable of such a feat?'

I hear his doubt, his sneering condescension, and meet it head on. 'Yes.'

He considers this for a moment. 'Why?'

'Excuse me?'

'Why are you here, wanting to help me? You want peace? Run away, I'm sure you'll find some. This isn't your fight, so I'm wondering why I should trust you?'

I look him right in the eye. 'He's made it my fight.'

The King holds my gaze and I tilt my chin in defiance. I will not be the first to look away. Perhaps he senses my resolve, because finally he nods slowly. 'Very well,' he says at last. 'You may have your ship. The rest? Well, I'm sure you will allow me some time to consider?'

He's throwing my own words back at me.

'It may take a few days to make the necessary arrangements, though. For now, stay. Consider my offer. Remember, I can give some measure of assistance to a usurper. But I can give everything to my queen.'

In other words his support is entirely dependent on whether I marry him or not. 'Thank you, but I'd rather keep moving. If my father finds out I'm here, none of us will be safe.'

'Nonsense, I insist,' he says.

'And Grace?'

'She will have to enjoy our hospitality from the dungeons for the time being, but she will be well fed and unharmed.'

Though I'm unhappy at the thought of Grace trapped in such surroundings, there's little I can do about it, and I'm more than confident she can take care of herself, so accept his offer. As if I had a choice.

The King escorts me to the door, but stops me before I can open it.

'I can be a generous man, Marianne,' he says, sliding his hand round my waist. 'Come to my chamber and perhaps you could persuade me to give you the Fleet along with your ship.' And his hand rises to my breast as he leans in to kiss me again.

If he were any other man, I would break him, would step over the pieces of his body lying on the floor without a second glance. But he is the King. He has all the power here. And he knows it.

Instead I move away slightly, putting some space between us, but looking up at him with what I hope is an alluring expression. 'Perhaps tomorrow. It's been a long day,' I say, forcing as much of a smile as I can. 'I really should get some sleep.'

For a second I think he might strike me, such is the burning fury in his face, but then it's gone, replaced with a cold smile. 'Of course.'

Without any outward sign from him, guards enter the room and I find myself flanked by armed men as I'm taken away from the food I've not touched and the King I wish I hadn't.

The day's light is fading, and servants are working their way along the stone corridors, lighting candles to illuminate the gloomy space. We spiral upwards until we reach a room where the guards inform me I'm to stay. I ask after Grace but they tell me nothing, just shut the door behind me, leaving me alone.

The room isn't as grand as the others I've seen; it has no luxurious furs or velvet cushions to soften the cold stone. But there is a bed with clean blankets and I sit down on it, trying to sort through the thoughts buzzing in my head.

That was a disaster.

Does the King truly want to marry me, or does he simply want to bed me? I shudder at the memory of his touch, his unwanted advances. Could I give him what he asks for the sake of the islands? Would it be any worse than being married off to Torin by my father?

I try to imagine kissing the King again and feel nothing but revulsion stirring inside me. Then I imagine kissing Torin and simply feel nothing. And then, entirely unbidden, I imagine kissing Bronn. His lips would taste like the sea, like laughter, like a thousand secrets shared between us. Like the wildest storm and the calmest ocean. Like a field of inkbells catching the breeze.

Like betrayal.

The reminder brings me up short. Pushing all thoughts of marriage aside, I force myself to focus on the biggest problem I face.

The King may have agreed to give me a ship, but for all my good intentions I have no idea how to overpower my father and bring him to justice. The Viper is not the most feared man on all of the waters for nothing. Perhaps there is my answer. He must be lured on to land, where he doesn't have the advantage of the *Maiden*.

And I'm as good a bait as any.

I can't sleep. The night is too humid for comfort, the air from my open window providing little relief, and my troubled mind is unwilling to rest. Whatever else the King may want, there's no point pretending he cares about the Isles or has the slightest interest in protecting his people. He cares only for himself. And what of his son? Where is Torin? What were his motives for marrying me? No one would endure the binding ceremony without good reason, and though I have no evidence, my instincts tell me he isn't working with my father. I need to find Torin. I have to know if I glimpsed something *more* the day we met, or if he's no better than his father. Only problem is I have no idea where in the Six Isles he might be.

Faint scratching noises are coming from somewhere close by, and I wonder if it's rats. I hope Grace isn't having to share her cell with too many unwanted rodents. I wonder how long she'll be stuck in her prison. I have a horrid feeling that might depend on how long I can keep the King's advances at bay.

The scratching continues and I roll over, hoping to ignore it, but then there's a barely perceptible shift in the atmosphere and I realise it's not rats. Someone's scaled the tower wall and is outside my window.

Cursing the fact that I've had my knives taken from me, I slowly reach my hand out towards the heavy brass candlestick by my bedside, glad to feel its weight. Better than nothing. Then I wait until I hear the soft drop of feet landing in my room.

And my heart sinks. There are two of them.

They're almost by my bed now and there's no time for doubt or hesitation. I swing the candlestick at the assassin closest to me, catching his temple. He crumples like a sail without wind, the knife in his hand clattering to the floor. But his accomplice is ready for me, her hand grabbing the other end of the candlestick and dragging me from the bed. I hit the stone ground hard, and roll fast to avoid her boot, which is aiming for my face. Adrenaline pumping, I spring to my feet, but she's too quick, and this time her boot finds its mark in the small of my back, knocking me down again. She grabs my hair and drags me to the wall, shoving me up against it with her fingers pressing firmly at my windpipe.

It's Choke. And I can tell from the look in her eyes that she knows about Briggs.

She says nothing, just squeezes my throat harder, and I know she doesn't care about returning me alive to my father. She wants to watch me die right here.

I try to claw her hands away from my neck, but she's too strong. I'm struggling frantically now, my lungs

178

screaming for air, as I feel around on the floor for what I hope is nearby. The tips of my fingers brush the blade that her companion dropped and, straining as hard as possible, I shuffle it into my grip – and then plunge it deep into her arm.

Immediately she releases me and before she has a chance to recover I slam her head against the wall, instantly knocking her out. Coughing, I rub my neck, gasping for breath. That was too close.

I check to see who was with her. A man named Turner. He once taught me how to fix the rigging, laughing kindly at my incompetence. Now he's trying to capture me for my execution. Charming.

How did my father find out I was here so quickly?

I don't have much time to wonder, because the scratching of boots on stone tells me there's another Snake on the way.

My fear is fast turning to annoyance. Really? Father sent three assassins for me?

After removing the dagger from Choke's arm, I climb up on to a table by the window. When the Snake drops in I launch myself on to his back, taking him by surprise.

My arm wraps round his neck and presses tight to cut off his air supply, and he slams me back against the wall, trying to break my hold. When he does it a second time the air is crushed from my lungs, and I'm thrown off, crashing to the ground. I scramble to my feet and turn round, facing my attacker, and my heart stops.

He's alive.

Relief is quickly outweighed by anger. Not only was he working with my father at my Initiation, but now Bronn's come to take me to my death and I lose all sense of calm.

'You bastard,' I cry, running at him, knife raised. 'You lying, treacherous, bastard.' I aim for his chest.

He defends himself, slamming my wrist so hard I drop the blade, but I don't need a knife to cause damage. I hit him squarely across his jaw, so that he swears loudly. Good. I want to hurt him. Want him to suffer the way he's made me suffer all these years. I strike again, but this time he's prepared, ducking out of the way and trying to grab hold of me. I'm fast too, though, and manage to land another blow, this time to the side of his ribs.

He recoils, and it gives me the advantage I need to unleash all my pent-up fury, pounding him again and again, so that he can do nothing but block my strokes, our arms moving with such swift synchronicity it's like a dance. For a moment I get lost in it, the rush of fighting him, matching him. I can almost forget where we are. I am solely focused on how my body is moving, how his is moving, the shift between me attacking, then him, then me again. He's good. So am I. It's almost as if we're trying to outdo each other, only to end up mirroring each other. I hadn't realised how much I've wanted to do this for the longest time.

And then his fist breaks through my defences and catches my chin, snapping me out of myself. Outrage flares quickly to the surface and I change tactics, kicking him in the gut. It buys me enough time to snatch the candlestick from the side of the bed next to the window, and swing it hard into his chest.

To my surprise Bronn buckles, staggering backwards. The blade I dropped lies close by, and I snatch it up before launching myself on to him, knocking us both to the ground. I hold the knife at his neck, our faces close, both of us breathing heavily from the exertion.

I didn't think it would end like this between us.

'Marianne.' His voice is a fierce whisper. 'Stop.'

I press the dagger closer to his skin. 'Make me.'

'I'm not here to hurt you. I came to help you.'

It's about the last thing I'm expecting him to say and it winds me as much as any beating. But it can't be true. He's just using my emotions to weaken me, and I won't oblige.

This time I push the blade so hard against him I break the skin, a bubble of blood forming at the surface. 'I don't need any help.'

'No, I can see that.' And to my utter surprise he smiles. He's impressed.

'How the hell did you know where I was?' I growl the words at him. He may be amused, but I am not.

Bronn's eyes flash at me. 'The King sent word. He wanted to use you as a bargaining tool, to get the Captain to stop his attacks.'

The King? That lying bastard. Did he always mean to use me as leverage against my father, or was it my punishment for spurning his advances? Either way, he certainly didn't waste any time betraying me.

Still, though his double-crossing stings it's nothing to the treachery of the man in front of me.

'The King is a fool. He should have known Father would simply send you to retrieve me.'

'He sent Turner and Choke. I followed them to keep you safe.'

The bloody nerve. He lost the right to keep me safe the day he cut me from his life.

'Well, you're a bit late, aren't you?'

'I'm here now,' he says, though I can hear it's an effort for him to speak and I loosen the pressure of the dagger ever so slightly. His eyes are searching my face, like he's trying to find an answer to some unasked question. Eventually he says, 'I saw Briggs. What was left of him.' I hear the concern in his voice. 'Was that you?'

The mention of Briggs's name sickens me. I have no desire to think about what he did, or how I retaliated.

And I certainly don't want Bronn knowing what I'm capable of.

'So you *have* been hunting me down?'

'I told you, I didn't come here to hurt you. I'm here to help.'

Our eyes lock, and I see something of the boy I knew, the friend I trusted. The friend I loved. I so desperately want to believe him.

But I don't.

'You're my father's man and this is a trick.'

He shakes his head. 'No.'

'Yes!' My father would enjoy nothing more than using my weaknesses against me. He must know my feelings for Bronn, complicated as they are. He knows Bronn's betrayal would hurt the most.

'We don't have much time,' Bronn says, indicating the unconscious assassins in the room. 'Trust me.'

He's right. They'll be awake again soon.

'Why? Why should I trust you? Make me believe you don't plan to hand me over to my father.'

'Because we're—'

'What? *Friends?* After what you did? You've barely spoken to me in years!' The full extent of my resentment towards him laces my words with venom, and he visibly flinches.

'To protect you! I thought you understood that.'

'Protect me?' I practically spit the words into his face. 'That's what my father used to say as he forced me to cut open my skin and purge myself of weakness.' I shove my palm in front of his face so he can see the scars. 'Those words mean nothing to me.'

We stare at each other, both hurt, both confused. But now is really not the time for this conversation.

'You're alive, which means you shot that man at my Initiation on my father's orders. If you were on my side, you'd be dead.'

'I did it to stop your father beating you to death. I did it to give you a chance to run.'

It's not the answer I'm expecting, but I'm too disconcerted by the momentary tenderness in his voice to form a response. He hasn't spoken to me like that in years.

I shake my head, both in disbelief and to clear my thoughts. 'No. He'd have killed you.'

Bronn sighs. 'I'm alive because I convinced him I was trying to show you up, but I was punished nonetheless. I can prove it.'

'Fine,' I say after a moment. 'Get up.' We manage to stand together, my dagger still firm at his neck in case it's a trap.

Then he lifts up his shirt. No wonder he went down when I hit him with the candlestick. His torso is etched with lacerations from where countless lashes have torn away flesh. They're not healing well.

'How do I know you're not planning to hand me over to ingratiate yourself with my father?' I can't bring myself to look at him, knowing how he's suffered, feeling bad about striking him on such painful wounds, yet not wanting to regret it because he damn well deserved everything he got.

'You don't. You'll just have to take my word for it.'

His voice is soft and I force myself to meet his gaze. On a face that's long been unreadable his eyes burn brightly at me. I tried to draw it once, his face. The slant of his cheekbones, the curve of his jaw. But I could never capture its everchanging beauty. His face told tales of adventure and hardship. Of secrets and lies. Of sadness and regret. Until it stopped saying anything at all, its stories as lost as our friendship.

But there's something in those fierce eyes looking at me now, almost golden in the moonlight, that reminds me of the face I once knew. A glimmer of something wild and unpredictable, but achingly familiar.

The next minute lasts an age as I make my decision.

'Do you have a way out of here?' I ask finally.

'Of course.'

'Fine. We'd better hurry then.'

Bronn smiles. 'So you trust me?'

'Don't push your luck. I'm choosing to believe you.' But I smile to myself as I lower my blade.

'We should take care of them.' He gestures to Choke and Turner.

'Tie them up,' I say, heading to the door. 'And get Choke undressed.'

'What? Why?'

I snatch fistfuls of my skirt and hold them up. 'Because I've officially had enough of wearing this.'

'Where are you going?'

'To get Grace.'

I'm out of the door before Bronn can voice his surprise, though perhaps he already suspected this is where she'd be after she disappeared from the *Maiden*.

I'm expecting there to be a guard outside my door, and am prepared to fight him, but the man assigned to my watch hasn't deemed it worth staying awake or sober for; he's slumped on the ground, an empty flagon of wine resting beside him. Which explains why he didn't burst in to help me during the commotion. I prod him with my foot and feel slightly resentful when he merely grunts in his sleep. Still, at least this waste of space isn't going to get in my way, and so I leave him to his dreams and creep off down the corridor.

The castle is mostly silent as I make my way along. I have to hide a few times, but stone pillars and plenty of shadows make avoiding the handful of guards on patrol relatively simple. I take several wrong turns, ending up in an opulent mirrored corridor and a pink-marbled courtyard, but assuming the dungeons will be far below I leave these behind and search for stairs. Eventually I find a hazardous spiral staircase that plunges into uninviting darkness. Looks about right.

I lightly step down, my feet making no noise, until a flicker of candlelight can be seen. There is one guard sitting at a table with a jug of ale, barely awake as he performs his duty. The useless guards here don't seem aware of the imminent peril facing the islands, and though their apathy angers me, right now it's incredibly helpful.

I wait for the guard's eyes to shut and then run towards him. He must sense movement because he opens his eyes in time to see me two steps away, but can only straighten up before I've jumped on to the table, grabbed the jug and flung the ale into his face. He splutters, staggering to his feet, but before he can take a single step forward I swing the jug round and send him flying to the floor.

I grab his vast set of keys, wondering how long it'll take to find the right one. 'Grace?' My voice echoes in the cold chamber.

The prisoners are waking up, disturbed by the fight, and are starting to make their presence known. I need to find Grace quickly before more guards arrive.

'Did I hear my name?'

I look up to see a cell door opening, and Grace emerges looking pristine as ever.

'How did you do that?' I ask in impressed disbelief.

She shrugs. 'They didn't take my hair pins. Idiots.'

I smile at her. 'So you could have walked out whenever you wanted?'

Grace nods. 'Was just waiting for you to give the word. So what's happened? Why the late-night escape?'

'Things haven't exactly gone to plan.'

Now she's the one to smile. 'They rarely do.'

'Bronn's here.'

Her eyes narrow as she reaches me, the smile quickly fading. 'Is he indeed?'

As we hurry back towards my room I fill her in on everything: my conversation with the King, his instant betrayal and my attempted capture.

'And you trust Bronn?' she says as we arrive back at my room undetected.

'I don't know.' I pause. 'Did you see what my father did to him?'

'Yes.' She falls quiet.

'You should have told me.'

'You didn't ask,' she points out. 'Besides, I wasn't sure you'd want to know.'

She's probably right. 'Well, if he's trying to double-cross us, I'm sure we can find our own way to punish him.'

'Now you're talking,' she says, and pushes the door open, barely acknowledging the still-snoring guard slumped on the ground.

Bronn has tied Turner and Choke to opposite ends of the bed. Unconscious and gagged, they'll be going nowhere fast. He looks relieved that we've returned.

'Grace,' he says with a nod. 'I wondered if you'd already caught up with Marianne.'

'The Captain must have been thrilled when I didn't return,' she says, unnecessarily checking Bronn's knots are tied securely.

Bronn raises his eyebrows. 'He's hoping you're dead. Better that than a deserter.'

'He'll be ecstatic when you don't come back then.'

'I think vengeful is a more accurate word.'

Grace fixes him with her most menacing gaze. 'I know what being a Snake means to you. And you didn't exactly hurry to join Marianne. You're sure you want to do this?'

'I'm here now, aren't I?' He easily holds her stare, until Grace relents and nods her compliance to his coming with us.

'Are you two done?' I snap. I don't want to hear about Bronn's reluctance to leave my father's crew or of his torn loyalties, and I instead turn my attention to changing into Choke's clothes, which Bronn has removed and laid out for me.

Painfully conscious of Bronn's presence, I face the wall to slip my dress off and pull on Choke's shirt and trousers – my first time in Snake uniform. Part of me feels wrong wearing something I haven't earned, but I'm sick of the impracticality of a dress, so manage to make peace with the situation.

When I'm done Bronn hands me Turner's knife, which he's clearly wiped clean on the bed sheets. Then with the merest nod towards the window he says, 'Let's go.'

We go back out the way he came in. Bronn has secured a rope to the bedpost, and Grace is first to climb down. Bronn and I wait together in silence, and I'm horribly conscious of his arm brushing against mine, the warmth of his breath on my neck. My body responds to his proximity in a way my mind cannot yet allow.

Grace tugs the rope to let us know it's safe for us to follow, and keen to put some space between me and Bronn I make my way out next. The night is still, but in the distance gunshots are being fired, and the roar of voices carries on the gentle breeze. It's hard to tell how far away the fighting is, but I wonder if the people arriving on the island desperate for sanctuary are using the cover of darkness to try to make it past the guards. If so, I don't like their chances.

One thing is certain. The fighting is getting worse as unrest grows. How much closer will it have to get before the King works out he's not safe in his castle? I doubt the realisation that assassins were able to easily creep in unnoticed and that prisoners have escaped will do much to reassure him. I have no sympathy for him – the treacherous bastard. In fact, I think I'd like to pay him one last visit. He did invite me to his chambers after all.

When Bronn joins us on the ground I ask, 'Do you know which room is the King's?'

Bronn frowns. 'Of course.'

'Show me.'

For a moment I think he's going to refuse, but perhaps he sees the determination in my eyes, because he beckons for me to follow him.

We move like shadows round the walls to the far side of the castle, and then Bronn points upwards to the second window, three floors above us. 'Whatever you're planning, make it quick.'

I nod and begin my climb. My fingers find nooks to cling to and I soon reach the window. It opens easily and I drop silently into the room.

For a minute I don't move, allowing my eyes to adjust to the gloom. The King is alone in his bed, which is a relief – I hadn't considered until now that he might have company – and sleeping deeply. A man without a care.

My steps make no sound as I gather his boot straps, and he barely stirs as I wrap them round his wrists. When I'm certain he's secure, I straddle his chest and press my knife to his throat.

'Wake up.'

His eyes open, then widen as he realises what's happening. I've gagged him so he can make no noise, and my restraints hold tight against his protests.

'Don't struggle,' I say, my voice barely a whisper. 'No one's coming for you. Not now, not ever. You may think you're safe behind your castle walls, but know this. You used to have only my father as an enemy, but now you've made one of me too. That was a mistake. You've abandoned your subjects to fend for themselves and for that I will make certain you don't emerge from the war that's coming unscathed. You will be held to account. So sweet dreams, Your Majesty. And enjoy your crown while it lasts.'

His fear is palpable, sweat beading on his upper lip, limbs trembling, and it would be so easy to end him, make him suffer, make him pay.

Now I'm the one with all the power.

I press my knife closer to his neck, just breaking the skin so a thin trail of blood escapes, my own darkness threatening to do the same, until I stop myself, scared by how easily the impulse came. Instead I raise the blade and, satisfied my warning has been heeded, render him unconscious with a quick blow to the head.

In a matter of moments I return to Bronn and Grace, who both seem relieved at my swift reappearance, and then Bronn indicates for us to follow him. We're invisible ghosts, passing unnoticed, until we reach the rear of the castle facing the waterfall.

Bronn turns to me. 'We have to swim.'

Grace looks sharply over, and I'm almost certain all three of us are remembering that day on the ship when Bronn drowned our friendship.

'I'll be fine.' I say it through gritted teeth, not wanting to live in the past when the present is dangerous enough.

He seems surprised, but nods his satisfaction. 'Head for the waterfall, then we climb.'

Despite my claim, my heart is racing as we slide into the water, barely making a sound. Grace lives up to her name as she glides forward, creating hardly a ripple. Bronn has clearly had a lot of practice moving unnoticed through water too. I'm somewhat less adept at appearing effortless, given every stroke sends a shiver of alarm through me, but still I manage to keep going, grateful that the waterfall's making enough noise to disguise my clumsy splashes.

In fact, by the time we're almost underneath it, the waterfall is deafening and my fear level starts to rise. Grace goes first, taking a deep breath and diving under the point of impact before appearing on the other side, hardly visible through the curtain of water.

Ignoring the panic pestering for my attention, I inhale and plunge under. The current is strong below the surface, the force of the falling water pushing me backwards while I struggle to move forward, resulting in me going nowhere.

My lungs are beginning to burn, but there's no going back. I have to make it through. Kicking and clawing, I try to break the invisible barrier, fighting my nightmares of drowning as much as the relentless pressure pressing down on me. And then a hand wraps round mine, and pulls me to the other side.

I come up for air at the same time Bronn does, but before I can say anything he's already moving forward towards the rock face.

Grace, however, pauses to look at me. 'You OK?'

'Yes.' I snap the word at her, because actually I'm shaking, hating the way water makes me weak, resenting Bronn's assistance, frustrated that I needed it. I'm so glad to escape the waterfall that I'm eager to start the perilous climb up rock that's slippery with moisture and algae.

Apart from the thundering of water there is no sound as we scale the cliff. When we're halfway up Bronn disappears above me. Seconds later I realise why. He's crouching on a ledge carved into the rock that leads into a cave mouth.

'You've been here before?' I ask, perching next to him and wringing out my sodden hair.

'The Captain expects us to know the way in and out of everywhere,' Bronn says as Grace climbs up on to the ledge.

'I'm not sure he meant the palace,' Grace says, giving him a sideways glance.

Bronn shrugs. 'I'm thorough.'

I suppress a smile. 'So where now? Into the friendly pitch-black cave?'

'Tunnel, but yes. If we follow it through, we'll come out the other side of the mountain, into the small town of Port Keath, where you can get a boat. Then it's up to you where you go next.'

I stare at him. 'You're not coming with us?'

He struggles to meet my eyes. 'No.'

There it is. There's the Bronn I've known for the past few years. The man who shuts me out, who tells me nothing. 'Then what the hell are you doing here?'

Bronn doesn't answer.

'It's a reasonable question, Bronn,' Grace adds. 'Adler's had Snakes hunting her for months and you've done nothing. Why now? Why are you here?'

'Do you realise what I've given up by coming here?' Bronn is furious as he turns to me. 'For you?' He spits out the words as if this is the last place he wants to be, as if I've inconvenienced him, and I flinch at his anger. I thought I was the only one full of rage. Looks like I was wrong.

He sighs, and turns away, as if he can't bear the sight of me. Instead he speaks to Grace. 'Until now they had no idea where she was. But this time they knew exactly where to go. Maybe I should have come sooner, but leaving has cost me my place on the ship. My life. Everything.'

The pain in his voice echoes into the darkness, silencing me and Grace. Because, despite everything, we know why Bronn is so loyal to my father. He doesn't talk much about his childhood, the memories are too awful, but I know enough. I know that he grew up with the rats in the sewers, lived off their dead bodies rather than starve. That most days he didn't know if he'd live to see the next. He was often beaten by drunkards, or by the older kids sharing the streets. Bronn lived to survive, until my father caught him stealing from our rations while we were in port and was impressed – not only that he'd had the nerve to try to steal from the Viper, but also that he'd nearly succeeded. My father saved Bronn from his misery and fed him, trained him, gave him a home and a purpose. All of which he's sacrificed. For me.

Bronn sighs. 'Now the Viper will hunt me for the rest of my life, so I'm planning on disappearing. I'm going to survive. I suggest you do the same.'

Growing up I always feared that I would wake one day and Bronn would be gone. The impulse to keep running, to stay alive was so deeply ingrained in him. I thought that over the years he'd moved beyond that, but I guess some instincts never leave you. He's thinking like a true Snake. About himself.

'Run like a coward if you must, but I'm going to find Torin.' I know it's cruel to call him that when he's just risked everything for me, but I can't help it. I'm so disappointed in him.

'Not sure wedding arrangements are a priority right now.' There's an edge to his voice.

'I'm hoping that unlike you Torin has integrity. That he'll fight for what's right.'

Bronn scoffs. 'You barely know the man.'

'True, which is why I need to find out if he's willing to do what his father isn't. Having the support of the King's Fleet is vital to the success of my plan.'

Bronn's giving me a strange look. 'What plan?' I realise in all the drama of our escape that I haven't actually told him about it yet.

'The plan to stop my father, of course.'

Bronn stares at me for a moment, before looking at Grace. 'Please tell me she's joking.'

Grace places her hand on my shoulder, clearly marking whose side she's on. 'Marianne's right. Adler has to be stopped.'

'He can't be stopped. No ship can match the *Maiden*, and he's destroyed over half the King's Fleet. The King's shown his hand, and now that the Captain knows he's afraid, he won't hesitate to take control of the islands. Your father didn't cause the accidents on the Sixth Isle, but you can be certain he's been exploiting them for his own gain. You do realise most of the bandits are working for him now?'

I didn't know that, and judging from Grace's expression she'd been kept out of that loop too. My father has quietly been moving his pieces into position with exceptional skill. The war I thought was coming has already started.

'So, what? We just let him destroy everything? Let him kill indiscriminately, rampaging over sea and land?'

Bronn holds my gaze, but he has no reply.

'I tried hiding, Bronn. He found me. He'll always find me. And I don't want to spend my life *running* while everyone else suffers at his hands.'

'There's a reason no one has stopped him,' Bronn says, still not willing to admit defeat, pleading with me to change my mind. 'He's surrounded himself with the deadliest fighters, has forged alliances throughout the Six Isles, and kills anyone he perceives as being even the slightest threat. He's the most powerful, the most feared of all men and has no equal on the waves. No one *can* defeat him.'

'I have to try.'

Grace walks towards the tunnel, staring into the dark. She's impatient to get moving again, and I don't blame her.

Bronn can also see Grace's impatience, but takes a step towards me. 'Whatever you think of me, I want you to be safe. Going against the Viper is anything but.'

Why does he do this to me? One minute he's cold, the next caring, and I hate the way he makes me feel like I'm drifting, like a ship without an anchor. I remind myself that I've survived perfectly well without him so far, that whatever he chooses I don't need him.

'I don't need saving,' I say firmly, doing my best to keep the resentment out of my voice. 'I'm not asking for your permission. I'm simply telling you what I'm going to do. Whether you come with me is entirely your choice.'

I hold my breath, waiting for his response. I want him to choose me.

After a moment he sighs. 'Torin has a residence on the Sixth Isle. Very few people know of its existence.'

'But you do because you're thorough?' Despite myself, I can't help but smile at him now and he's quick to return it. So there is some of the old Bronn still in there.

'Precisely. I'm almost certain that's where he'll be.'

'Can you two hurry up?' Grace snaps from the shadows. She's already gone far enough along the tunnel that I can't see her. 'Ship full of assassins looking for us, remember?'

Bronn touches my arm. 'This doesn't mean I'm coming with you.'

'I know.' But it's enough for now.

A rush of warmth sweeps over me. There's so much to be afraid of, but I'm unbelievably glad that they're both with me. Though there are many reasons why I shouldn't trust either of them, I do. And so when Bronn gestures for me to lead the way, I walk without hesitation, allowing the darkness to swallow me whole.

The tunnel winds endlessly through the mountain. I walk beside the wall, running my fingers along slime-covered rock, trying not to stumble over stones I can't see. We don't speak, all sensing that silence is our friend at this point, just in case anyone else has sought sanctuary in the darkness.

It's several hours before the first glimmer of light tells us the opening is nearby, and when we finally emerge from the tunnel and on to another cliff face it's early morning. The air feels wonderfully fresh after being in such dank murkiness and carries salt on it that clings to my lips. We are near the sea, just as Bronn said we would be.

Our descent is far easier than the way up. Once we've scrambled down from the ledge, waging war on the thicket of thorns covering it from prying eyes, we take a dusty path towards the town. A quick check of my compass tells me we're facing west, nothing but the vast expanse of ocean in front of us until the Western Isles – a thought that makes me prickle with unease as I remember Grace's claims. I tuck the compass into my pocket, glad to still have one of my birthday gifts. Bronn's dagger is somewhere at the palace. The King may as well have buried it in my back after selling me out to my father.

The betrayal still stings, even though it shouldn't. Our dinner together left me in little doubt of what kind of man the King is. I just hadn't wanted to believe he was such a coward that he'd rather make a deal with his enemy to protect his own skin than work with a willing ally to restore peace. And now I'm gambling everything on his son. Bronn is right: I don't know anything about Torin, have no real reason to believe he'll help, only a momentary connection forged in the melding of flesh. I could be making a terrible mistake.

We walk for about an hour and hear the town long before we see it. Though it's still early the thrum of voices reaches us, and I glance over at Bronn.

He's frowning. 'Thought this side of the island might be quieter. Obviously not.'

'The more people, the more cover,' Grace says.

'Maybe.' Bronn isn't happy. 'We'll split up. I'll sort out boats; you two send word to Torin you're on your way. The sooner we're off land the better.'

And once we're back at sea he'll be gone. The thought makes my insides tangle together. But if he's determined to leave, then there's something I want to do before he goes.

I fall into step beside Grace, and pull her back a little, so Bronn can't hear me. 'Can you take care of the message on your own? I have an errand to run.'

She gives me a curious look, but nods.

If the main port had seemed busy, this is mayhem. Hundreds of people have flocked here, hoping to land unnoticed on this quiet part of the isle. Crowds of desperate islanders are beseeching the regiment of the King's Guard blocking their way, and judging by the bodies strewn about there has been fighting overnight. I realise this was probably what I could hear when we were leaving the palace. My instincts that it wouldn't end well appear to have been horribly right.

The moment we arrive we're besieged by people clawing at us for money, for food, for shelter. Bronn shakes them off like flies, determined to secure both him and us passage off the island. Grace pushes through them in the opposite direction, searching for a stall with sea vultures ready for service.

These exceptionally intelligent birds are the quickest way to deliver messages around the Isles. Simply tie a note to their leg and whisper the location you want it taken to and they will fly there with haste. Few people have their own sea vulture, and Talon is another symbol of my father's power. Their amazing understanding of our words has always seemed to me a remnant of the magic we once had, a link to a lost past, and normally I would welcome any opportunity to see a flock of them lined up on their perches.

But it is not the sea vultures I'm interested in today. My mission involves finding an apothecary. The town isn't big and most of the merchants have packed up, afraid of being robbed by desperate people, but healers don't disappear, not even in the darkest of places. That's where they're needed most.

I ask several of the people rushing past me, until eventually one man pauses long enough to point me in the direction of a tiny cottage. Crooked and neglected, it looks just right to house what I'm seeking.

I have to knock twice before an old woman appears at the door. Two gold coins is all I'm required to part with to get what I need. I slip the bottles into my pocket, then set off through the throng of bodies again in search of Grace.

I haven't walked far before someone tugs low down at my trousers.

A small girl stares up at me with eyes that remind me painfully of Tomas. 'I'm hungry,' she says.

I bend down to lift her up, worried such a little body will get crushed in this tide of panic. 'Where's your mother?'

'I lost her.'

I don't need this. But I can't just leave her. 'Let's get you some food, then I'll help you find her, OK?'

The girl nods, looping my hair round her finger.

We push our way into the inn where I buy her a bowl of gruel – the only food on offer – at a ridiculous price. I watch her, very intentionally not asking for her name.

I mustn't get attached. Grace will have the bird sorted soon, then she'll come looking for me, and won't be pleased to find me saddled with a child.

Fortunately the girl eats quickly, so hungry she practically inhales the sludge, and when she wipes her mouth clean on her sleeve I smile at her.

'Where did you last see your mother?'

'I don't know. There were horses.'

'The blacksmith's?'

She nods, though a little uncertainly.

'Come on then, let's check there first.'

I hold her tightly as we fight our way through the crowds. The shouting's getting louder, and then a gunshot blasts through the air. I turn round in time to see a man fall to the ground. It looks as though his crime was attempting to run past the guards, as they stand over him, kicking his legs to see how injured he is. While I watch him lying there, his body shuddering in the grip of death, someone tries to pull the girl from my arms. I spin round, ready to attack, fighting to keep hold of her, but the woman is screaming at me.

'You stole my child! You stole my child!'

Releasing my hold on the girl, I stare in confusion as her mother snatches her from me, accusing me of terrible things. The girl says nothing, just watches me as the two of them disappear into the crowd. It all happens so fast that I don't have time to say a word, and so I go after them, wanting to explain, searching every face, trying to find the woman's.

And then my blood runs cold.

My father is striding towards me flanked by Cleeve and Nestor. Behind them are a dozen other members of the crew and, even consumed by their plight, the crowd parts fearfully out of the Viper's way. By some miracle none of them have seen me yet, so I lower my head and walk quickly the other way, hoping not to draw attention to myself.

I see Grace up ahead whispering the coordinates Bronn's given her to a sea vulture, before releasing the magnificent creature into the air.

I run towards her. 'My father's here.'

She's instantly alert. 'Where?'

'To my left, and he's not alone.'

'They must know we're here,' she says, grabbing my arm. 'Come on.'

We move quickly to hide ourselves behind the stall, keeping low as we run in the direction Bronn took, towards the jetty. The crowds thin the closer we get to the water – most people want to get on the island, not off it – and we start to lose our cover.

I see Bronn the same moment my father does, the same moment my father pulls out his pistol and shoots.

Everyone close by screams.

For me, though, it's as if time stands still while my brain processes my options. My father is right there. I could end this all now if I confront him – if I kill him. But even after everything he's done to me, I don't know if I can do it. Not him. Not my father. Besides, the more rational part of my brain screams at me that with the rest of the Snakes here we're outnumbered, and trying to stay and fight will just result in our capture and death, which will help no one.

And so I run. I sprint as fast as I can towards the jetty, dodging the shots being fired in my direction. Bronn is unharmed, my father too far away to aim accurately. He's in a rowing boat, hastily untying it as he shouts for Grace and me to hurry.

As we pound down the jetty Bronn starts to row, deep strokes taking him quickly away. I don't hesitate. I leap from the edge and fall into the boat. Seconds later, Grace tumbles on top of me.

'Keep down,' Bronn says as several more shots are fired in our direction.

'You coming with us then?' Grace says, sitting up.

Bronn gives her a withering look.

'Which one are you heading for?' Grace is looking at the ships, trying to figure out Bronn's plan.

I'm more interested in how close behind my father is, and to my horror he and his men are already jumping into other boats in pursuit.

'A skerry-cutter?' Grace sounds confused, and then her mouth falls open with disbelief. 'The fiord?' She's worked out what Bronn has in mind and is not amused.

Bronn isn't interested in debating this. 'It's the only way to outrun them.'

'You're a bloody fool,' she says, but I can tell she's impressed with his gutsy idea. She leans forward to take Bronn's pistol from his belt, turns elegantly and shoots at my father. They're out of range, Bronn a stronger rower than the others, and so knowing we can't be hit either I stand up, ready to leap aboard the vessel we're pulling up alongside.

We scale the side of the sailing boat and drop on to the deck. Small and narrow, designed for speed and agility, the skerry-cutter is used by trade carriers to deliver goods around the islands, enabling them to stay close to land and avoid the small clusters of rocks beneath the surface known as skerries. No one in their right mind would think of using them to attempt the route Bronn intends, though. A route only desperate people would take, which just about sums us up.

I weigh anchor as Bronn runs to the wheel, and Grace releases the neat triangular sails that immediately catch the breeze.

My father is firing again, as are most of his men, and we duck low to avoid their shots as our cutter sweeps hard to starboard, taking us out of their reach. There are several other skerry-cutters anchored offshore and it'll only be a matter of time before they've commandeered them and make chase.

We sail north, hugging the coastline as we head towards Skerrikut Fiord, the narrow waterway that crosses the island. Centuries of strong currents have carved their way through the rocky land, creating a channel that will lead us to a tunnel in the cliff face at the far end of the fiord, and into the open sea on the other side. It's a faster route than going round the island, but it's obstructed by so many small skerry formations that it's virtually impassable.

As we approach it my eyes widen with horror. Even from here I can see the tips of the rocks breaking the water's surface and cannot fathom how we'll make it through, but if ever there was a sailor mad enough to attempt it, then it's Bronn. Without hesitation he takes us in, spinning the wheel with apparent ease to weave round the hull-tearing masses as though they were nothing more than foam. I glance behind to see three other ships in our wake. Despite the fact that none of the other sailors are anywhere near as accomplished as Bronn, they're keeping pace with us by mimicking exactly what Bronn does.

No one asks the obvious question: how did my father find us? There'll be time for that later if we manage to escape.

Because if we somehow make it through the skerries, we'll pass into the fiord – a twisting narrow channel of water flanked on either side by steep cliffs. Scores of islets are scattered through the deep fiord, as well as further skerries that catch you unaware if you're brave enough to attempt its undulating passage. Or foolish enough.

But if we can lose my father and his Snakes in these almost labyrinthine waters, then we can break clear into the Eastern Sea and make our journey towards the Sixth unhindered. At least that is what I assume Bronn intends to do.

Grace and I start emptying chests, searching for weapons. I find a pistol, which I toss over to Grace.

While she checks the powder charge I turn to Bronn. 'What can I do?'

'Take the wheel.'

'What?' He may be crazy enough to attempt this, but I'm not.

'There's too much tension in the sails,' he says. 'Just keep us in one piece while I loosen them.'

There's no time to argue. I grasp the wheel and swerve left and right round skerries, impressed with how quickly the boat responds to my requests. There are rocks everywhere, and I'm concentrating so hard on my steering that it's only when Bronn appears back beside me that I realise I've been holding my breath.

'They're gaining on us,' he says, taking over the wheel again. 'We're buffering the wind for them. We're going to have to get closer.'

'Closer to the rocks?'

'It's that or get caught.'

The boat creaks in objection as Bronn careens through the gaps between skerries, doing it so skilfully the wood itself seems to curve. For a moment I think my father's boat is going to get caught on one of the rocks, but Cleeve manages to scrape out of trouble just in time. One of the other boats isn't so lucky. The vessel furthest from us, helmed by Lynx, crunches hard on her port bow and they immediately start to sink. All four on board abandon their pursuit as they focus on survival.

The closer we get to the fiord, the denser the skerries become, and we bump and scuff a few corners, but the boat holds. For now. As soon as we reach the fiord there'll be nothing to stop my father catching up with us.

'They're coming alongside,' Grace says, leaping to stand next to me.

She's right. My father has taken over steering his skerry-cutter and has pulled to our starboard side, taking a parallel route that intermittently brings us closer together. We're going to have to do this the hard way.

Grace raises a pistol in each hand, while I pull the dagger from my belt. I'm happier with knives.

There are four other Snakes in addition to my father on his cutter – Cleeve, Nestor, Ruby and Agnes – and our main priority is to stop them crossing over to board us, and so we stand with weapons raised. As the two parallel paths our cutters are on swing together, so does our steel. Nestor, Ruby and Agnes target Grace, presumably deeming her the greater threat, leaving Cleeve for me. I can tell he's still seething from our last encounter on the *Maiden*, that he feels this is his opportunity for revenge. He's hated me all my life, resented my presence, my claim to the ship. I've always known of his desire to crush me like a troublesome roach, and now he senses it's time. Not to mention the glory he'll receive for being the one to capture me for Father.

But his hatred is nothing compared to mine, and just the memory of him beating Toby – for no reason other than sport – fans the flames of my pain. I launch a vicious attack, thrusting and slicing with menacing accuracy so that Cleeve struggles to parry my blows.

And then in my mind I see him beating Toby, only then it's not Toby, it's Tomas, and then it's not him doing the beating, it's me, and it's not Tomas, it's Briggs.

The flashback to Briggs's death is so unexpected that I can't breathe, traumatised by the memory of how flesh and bone felt breaking beneath my fists.

Cleeve takes full advantage of my lapse, and now his every blow is more savage, more violent, and soon I'm struggling to hold him back. When Bronn tilts us unexpectedly to port I momentarily lose my balance.

'Get her!' I hear my father shout as he pulls their ship about, and Cleeve obeys, lunging for me. He grabs my arm and tries to drag me across. I have to drop my blade so my hand can clutch at the side of our boat, but I can feel I'm going to topple soon, so I do the only thing I can – sink my teeth into his hand.

He cries in pain and releases me, but instinctively he lashes out and a sudden heat streaks up my cheek, followed by wet warmth. 'Consider that a taste of what's to come!' he shouts at me with a cruel laugh as I fall hard on to deck.

Bronn's managed to steer us further from them, and so Grace takes the chance to drop to my side.

There's blood everywhere, and I try not to panic. I know faces bleed badly, so it probably looks worse than it is.

Grace rips a strip off her shirt and presses it hard against my cut. 'Bronn, get us out of here!'

'I'm working on it.'

'It's OK,' I say. 'I'll live.'

She nods. There simply isn't time to fuss. The second ship full of Snakes is catching up and its occupants are openly firing at us.

'Are your pistols loaded?' I ask her. I realise I've no idea whom she's dispatched and how.

'Yes, what do you have in mind?'

'Just cover me as best you can.'

And I take Bronn's pistol from her and stand up, targeting the rigging of the offending skerry-cutter. It's an almost impossible shot and even if I make it there's no guarantee it'll work, but I have faith in my aim. My finger squeezes hard on the trigger and I hit my mark. The rope securing the boom is split by the bullet and begins to unravel, making the boom swing loose, knocking two men who are standing in its way immediately overboard. The other Snakes struggle to regain control, and in a desperate attempt to avoid hitting the rocks their helmsman misjudges his steering and the small boat flips over as they spin in the wrong direction. They are no longer a problem.

Blood is still spilling down my face and I wipe away at it furiously. That's two ships down, but my father's boat is still close in its pursuit and, though both Ruby and Nestor have been disposed of, he's not dissuaded from his mission.

'Nice shot,' Grace says with an impressed smile as she takes the pistol back from me to reload it. 'Reckon you can make it twice?'

But even as I nod, the skerry-cutter pitches in the turbulent waters, and I know I won't get a sure enough aim.

Grace knows it too, and shouts at Bronn, 'Whatever you're doing, do it faster!'

'We're through to the fiord,' he calls back. We run to join him at the wheel, but the stretch of clearer water ahead does nothing to reassure me. At least the skerries got in their way as much as ours. Now it'll be harder to stop them drawing alongside us.

'You can't outrun me.' My father's booming voice carries on the wind, echoing my thoughts. 'You've already led me straight to her, Bronn. So predictable. I'll spill your guts and eat them raw for this betrayal. Do you hear me?'

I look up at Bronn, whose jaw is clenched so tight it must hurt. What has my father seen in his behaviour these last years that I have not?

'Please tell me you have a plan,' Grace says to Bronn.

'Of course,' he says. 'Just make sure you two don't fall overboard.'

We don't even have time to ask him what he means, because he turns so hard and so suddenly that our boat tips horizontally and I think we're going to capsize.

There's a crash of wood on rock and for a moment I think it's us, but then we're righting ourselves and I spin round to look behind. Bronn had seen a skerry lurking under the surface of the water and lured my father straight into it by turning at the last possible second.

My father's ship has smashed its hull on the sharp rock and they're going nowhere fast.

I can feel the force of his fury from here.

'Marianne!' he bellows towards me, his voice a curse on the wind. 'Everything that happens from now on is on your head. I will make them suffer. I will make them all beg for death. Because of you!'

I snatch a pistol from Grace and fire towards my father. I know it won't reach him, that's not my intent. I just want to give him a reply he'll understand.

Grace touches me gently on the shoulder. 'Come on, let's sort you out.'

While she roots through the chests, I collapse to the deck, the blood loss making me light-headed. But it's more than that. My father's words have shaken me. I know he meant every one of them; his threats are never empty. I hate to admit it, but I'm afraid.

Grace squats next to me. 'I've found a needle and thread, but there's nothing to clean them with.'

'Just do it.'

She gives me an apologetic glance, and then pushes the needle into my skin. I bite back the expletives, not wanting to make this harder for Grace than it already is. Though we've lost my father, Bronn still has to outmanoeuvre all the hazards of the fiord and we're pitching from side to side. This scar isn't going to be pretty.

By the time Grace is finished I have to lean over the side to vomit. But at least the bleeding's stopped. Grace sits beside me, both of us redundant for the moment. All Bronn needs from us right now is not to distract him.

'Are you OK?' She's not asking about my cut.

I close my eyes and consider my answer. Of course I'm not. I've just seen my father for the first time in months and he was trying to kill me. Even though I knew he was after me, it's substantially more painful to be confronted with the reality.

'What happened back there?' she asks, sounding concerned.

Oh. She's talking about my fight with Cleeve. The images that made an unwelcome appearance in my head couldn't have come at a worse time and nearly cost me dearly. I don't want to think about Briggs, not now, not ever.

'Nothing, I'm fine.' The lie slips out easily as I squash the mixture of horror and shame away.

'It's OK to hate them,' Grace says softly. She looks pointedly at my scabbing knuckles. 'And it's OK to admit you killed Briggs. I understand. He stole something precious from you. But you need to make peace with it before you get yourself killed.'

Has she always known me this well? To have seen straight into my soul full of its darkest deeds? Such perception leaves me raw, exposed, and that combined with my guilt over Briggs makes me defensive. 'Why do you care?' I snap. 'You're a Snake, whose entire purpose was to train me to kill. Well, I've done it. I took a life. You succeeded. You should be happy.'

I regret the words the moment they're out of my mouth, especially when I see the hurt flash across Grace's face.

She is no Snake.

She takes a moment before she replies, and her voice is warm with kindness. 'We both know you've been capable of killing someone for years. But you always chose not to and I have both admired and respected you for it. An assassin with a conscience. So I know that crossing the line won't have been easy for you. And I'm here if you need to talk about it. Trust me, I know it's hard to live with.'

I lean my head on her shoulder and slip my fingers into hers. Grace understands me better than I understand myself sometimes. I, on the other hand, have failed to consider the toll that killing has taken on her. Hearing the trace of sorrow in her voice is disconcerting.

And after everything she told me just days ago about her heritage I can't help but feel responsible. She's stayed with Father for me. Committed terrible acts to do so. And for nothing, because there simply can't be any truth in her belief that I'm somehow descended from the lost royal bloodline.

And yet . . . the desire to head West has been with me as far back as I can remember, a longing that has always been inexplicable. Until maybe now. Is it possible I've wanted to travel there because of some deep and powerful sense that I'm a descendant? It's an unsettling thought and I'm more than grateful when Bronn saves me from it.

'Hate to interrupt,' he says, not sounding the least bit sorry. 'But we're nearly out of the fiord and there's nothing good waiting for us.'

Grace and I are instantly on our feet and join Bronn as he steers us through the last of the strait. Ahead is a tunnel, a natural gap in the island's rock that will lead us to the open sea. What awaits beyond is far from welcoming. The sky is black, the wind strong, the waves swelling.

'There's a storm coming,' Bronn says.

There certainly is, in more ways than one.

To start with the wind works in our favour. The triangular sails billow wide and we fair fly along the east coast of the First Isle. But the skerry-cutter is a small boat, not designed for ocean sailing, and it was always going to be a challenge to reach the Rock Island in it, even in calm seas.

We've almost managed to pass the First when the dark clouds finally obliterate the sun and cast an ominous gloom over our position. And then the heavens open, the rain instantly stinging my face like a thousand wasps and soaking me through. The wind whips up a gear, and used to the *Maiden*'s steadiness in such weather I'm panicked by how this ship dances to the waves' tune, swaying in a frightening rhythm.

'Drop the sails,' Bronn shouts across the squall, his wet clothes sticking to his skin as tightly as the hair is plastered to his face.

I run to help Grace, who's already made a start.

She blinks at me through the rain. 'We're going to run off downwind.'

I nod my understanding, hiding my fear, and race to the stern where long, heavy lines of rope are fastened. Though it takes an enormous effort I throw them overboard so that they trail behind us in the water, slowing us down.

It's a risky tactic, sailing with the wind. If all goes well, we'll travel quickly along, blown in the direction we want to go. But the wind is only going to get stronger and then we're in danger of going too fast and ending up with the ship's bow submerging beneath the wave in front, which would cause us to pitchpole, somersaulting until we capsize.

Grace is tying a rope round Bronn's waist and I see the other end is attached to the helm. Then she comes over to me and gives me my own length.

'Don't want to lose any of us overboard,' she says with a grin, as she fixes my end to one of the two masts. There is no fear in Grace's eyes. She lives for this kind of danger.

The ship is soon taking a battering from the ferocious wind, emitting creaks and groans that do nothing to reassure my pounding heart. Bronn is steering with his usual skill, keeping the stern perpendicular to the approaching waves to prevent us from tipping too far to one side. A broach at this speed would be catastrophic. We're moving at an incredible pace and Grace whoops and hollers into the gale. Waves roll rampantly over us, but we're already as wet as we're going to get, and I'm beginning to think our little cutter is going to survive this beating when there's a deafening crack like a gunshot. For a moment I'm not sure what's happened, but I look up in time to see the snapped foremast come sweeping down, bringing with it a wild tangle of rigging. I have to duck to avoid having my head smashed.

The ship instantly spins, Bronn's control all but lost, and both Grace and I run to help him stabilise the wheel, which is whirling chaotically. We're being thrown about like driftwood and it takes all our strength to keep the boat upright, while the broken mast swings from side to side, threatening to decapitate us at any moment. If this storm doesn't break soon, we're not going to survive.

And then it does. The wind drops almost as suddenly as it arrived, and though the rain outstays its welcome it's far from our biggest problem – that honour is reserved for the destruction wrought by the mast, which has ended its rampage by smashing into the deck.

We need some pitch to patch up the holes before we take on too much water, but there isn't any. We're not going to progress quickly like this.

'Where do you think we are?' I say, looking around at the expanse of ocean.

'Hard to know,' Bronn says, squinting at the skyline. 'If I had to guess, maybe a few miles away from the Second? We covered a lot of distance at that speed.'

So we're still a long way from the Sixth, with only one mast. Great. How long will it take my father to return to the *Maiden* and set off after us? We couldn't be an easier target.

'Can we create a makeshift mast?' I ask, my eyes searching around the small ship for anything that could be used to make a temporary pole.

'What about the bowsprit?' Grace suggests, staring at the spar extending out at the prow of the ship. 'We could set it upright and tie it to what's left of the original mast.'

Bronn nods. 'That might work. Give me a hand.'

While Bronn and Grace put the plan into action, I spend the best part of the day detaching the sail from the defunct mast and salvaging what I can of the rigging to use in our substitute construction. The sail's been ripped in several places, so when I finally make sense of the mess on deck I set about repairing the canvas, trying hard not to think of all the many reasons I should be panicking right now.

I could worry about the fearsome Viper ship that's bound to be close on our tail, or the father who wants not only to kill me but also to make me suffer. I could be concerned about my friend who's been hiding secrets from me since we met, or her assertion that I'm the last of a royal bloodline supposed to rule the lawless West. The burning throb in my face reminds me I could just worry about the slice down my cheek and the risk of infection it carries.

I fight those thoughts away and instead focus on what we need to do next. We'll get our replacement mast up, then make it to the Second Isle and switch ships. From there we'll carry on to the Sixth Isle and meet up with Torin, who will immediately declare his intention to help me and send out his Fleet in defiance of his father. We'll bring the Viper to account for his crimes, with Torin becoming king for good measure. And I'll live happily ever after.

Simple.

By the time night falls we've got something resembling a mast in place, with a sail attached, and we're moving, albeit slowly, in the right direction. The rain has finally stopped, the wind once again kind, as if apologising for its earlier transgression, and we've decided to take it in turns at the helm so we can get some rest.

Bronn is sitting beside me, watching as I mash the herbs I bought from the apothecary what seems an age ago. I had planned to do this back on the First Isle before we went our separate ways. I hadn't expected my father to appear and throw us into chaos. And back together.

I couldn't get any earthenwort, but I have mettleroot and I'm mixing it with carrowseed and wolfbalm to create a dark paste, which despite its foul smell I'm certain will prove effective.

'Please tell me that's not our dinner,' Bronn says, wrinkling his nose.

'In a couple of days' time when we're still stuck on this boat with nothing to eat you might be wishing it was,' I say with a wry smile. 'Take off your shirt.'

He raises his eyebrows, but we're no longer close enough for him to make the suggestive joke he would have a few years ago. We haven't teased each other like that for a long time, too many words have been spoken in anger since, and the silence where his retort should be feels empty.

Though I only have moonlight to work by, I can see the lacerations on Bronn's torso caused by the cat-o'-nine-tails are deep and infected. He must be in constant pain from them.

'Did Milligan give you nothing for these?'

Bronn shakes his head. 'I'm not one of her favourites.'

'I'm sorry.' This is all my fault.

'Could have been worse; at least Adler didn't have me keelhauled.'

'He may yet,' I say quietly as I start to smear my concoction on Bronn's wounds. He flinches at my touch, but doesn't protest, though I know it must be burning like fire.

It takes quite a while to tend to each cut, my indignation rising with every minute at the fact Milligan had refused him any salves. Even the injuries of punishment should be treated if my father wants his crew to perform to the best of their abilities, and I can't help but wonder if Milligan's dislike of Bronn is linked to her hatred of me.

The quartermaster always administers any floggings that require the cat, and the thought of Cleeve enjoying each barbaric stroke, every strip of skin torn off, is more than I can bear. It was a severe punishment for my father to choose, and the words he shouted at me back in the fiord come to my mind. Many sailors throughout the King's Fleet refer to the cat as the 'captain's daughter' and I wonder if this castigation meant more than I first realised.

'What did my father mean when he said he knew you'd lead him to me?' I can't even bring myself to look at Bronn when I ask this, scared of what his answer might be.

He doesn't reply immediately. I'm clearly not the only one afraid of this conversation.

'You weren't at my Initiation,' he says eventually in barely more than a whisper. 'It was nothing like yours.' He pauses and it's surprising to hear him sound haunted by the memory. I thought Bronn feared nothing.

'You've never spoken about it.' Not to me anyway.

Bronn turns away, as if he can hardly bear to think of it. 'For good reason.'

I wait, not wanting to say anything that might make this harder for him.

He can't look at me. 'It lasted several weeks.'

I'm shocked. How is that possible?

'It started much as I expected. Tests, challenges, proving my knowledge of the islands, the lore. Then came the first kill. I was to assassinate a diplomat from the Mist Island who was causing the King a headache. It needed to look accidental.'

Bronn has never spoken to me about his assignments before and I realise I'm holding my breath. 'How did you do it?'

'Caught a venomray in the southern shallows of the Fallow Island, extracted its poison and dipped a stiletto blade into it. Then all I had to do was push past her in a crowd, at the market. Prick her neck. She probably thought she'd been stung by a wasp. Two minutes later she was dead. No questions, no suspicions. A perfect execution. I thought that would be the end. I honestly thought that was all there was to it.'

'That wasn't enough?'

Now Bronn meets my gaze. 'The thing about Initiations, as you of all people should know, is Adler tests our weaknesses. He knew both of mine.'

And that's when I realise how much I still view Bronn through younger, innocent eyes. Growing up he was perfect to me. I wouldn't have known what flaws to put on trial. Clearly my father knew him better.

'The night after I'd celebrated what I thought was the end of my Initiation, I was taken from my bed, blinded with a sack over my head, bound hand and foot, and shoved in a barrel. They tossed me overboard. I didn't know the barrel was still attached to the ship. All I knew was darkness and rising water. I thought I'd been left to drown.'

My heart hurts for him. As an orphan who doesn't even know what island he was born on, it makes sense that one of the things Bronn would fear above all else was losing his home, the place he'd found on the ship, the family he'd made in the crew. Dying alone, rejected. He must have been terrified.

'I don't know how long I was left there,' he says, 'but when they brought me back on board, I was weak, disorientated. Which is just what your father wanted.'

He pauses, and then surprises me by asking, 'Do you remember Dart?'

The name sounds familiar and I cast my mind back. Crew come and go frequently, and when I was younger I didn't pay much attention. But I do recall a spindly lad, similar in age to Bronn, who always seemed a bit out of place. Too nice for the *Maiden*. I don't remember him staying with the crew long. I have a horrid feeling I'm about to find out why.

'When they dragged me from the barrel the crew were watching. Surrounding me, like they were you. Your father stood in the middle with Dart, who looked confused. And then the Captain explained the final test. Only one of us would pass our Initiation – whichever one of us was still alive at the end of the fight.'

Oh.

'At first we thought it was a trick. Maybe a joke. But it wasn't.' Bronn's eyes flash with anger now. 'I liked

Dart, had taken him under my wing when he came aboard. And I had to kill him. With my bare hands. Like he was nothing more than an animal. I tried to make it quick for him. Snapped his neck. But I hated myself for it. Still do.'

I want to offer some comfort, but there's none to give.

'Afterwards your father took me to your cabin. You were asleep. And he told me that my weakness was getting attached to the wrong people. I had to show him I could sever those ties, and be loyal only to him. I'd proved I could do what was necessary with Dart. Now I had to give you up too. If I refused, then I'd go back in the barrel, this time with rocks for company. I was selfish. I chose to live. Passed my Initiation at the highest possible cost.' He pauses, and his guilt is laid bare before me. 'That day I pushed you overboard? Your father was watching. I don't know if you saw him, but he was observing me. I went too far, so desperate to appear indifferent to you, and I have hated myself for it ever since. But it worked – for a while. Until the minute I shot that man on the Black Island. Then the Captain knew. He'd underestimated my feelings for you, and I'd overestimated my ability to hide them.'

His honesty hurts in every way. For years I've been so angry with him and now I understand why. Because I loved him as a child and never stopped. I should have known him better, should have seen what was happening, but I was as blind to that as to everything else around me. We're both products of my father. Both of us broken into pieces and stuck back together all wrong.

I nod at his wrist, where the string bracelet has slipped into view again. 'You kept it.'

'Of course.'

I can feel the tears forming behind my eyes, an overwhelming sense of relief that I never lost my friend at all. And then I notice his expression, burdened by guilt and regret for all he's done. How I wish he could have told me why we couldn't be friends, spared me the pain of rejection and humiliation. But I understand why he had to be cruel. Because I wouldn't have accepted it any other way; I loved him too much. It is not him I blame, not any more. It is my father.

'Do you remember when we were young and you used to sneak into my cabin during a storm? You'd lie on the floor beneath my hammock and when I reached my hand down you'd take it, holding it until I fell asleep?'

Bronn nods, a nostalgic smile forming at the memory.

'Every night since your Initiation, I've reached my hand down for you. I will always reach out for you.'

But he's the one who gently takes my hand in his. His eyes meet mine, and they seem to overflow with sadness. So many wasted years, our unhappiness the price of his survival.

'Looks like I'm stuck with you after all,' I say, cautiously hoping I'm right, and that he's not planning to leave us once we're safely ashore.

'Looks like it.' It's as much commitment as he's going to give, but this time I believe it. He's starting to shed his Snake skin.

I rest my head on his shoulder, and fall asleep with my hand still in his, stirring slightly when he swaps with Grace during the night, the loss of his touch suddenly exposing me to the bitter air. It's dawn when Bronn wakes me for my stint at the helm and I'm shivering, still cold from yesterday's soaking.

'Any sign of the *Maiden*?'

'None.' Bronn doesn't sound pleased, though.

'You think that means he's decided not to come after us?' It doesn't make any sense.

'I'm not sure what it means, but it's nothing good. I think we should keep going.'

I stare at him in surprise. 'What about the mast? Shouldn't we find a better ship?'

'I think landing's too much of a gamble. If he's decided not to hunt us down, your father will have spies on the lookout. We don't want to risk being seen. Besides, this mast is holding. I say we stay our course.'

He's right, there's definitely something suspicious about my father's absence, and yet I'm relieved not to have to try to escape from the *Maiden*. And honestly, if

Bronn thinks he can get this boat to the Sixth in one piece, I trust him to do that.

'OK, if Grace agrees, I'm happy. But can we risk going a little closer to shore? There are plenty of other things out here as dangerous as the Viper.' A merbeast could swallow us whole if we're unlucky enough to stray into its path.

'Agreed.'

Neither of us says anything about last night, but before he goes to rest he slips a blanket round my shoulders and the gesture warms me every bit as much as the thick wool.

The next few days pass without any incident. The three of us fall into an easy routine, taking it in turns to sail then rest, surviving on raw fish and seaweed caught in a net from one of the chests.

None of the conversations of the first day are revisited, all of us too tired to do much beyond survive, but Bronn and I are rarely far from each other's sides, a sort of unspoken intimacy returning to our relationship that is mirrored in our physical proximity. We find excuses to touch, a brush of skin here, a grazing of fingers there, and the thrill of his closeness astonishes me. I hadn't realised how strongly I'd missed him all these years.

To her credit Grace makes no comment, although on one particularly clear day with the unforgiving sun beating down on us, she sits beside me during Bronn's shift.

'You seem cheerier.'

I laugh. 'We're on the run, facing a hopeless mission. What could I possibly be cheery about?'

Grace nods pointedly in Bronn's direction. 'He used to ask me, you know. How you were, if you were happy. Never able to forget you no matter how hard he tried.'

I attempt to hide the delight threatening to turn me giddy and feign indifference. 'Oh?'

Her face breaks into a smile. 'Yes, oh.' And then instantly the smile is gone. 'What is that?'

She's looking beyond me and I turn to see what's concerned her. Smoke is filling the sky in the distance, thick and black.

Bronn's seen it too and he's squinting in disbelief. 'It can't be.'

But it is and I think I'm going to be sick.

The Floral Island is on fire.

We immediately change course to make for land, and the closer we get the greater the horror. The fire is spreading from the west and heading in our direction, preceded by a crowd of islanders all desperately fleeing to the sea. Flames are destroying the island, homes and livelihoods being obliterated in heartbeats, and it's all too clear there aren't enough boats.

'We have to help them.'

Bronn frowns at me. He doesn't believe this is a natural fire any more than I do. 'It's a trap, Marianne.'

I shake my head. 'No, it's not. He's taunting me. He said he'd make them suffer – said he'd make them beg for death. This is it, this is his way of punishing me.'

'All the more reason not to go,' Grace says gently, and I know they're trying to protect me, probably with good cause, but I don't care.

'He's wiping out an *entire* island, Grace.'

'They're already as good as dead,' Bronn says. 'We should keep going.'

I stare at him. His indifference is a painful reminder that despite all our feelings for each other we're very different people. It hurts more than I expected.

'There is no way I'm standing by and simply watching.' My voice is soft but deadly. I am not asking.

Bronn and Grace exchange a look.

'All right, you win. What do you want to do?' Though Bronn sounds far from enthusiastic, I'm relieved not to have to argue any further.

'We'll assess the situation when we're closer. But at the very least there's room on our boat for islanders.' Not many, though. Not enough.

What awaits us is chaos. The screams and frantic cries of fear can be heard long before we land, and with the heat at their backs I'm not surprised. The fire is charging hungrily towards the shore and the survivors are running out of safe ground. People inland will have struggled to escape at all. I think of Joren's little cottage and a knot of sickness forms in my throat. I hate my father and his sick depravity. This is a new low even for him.

'Stay with the boat,' I say to Grace as we pull up alongside the jetty. 'Or we'll never see it again. Get as many as you can on board – children first – and then pull away. Bronn and I will catch up with you later.'

'What are you going to do?'

'I'm going to stop him,' I say, and as soon as we're close enough I jump ashore.

The smoke in the air is overpowering, and it stings my eyes and irritates my throat before I've taken more than a few steps. Panic has tightly gripped this peninsula, fear rendering people senseless, so I look about for anyone who might be in charge, my eyes falling on a group of women who are helping injured people make it to the sea. I run over to join them.

'I have a boat,' I say to get their attention, and point in its direction. 'My friend is ready to take as many on board as we can.'

The oldest of the women, her hair as white as her skin, glances over to where Grace is already lifting children aboard. 'Thank you.'

'How did this start?'

'I don't know . . .' she says before trailing off.

Bronn has come to stand beside me and perhaps it's because we're together but the woman seems to have realised we're in Snake clothing.

'This is my friend,' I say, hoping to convince her we mean no harm. 'We're here to help.'

The woman gives me her full attention now, her startling red eyes brimming with anger. 'They're saying people are attacking our settlements. They say they're burning our crops to the ground.' She glares at Bronn. 'People like you.'

'We are no longer in the Viper's service.'

She considers me with a fiery gaze. 'Then stop them destroying what's left of our home.' And then she's done with me, returning her focus to helping her kin.

I tug at Bronn's sleeve pulling him to one side. 'We need to find them – if they're still here, we can stop them doing more damage.'

'Or they can catch you.'

'There's a time for running. This isn't it.'

I see something flash in his eyes – a spark of respect? Or affection? Either way, he abandons his futile attempts to dissuade me and switches into fighting mode. 'They're still here – probably in groups, and I wouldn't be surprised if there are bandits as well as Snakes. They must be fuelling the fire for it to burn so ferociously. If it were me, I'd be staying close to the sea to avoid getting trapped, and feeding it from the outside in. Given how close the fire is I doubt they're far away.'

An explosion in the distance shudders through the ground, and as people around us scream Bronn and I exchange glances.

'Gunpowder.'

'He's pulling out all the stops,' Bronn says, almost impressed.

Father certainly is making a statement. 'We should split up. Less likely they'll see us coming.'

'I'll go south, you take north. Be safe.'

And to my complete astonishment he leans forward to brush a light kiss on to my good cheek before he's off, shielding his face from the smoke as he takes the long route round the island.

There isn't time to linger and I start my own sprint towards danger. No one else is running in this direction, and I have to weave to avoid the people fleeing the fire as I plunge head first into its path. As I get closer to the blaze I see more and more injured people struggling to flee, and one man hurtles past me, clothes alight, his screams of agony unbearable. I shout at him to drop and roll on the ground, but he's beyond hearing. He stumbles and falls, and I run over to him, not sure how I can help, yet unable to leave him to suffer alone. But by the time I reach him his screams have stopped and his eyes are open and empty. At least he can no longer feel the flames devouring his flesh. No one should have to endure such a horrific death, and I'm more determined than ever to stop my father as I head towards the woodland that separates the meadows from the sea. From this angle I can see the wood conceals a small river, the end of which runs directly back towards the ocean. If I wanted to stay safe while fuelling this monster, then I would definitely be keeping close to a water source.

The moment I enter the trees an eerie silence falls. The screams are dulled by the dense nature of the branches and leaves, and the smell of smoke and burning flesh has only vaguely penetrated the sheltered atmosphere. My knife is firmly in my hand as I creep silently into the heart of the wood, tracing the bank of the river – I'm certain I'm not alone.

The sun is at its height in the clear sky and it's fiercely hot even in the shade of the trees, though I suspect a large part of the heat is the wall of fire heading this way. When it hits this woodland it'll devour it quickly, so I want to be long gone by then.

In the corner of my eye I catch a flicker of movement and press myself up against the nearest tree. Slowly I peer round and see one of the *Maiden*'s crew walking boldly towards me, pouring fluid from the barrel he carries. How my father convinced the Snakes this venture was worth sacrificing their supply of rum for I have no idea.

I watch for a moment, weighing up the best time to strike, and then with a sinking heart realise it's Gustav, a boy only a year older than me. I don't know him well – all I know is his name and that he doesn't have friends – but if I have to take another life, there's no way it's going to be him. I slide my knife back into my belt. Grace has taught me well in unarmed combat and I know how to take down an enemy without killing him.

As Gustav passes my tree I strike. I bring one arm firmly into his gut, winding him, and before he can even blink I hit him hard under the chin with the heel of my palm, snapping his head back and rendering him unconscious. It's all over in an instant, and despite the horror of being on a burning island I'm relieved. I stayed in control. No darkness, no flashbacks. I crouch down to check his pulse. He should come round in time to flee the fire.

I'm about to stand up when a cold and very sharp blade presses on my neck.

'Well, well. This *is* a pleasant surprise.'

Of all the men my father might have assigned to this mission I wasn't expecting Cleeve to be one of them, and the pride I'd felt after my quick defeat of Gustav evaporates. This won't be so easy. He'll be wanting to finish what he started on the skerry-cutter.

The blade at my neck is drawing blood, but nothing life-threatening. He just doesn't want me to run. He hauls me to my feet by grabbing my hair and slams me against the tree, his arm wedged under my chin, causing me to choke. He pulls my knife out from my belt and throws it far from my reach.

'I'd rather hoped you'd drowned in the fiords,' I manage to hiss, though it isn't easy to speak when I can barely breathe.

My 'uncle' gives me a leering smile. 'Now, now. You know you've missed me.'

'Like the plague.'

'Your father can't wait to have you back home. You have no idea the welcome he has planned for you.'

His breath is foul and it's not helping the lack of air situation. I need to break his hold on me, or I'm going to black out. 'Think I'll pass.'

Cleeve laughs. He's enjoying my retorts, relishes the game. 'He's promised us all a turn to show you how much you mean to us. Milligan's claimed first go and is most excited. Says she never did finish teaching you all she could, and you were such a willing student.'

The prospect of being Milligan's plaything is the stuff of nightmares. I have to get out of here. Now.

My knee slams hard into his groin, causing him to loosen his grip enough for me to break free, but he's only stalled for a second and grabs me back immediately, harder, his eyes bright with bloodlust. All I've done is whet his appetite.

It's now or never. Fight or die. And so I whip my leg up, striking out with my foot and catching him in the neck. He releases me and before he can grasp me again I immediately bring my hand round in a fist to his stomach. He stumbles backwards, the attack taking him by surprise, but he rallies quickly, parrying my blows, until he's back in control of the fight and I'm the one blocking him.

My eyes rest on my knife lying discarded in the dirt. I try to manoeuvre us closer to where it lies, hoping to snatch it up and give myself a chance. But then Cleeve realises what I'm doing and roars with fury.

He's through playing games; my retaliation has angered and humiliated him, and he lands a strike clean across my face, then pushes me into the river before I can regain my balance. It's not deep, in fact, I'm only submerged because I'm lying flat, but panic makes me irrational. Air becomes the only important thing in the world. But the moment I break the surface and inhale deeply, his lethal hands have hold of me and are groping every inch of my body as I kick, bite and writhe – anything to fight him off. He has the advantage, though, and pins me to the riverbed, straddling my chest, holding my head above water, with his knife at my throat so I'm forced to stay still.

'You think you're a match for me? Your father's only stipulation is that you're returned alive. He never said you had to be in one piece. Milligan will be disappointed, but then I never did like her much.'

Cleeve looks fondly at the gash he previously marked my face with, and leans forward to lick it. I try again to pull away, but it's impossible. He grazes the blade to and fro on my neck, sliding it down over my collarbone, his skin glistening with sweat as he focuses on the prize he's about to claim. I wonder what part of me he'll remove first. A fingernail perhaps, to build up slowly? Or maybe he'll take the whole hand to leave an indelible mark.

But he takes nothing, because at that moment he topples forward and I'm smothered by his weight, going under the water again. Frantically I push him off me and manage to sit up, only to see an axe protruding from the back of his head.

My saviour stands over me and once I recognise who it is my gratitude is replaced by renewed fear. Ren. The boatswain is well known for his loyalty to his fellow Snakes. For him to have killed Cleeve can only mean that he wants to present me to my father himself. When he offers his hand to pull me up, I ignore it, unsure of his intentions, and scramble to my feet myself. He retrieves his axe from Cleeve's limp body, kicking him hard. 'Piece of filth.'

'What are you doing?' If he means to harm me, I may as well find out sooner rather than later.

'Saving your skin.' He grabs a handful of grass and wipes the blood from the blade. 'The fire has already entered the woodland; it's only minutes away from here. There's gunpowder scattered all over this area. You need to run.'

I'm stunned into silence, confused and relieved all at once. He turns to leave but I grab hold of his sleeve. 'Wait. Why are you telling me this? Why help me?'

'Because you stood up for my boy. Against this scum.' He spits towards Cleeve.

I have no idea what he's talking about, but then it hits me. 'Toby?'

'He's my son. And this rat's made his life a misery.' He swings his axe over his shoulder, watching me closely. 'I'm not the only man aboard who'd switch his allegiance should the right person challenge the Captain.'

It takes me a moment to realise what he means and when I do I can scarcely believe it. 'Are you saying *I* have your allegiance?'

He stares at me a while longer before spitting once more. 'Try to stay alive.' And then he's off, running towards the coast to escape the approaching furnace, and the only company I have is Cleeve, whose blood is turning the river red. The sight of his mangled head is pretty nasty. Still, the approaching crackle of burning leaves means he'll soon be cremated by his own fire, and if I don't want to join him I'm going to have to hurry.

A twig snaps and my eyes dart up to see Gustav pause in mid-run. He takes in the scene: me standing over Cleeve's butchered body. If I let him go, he'll tell my father. But there's no time to fight him without risking the blaze. My hands twitch in anticipation, wondering what Gustav will choose to do. Our gaze is locked and I realise he's thinking the same thing as me – that if we stay we'll both be engulfed by a fire that kills regardless of whose side you're on. He makes the decision first and almost trips over himself as he flees towards the sea.

I'm not going to argue, and hurtle back the way I came, no longer making any effort to be quiet. There's no halting this fire now. It's self-feeding, hungrily consuming the flowers and woodlands that made this island so beautiful, turning it to ash.

I've failed. The first time I tried to take on my father, and I couldn't stop him. Couldn't protect the island any more than I could protect Tomas. Couldn't defend the flowers any more than I could defend Joren. Couldn't save the people any more than I could save Clara.

Maybe Bronn was right. Maybe I shouldn't have come here.

The force of another explosion nearby throws me to the ground and with my ears ringing I clamber back to my feet and press on.

As I near the shore where we landed, I come across a small family making their escape far too slowly. The youngest child is struggling to carry a mangy hound, and refusing to leave it behind despite her mother's pleas.

'There are ships waiting, but you have to go faster,' I shout at them as I approach, hoping it's still true. 'Let me carry the dog.'

I reach out my arms and the child considers me, weighing up whether I'm trustworthy. I don't wait for her to decide, and snatch the dog. 'Run!'

I only glance back long enough to see them in pursuit, the father now carrying the child who just wants to catch up with her beloved companion. Whether or not there'll be any space for them on a boat still remains to be seen. It wouldn't surprise me if the ships had all gone, leaving the remaining islanders to their fate.

So when I reach the brow of the hill and see the cove beneath me I pause in disbelief.

Four large ships are anchored offshore, smaller boats ferrying people to them with organised urgency. Though the flags flying leave little doubt, I can't quite believe it. They're from the King's Fleet.

The family overtaking me reminds me to keep moving and I run so fast down the hill I almost lose my footing. When I reach the bottom, my lungs burning from the exertion, I reunite the girl with her dog and point them towards the orderly gathering.

'Go, quickly, someone will get you to safety,' I say, and once they're gone I cast around for any sign of Bronn.

My eyes fall on someone else instead.

Looking as gorgeous as the day we met, his unkempt appearance only improving on perfection, my fiancé is helping an elderly couple towards the boats. Well, that explains the presence of the King's Fleet then. As if he can sense my eyes on him, Torin looks up and meets my gaze.

His lack of confusion upon seeing me suggests he's already found Grace and I raise my arm in greeting as I run towards him.

The warm embrace he gives me is utterly unexpected. 'Grace said you went after Adler's men? I was worried.'

I think of Cleeve, his breath on my face as he threatened to mutilate me, and hate to admit his worry was nearly justified. How can I expect to take my father down if I couldn't even handle Cleeve? Instead I ignore my anxieties and say, 'What are you doing here?'

'I got your message and thought it would be best to sail out to meet you. Just as well, or we wouldn't have got here in time.' He pauses, his eyes lingering with concern on my cut cheek and the fresh mark on my neck. 'It's good to see you, Marianne.' And he seems wholeheartedly genuine.

'You too.' Which is quite probably the biggest understatement I've ever made.

But there's no time for anything more as one of Torin's men runs up to us, staring at me suspiciously as he does so. I recognise him immediately as the bodyguard who accompanied Torin on the day of our engagement. He seems no happier to see me today than he did then.

'We need to hurry, sir,' he says. 'The island's lost.'

Torin nods his agreement. 'Marianne, this is Sharpe, my most loyal commander.'

'It's a pleasure to meet you,' I say but he doesn't return the sentiment.

'Sir?'

'Right, come on.'

'Wait,' I say, looking around. 'Where's Grace?'

'She's safe,' Torin replies. 'Helping people on to my ship. I'll take you to her.'

Torin's hand rests on my back as we jog over to urge the remaining people on to boats, but my eyes are still scanning for Bronn. The fire will reach us soon, and his absence is making me nervous. If he doesn't show up quickly, he's not showing up at all.

'Were there many others behind you?' Torin asks me and I shake my head.

'This is it, from this part of the island anyway.'

We share a grim expression. The death toll will undoubtedly be high.

'We'll make him pay for this,' Torin says, and despite the circumstances something inside me lifts. Though there's still so much I don't know about this man, he came to help. Which is more than his father was prepared to do. It's the first glimmer of hope I've had in the longest time.

Everybody's on a boat now, only one boat remaining for us. Sharpe boards, followed by Torin, but I hesitate.

Torin holds out his hand and when I don't take it he frowns. 'What's wrong?'

'Bronn's out there.'

An understanding passes between us as Torin comprehends that Bronn is someone important to me. 'We'll wait.'

'Sir!' Sharpe objects.

'I said we wait.'

I nod my thanks to him, then turn anxiously round. Black smoke stretches high as if it hopes to obliterate the sun, and the air is increasingly hard to breathe. Or perhaps it's just my heart struggling to beat properly as worry fully takes hold. I can't lose Bronn, I can't. I've only just found him again.

Minutes pass. Nothing. Only the shrieking of gulls overhead and the roar of the approaching inferno.

Torin touches my shoulder. 'Marianne, we have to go.'

I ignore him, staring, willing Bronn to show up. I'm not leaving without him.

'If your father decides to come and join us, we're all going to die,' Torin says, trying to pull me towards him, and I hate that he's right.

'Bronn!' I scream his name into the air, hoping he'll hear me. 'Bronn!'

'He's not coming.' Torin is gentler this time.

Tears that have nothing to do with the smoke prick my eyes, and when I see the blurry image I think I must be imagining it. But I'm not.

Bronn is struggling towards us, a body slung over each shoulder. I sprint towards him, Torin close behind me, and when we reach him Bronn drops to his knees so that he can unload one of his passengers for Torin to take. The unconscious man is badly burned, and Torin quickly scoops him into his arms.

'What happened?' I ask.

'Found Davies and Roach.'

I know Bronn was friendly with both of them, and won't have taken any pleasure in their deaths. 'I'm sorry.'

He doesn't react. 'Picked up these two on my way back, and they slowed me down.'

Take two lives, save two others. Perhaps that's how Bronn deals with killing.

We don't talk any more; there'll be time for that later. Now our only focus is on getting off this doomed island. As soon as we're all in the boat Sharpe begins to row us away.

Once I know we're safe from the fire, exhaustion hits me hard and I lean against Bronn's shoulder. He takes my hand, but his fingers pause as they run over my wrist, over my burn. I catch Torin looking briefly before he turns away and realise this could get complicated.

I close my eyes. It's the least of my worries. The Fourth Isle has been destroyed in the cruellest attack in the history of the Twelve Isles. All trace of Joren's fields will be gone, his beloved crops reduced to ash, and my chest aches with grief. It hurts like I've lost them all over again, an agony I can hardly bear.

What's more, not only did I fail to stop the crew, Gustav will report that I murdered Cleeve when he returns to the *Maiden*.

If my father was angry before, this will only fuel his rage. The Fourth Isle was just the beginning. What worries me now is what he's going to do next.

16

There was a time mere weeks ago when I'd hoped never to return to the Sixth Isle, but after the journey to get here even the ominous low clouds and deadly rocks look inviting. Though Torin's frigate is vast by any standard, in some ways it has felt smaller than our little skerry-cutter.

After we left the Fourth to burn – its once vibrant colours now turned to black, any remaining magic that lingered there purged – we transported our refugees to the Sixth, while the other three ships from the King's Fleet took passengers to the Second, Third and Fifth Isles. Given the fragile state of all the islands, more displaced people will only add to the burden.

I've spent the best part of the journey tending to the wounded. The ship's surgeon, glad of my assistance, provided me with various tonics and an abundance of second-salve to administer to the injured. Unsurprisingly there are many burns of varying degrees, and the second-salve especially has been well used. I try not to think about how many vital medicinal ingredients have been lost to the flames, and the long-term impact that might have on the Isles. From now on I shall have to be frugal with certain supplies, but at least the invasive black bramble that farmers on the Fallow Island cut and sell to be used for second-salve is in no danger of running out.

It's been good to have something to keep me occupied because all that awaits me otherwise are difficult conversations and awkward situations.

The night we joined Torin on the ship he had invited me to dine with him in his quarters – a dinner that, to my relief, was entirely different to the one I'd had with his father. We'd spoken of many things. I'd told him all that had happened since our binding ceremony, and why I had been coming to find him.

'I want to know if you'll do what your father is too afraid to?' I'd asked, thinking it was wisest to get straight to the point, and feeling far too tired for anything other than complete honesty.

Torin had downed a large mouthful of rum. 'There's one important thing you need to know about me,' he'd said, leaning forward to fix me with his earnest gaze. 'I am nothing like my father.'

'Likewise.'

'Do you know why I came to your ship? Allowed myself to be bound to you?'

I'd considered him closely. 'Honestly? No. I know nothing about you beyond rumours.'

He'd smiled, not a false one like he'd had when surrounded by enemy crew, but a real one. It was open and warm and lovely. 'Ah, yes, the rumours. Last I heard

I was a snivelling coward hiding away from danger.' He'd shrugged, unbothered by the implication. 'My father and I aren't close, you see, so people talk.'

I knew enough about complicated father–child relationships to guess that was a massive understatement.

'Is that why you schemed with my father to marry me? To get back at the King?' I'd wanted him to know I was aware of his duplicity. I'd wanted to know what explanation he had.

'I came because I was furious with my father. His Viper was attacking our ships and killing our men, and though the Fleet belongs to my father in name it's always been my dream to captain it. My father has forbidden any such thing, denying me any future I might actually desire, but it doesn't change the fact that I'm the one who's grown up training with them, who sails with them. Without us there's no one to monitor the trading channels, maintain law and order among the many people who rely on safe passage from isle to isle. And when they were being attacked my father did nothing, made plans only to protect himself, while our men, my friends, were dying. While the islands were put at risk. So when your father contacted me suggesting our union, I decided what better opportunity to find out for myself what was going on than an invitation to the Viper's table. It's a rare thing indeed.'

I'd bristled slightly at the thought that he was there spying on us, yet another person playing the game while

I knew none of the rules. 'And did you learn everything you hoped to?' I'd heard the bite in my voice.

'Not everything,' he'd said. 'But I found something unexpected. You.'

When I'd frowned at him he'd added, 'I'd imagined you to be working with your father, but instead I found a bird in a cage desperate to fly. I hoped then that we could become allies – in time.'

'Time is no longer a luxury we possess.'

'I agree. But we're both here now, are we not?' He'd given me another of his warm smiles, and I wasn't sure I'd ever get used to such transparency – his willingness to reveal himself to me. 'Look,' Torin had continued, 'your father orchestrated our marriage to try to achieve power. I went along with it for information. But that was then.'

'So you think we should sever the promise between us?' I'd tried hard to keep the hope from my voice. Because though I'm fast growing to like Torin, he has one flaw. He's not Bronn.

'On the contrary,' Torin had said. 'I think together we could reunite land and sea.'

This time I'd failed to mask my disappointment. 'Surely we can do that without getting married?'

Torin had reached his hand across the table and taken mine. 'Our duty never leaves us, no matter how greatly we disappoint our fathers. The islands, the people – they have never been in greater need of a strong show of power. After all that has been done, I believe only a marriage will be enough to restore their faith in the King and his Viper. And only if we two assume those titles.'

I'd known he was right, of course. I'd always known it. I'd just hoped . . .

'I'm not asking you to love me,' he'd said with a small smile. 'I know when a heart is already spoken for.'

I'd hated how easily I blushed. 'And what of your heart?'

Then it had been his turn to look away. 'I lost it to another a long time ago, to a person my father disapproved of. Our union wasn't in accordance with my duty.' There had been so much bitterness in those words that I couldn't help but feel sympathy for him. But I'd also been intrigued as to who had claimed his affections and why the King had forbidden their match. For all his honesty he hadn't been willing to share that with me. Instead he'd looked up at me with shining eyes. 'This is bigger than either of us, Marianne. Our desires, they're irrelevant. Only the future of the Eastern Isles matters.'

I'd nodded, crushing my sadness with necessary resolve. 'Then we overthrow our fathers and restore peace.'

'I'll drink to that.' And he'd raised his glass.

But what had seemed so simple in the privacy of his quarters was less so when confronted with Bronn. He'd sought me out later that same night when I was lying on deck watching the stars.

Wordlessly he'd lain down beside me, just as he had when we were young, and for the longest time we stayed like that in silence.

'You're going to marry him.' It hadn't been a question.

'Yes.'

'It's the right thing to do.' His resignation was barely audible, but hearing it made my heart ache.

'Just the small matter of stopping both our fathers first.' I'd tried to make a joke about the least funny thing ever.

'You're going to have to kill him, you know.'

I'd turned to look at Bronn, the lanterns illuminating his cheekbones and brow, the rest of his face lost in shadow.

'Who?'

'Adler. He'll never allow himself to be captured.'

I'd said nothing, a worm of unease burrowing into my chest. 'You don't know that.'

'Yes I do.' He'd turned to me then, his fingers brushing across my neck where Cleeve had drawn blood. Though Bronn was gentle, the bruises left by Cleeve's arm as he'd crushed my windpipe were still tender under his touch. 'What happened?'

Though I didn't particularly want to relive it, I'd told him everything, including what Ren had said about switching allegiance.

He'd considered this carefully. 'It's not enough that you're his daughter. The crew will only recognise you as the Viper if you kill their captain.' When I'd said nothing he'd tucked a curl of hair behind my ear. 'What is it?' he'd whispered gently. 'Is your love for him so great, even after all he's done?'

I'd shaken my head, trying to rid it of conflict.

'Then what?' Bronn had continued to coax the truth from me. 'I know you've done it before.'

So he'd known I was responsible for Briggs then. 'I never wanted to kill anyone,' I'd said. 'I want to save lives, not take them.'

He'd given me a sad smile. 'Sometimes they're one and the same thing.'

I wasn't being completely honest, though. I couldn't admit to Bronn – could barely admit to myself – that when Briggs had murdered Joren and Clara and Tomas, a thirst to inflict pain had awakened in me. The truth is death wasn't enough for Briggs. I wish he was still alive because I still want to hurt him, still want to punish him. The force with which I desire that suffering is powerful and only growing over time. The realisation that I'm capable of such darkness terrifies me.

'I don't want to become my father.' It had come out a frightened whisper.

'You are nothing like him,' Bronn had assured me. 'But one of you is going to die.' His eyes had shone fiercely. 'Don't let it be you.'

Did he know what he was asking? To win this fight I will need to marry a man I don't love, and kill my own father. Who will I be after that? How much of myself must I sacrifice for the islands?

'The diplomat at my Initiation?' Bronn had looked away from me, staring up at the night sky again. 'She wasn't my first kill.'

He was an endless well of secrets. 'What? Then who?'

'Do you remember Scurve? You'd have been about thirteen.'

I'd tried to recall, and a hazy image of a pencil-thin, greasy-haired man had floated into my memory. 'Did he have a scar on his nose?'

'Yes, a big one. He was my first.'

That had made no sense at all. 'Had he crossed my father?'

'Not exactly.' He'd paused. 'We'd been drinking one night, after a good day's haul. Everyone was in a good mood, apart from old Scurve. Drink made him even crueller than usual, and that particular night he decided he'd like to pay you a visit.'

I'd looked over at Bronn, confused. 'Me? What would he want with . . . Oh.' My blood had run cold as I realised what he'd meant, and bile crept unbidden to my mouth.

'All the men knew you were off limits, being the Captain's daughter, not to mention a child. Scurve was

258

too drunk to care. I tried to reason with him, but he was having none of it, and started making his way to your quarters. Things turned nasty when I stopped him. He got violent; I won the fight. Captain didn't care because I'd prevented an incident that would have shamed him.'

He'd sighed, not enjoying reliving the memory.

'The reason I'm telling you this is because I understand how you feel about killing Briggs. I know the difference between killing on orders, killing in self-defence and killing in anger. You lost control with Briggs. I lost control with Scurve. And yet it's the one kill I don't regret, not for a second. It was him or you. And it was always you.'

My breath had caught in my throat, something between a sob and a laugh, strangling me with its intensity.

He'd brushed his finger lightly down my cheekbone, his breath warm on my skin, and I'd slid my hand across his chest, lingering where I could feel his heart beat.

'You will find a way to do what you have to do,' he'd whispered. 'And you'll restore the honour of the Viper. I know you will.'

I'd blinked salty tears away. 'And you?'

'I'll do whatever you ask of me. But when we reach the Sixth Isle I think I should leave. For both our sakes.'

Just as I'd always feared he was going to run. But this time he wasn't just protecting his heart – he was protecting mine too. The sickness I'd known would come at this inevitable conclusion flooded through me, but I'd nodded in agreement. 'Maybe you can find me a ship? Something that'll give us a chance against the *Maiden*?'

He'd laughed. 'I'd have to build it from scratch.'

'The *Maiden* no longer has her best sailor. With a good ship we have a chance. Find one you can captain.'

'Consider it done.'

And then he'd gone, leaving me with only the loneliness of my thoughts.

Since then I've spent the remainder of the journey hidden away, losing myself in the troubles of others. Any time I've not been tending to burns or wounds I've managed to keep my conversations with Torin superficial, and have avoided Bronn almost entirely. Or he has avoided me. I'm not quite sure which.

One of my patients, a young man with severe burns to his torso, is in particularly bad shape. I've stayed up two nights nursing him through his fever, hoping it will break, but the surgeon's medicines are limited and I'm beginning to think I'm just prolonging the poor man's agony. Still, I'm hopeful that when we land I will be able to move him to Torin's castle, and perhaps do something for him there, though I'm not entirely sure what miracle I expect to perform.

As the ship slowly makes its approach to the island, keeping to the invisible path that will lead safely to Torin's concealed cove, I stand near the bow, breathing in the saline air.

'Hi, stranger.'

Grace appears beside me, and I immediately sense she's been deliberately keeping out of my way these past few days. She knows me well enough to give me space when I need it, but my time is up. The journey's over and we need to focus.

'Some of Torin's men think they have a ship that'll be suitable for Bronn to modify,' she says without preamble, for which I'm grateful. 'They'll take him straight there when we land.'

'OK.' I really can't bring myself to say anything more than that. He's only doing what I asked.

She obviously has more to say on the subject, but we're interrupted by Sharpe approaching, the usual scowl he reserves for me firmly in place. 'The Prince requests you join him in his quarters.'

'Of course, I'll be there in a minute.'

When he's gone Grace turns to me and smiles. 'Not your biggest fan.'

'I don't know what his problem is,' I say, shaking my head. 'Is he like that with everyone else?' Whenever I see him he's watching me, always suspicious, always glowering. I can't think what I've done to earn his dislike.

Torin clearly values Sharpe highly as they're rarely apart, but I can't understand why he's friends with him. And I dread to think what Sharpe says about me behind my back. I can't imagine he is an advocate of my future marriage to Torin.

'No, he's one of the most popular men aboard the ship, hard-working, kind, thoughtful . . .' Grace says, cutting her list short when she sees my expression. 'Perhaps he just confuses you with your father.'

'Perhaps.'

She walks with me towards Torin's quarters. 'Should I ask what's going on with you and Bronn?'

'Nope.'

'Fair enough. But I'm here if you want to talk.'

I shrug. 'There's nothing to say.'

She slings her arm round my shoulder. 'Been a strange few months, hasn't it?'

I laugh. 'That's one way of putting it.'

When we reach Torin's quarters, Grace makes to leave but Torin calls her in. 'Join us, please. It's nothing private.'

The Prince is looking distinctly scruffy, his smooth face now hidden under stubble, his clothes a little worse for wear. I find myself liking him more every day.

'How's your patient?'

Even with a ship full of wounded people I know he's referring to my dying man.

'Not good.'

Torin doesn't look surprised. 'If anyone can help him, you can.'

He has absolutely no evidence to support this, but I appreciate his faith in me.

'What can I do for you?' I ask.

He picks up a box from his desk. 'I was wondering if you'd do me the honour of wearing this.'

I take it from him and open it to discover a small crystal pendant on a delicate chain. It's beautiful.

'It was mined from this island,' he says with a gentle smile. 'It was my gift to my sister upon her birth, but she died in the cradle, long before she could wear it.'

'Thank you.' The gift feels too intimate, too personal, but I remind myself that he is my fiancé. Intimate and personal are things I'm going to have to get used to.

'May I?' He gestures an offer to put it on, and I nod, turning round and pulling my hair up, not giving it a second thought until I catch Grace's widening eyes and sense Torin pause as he sees my neck.

There is a short but astonishingly awkward silence.

'It can't be,' he says under his breath as I hold Grace's stare.

'It is,' she says after a moment.

I let my hair fall back down as the three of us all try to work out where this conversation is going.

'You bear the mark of the crescent moon.' He looks at me in disbelief.

'You've heard of it then?' So Grace truly hadn't made it up.

'Of course, but there's no one left alive who should have it.' He switches his scrutiny between Grace and me. 'How is this possible?'

Grace raises her eyebrow at me, seeking permission to tell him everything. I shrug my agreement.

She fills him in on who she really is and what she believes. Somehow hearing her say it to someone else and seeing that he actually believes her, brings home the gravity of the situation.

'You're Western royalty?' Torin actually has to sit down.

'It's a tiny, slight possibility,' I concede.

He shakes his head. 'You bear the mark,' he says, and it's disconcerting to hear him sound awestruck. 'It's more than a slight possibility.' He rubs his stubble, deep in thought. 'This changes everything. An alliance between land and sea was one thing, but this? This would be an alliance between East and *West*. The restoration of the Twelve Isles.'

'The Western Isles are lost,' I say. 'And I have no interest in claiming that poisoned throne. Stopping my father is all the madness I can take.'

Grace smiles. 'So you finally admit the throne is yours to claim?'

'No, that's not what I meant,' I say, but I'm no longer sure. Torin's conviction in Grace's theory has rattled me.

Torin stands up and this time succeeds in putting the necklace on me. 'I knew there was more to you than met the eye,' he says with a chuckle.

'Don't tell anyone,' I say, turning to him, increasingly scared at how real this is becoming and wanting it to stop. 'We're already facing an almost impossible fight against my father – and yours. Things don't need to be more complicated.'

'Of course not. But I don't think this is something you can ignore for ever.'

Just then Sharpe knocks on the door, finally doing something helpful by saving me from this awkward conversation.

'We've dropped anchor.' His eyes linger on the pendant resting round my neck and narrow with displeasure.

'Thank you, Sharpe.' If Torin notices his commander's lack of civility towards his betrothed, then he doesn't mention it.

'Right then,' Grace says to Torin, her voice bright. 'Time to show me how you've managed to keep your castle secret on this island.'

'Will you excuse me?' I say. 'I'm going to help bring the wounded ashore.'

I leave them as quickly as possible. The necklace may as well be a choker round my neck – I can barely breathe.

The Western connection isn't something I can dwell on right now; I have to keep focused.

My father hasn't been sighted since the Fourth Isle, and it's not because he's feeling in any way thwarted. He's plotting something, some hideous revenge for Cleeve. I know he is. Luring us into a false sense of security, so that we lower our guard. I can't let anything distract me, especially not some ludicrous notion of bringing peace to six desolate islands.

I have far more immediate problems. I've had nothing but time to think about what Bronn said, and he's right. I have to kill my father before he kills me. And I have no idea how I'm going to do it.

17

The moment we arrived it was immediately clear how the castle had remained so successfully hidden over the years. It's built right into the rock face, disguised by the high walls of the crater it's nestled in, so that at a glance you would never suspect a thing.

When I'd asked him how he came to live in such a fortress, Torin told me that his ancestors had built it during the war against the West. His grandfather had told him about it, but his own father knew nothing of its existence and so when he needed to escape from the King, Torin had claimed it as his own.

It's a dark place, with no natural light penetrating the rock, and lanterns casting eerie shadows in the corridors and rooms. But there's something about being deep in the heart of the island that creates a feeling of security. At the castle's centre is a cavernous hall, the walls glistening with moisture from a natural spring. In the middle of the cave is a circle of twelve standing stones, one to represent each of the Isles. Torin told me that his ancestors never gave up hope of reuniting the two kingdoms.

Subtle.

When we first arrived, sea vultures were immediately dispatched to those loyal to Torin in the remnants of the King's Fleet, advising them to stand by for action. Most of the refugees from the Floral Island have been taken to the nearest settlement, which is already overpopulated by other Sixthers displaced by mining accidents and bandit attacks. I've spent several days down there with Torin and Grace doing what we can to help. But there's only so much food and only so much medicine.

Still, a regiment of the King's Fleet guard it, so it's the safest the people are going to get, and word is that more islanders from the Sixth are making their way towards it.

I've kept my sickest patient at the fortress, wanting to move the poor man as little as possible. Four days we've been here and it was only last night, while he screamed in feverish torment, that I admitted to myself he was going to die. His burns are too severe.

I mixed up a tonic to knock him into the deepest sleep I could, and have sat by his bedside in a gloomy small room ever since. I'm supposed to be attending a council meeting that Torin's called with his advisors, so we can draw up our plan of action against the Viper, but they'll have to wait. I won't leave this man to die alone.

He's in a bad way, his skin oozing and infected over the burns, his eyes sunken into his skull, his breathing rapid but shallow. I can do nothing but keep him comfortable, changing the poultices on his wounds and keeping the dressings fresh, though I know it won't save him.

I'm not surprised when there's a knock at the door. I knew they'd try to drag me away to this meeting. But I'm a little disappointed by who's been sent.

Sharpe stands in the doorway, but rather than insist on my accompanying him, he comes in to sit opposite me.

'How is he?'

I'm so surprised by his civil tone I almost forget to answer. 'He's not got long.'

'Is there anything I can do to help?'

I stare at him, confused. Is this the same man who's been nothing but unpleasant to me since we met? 'No, it's fine. Thank you, though.'

'When did you last eat? Can I bring you something?'

That's it. I'm far too tired to pretend this is normal behaviour for him. 'What are you doing?'

Sharpe looks up at me. 'Offering you food.'

'No, I mean, why are you suddenly being nice? I thought you hated me.'

He winces, shame reddening his cheeks. 'I guess I deserve that. I think an apology is in order for my earlier conduct towards you. I'm ashamed of myself. I hope you can forgive me?'

I consider him carefully, noting his complete sincerity and wondering at it. 'Apology accepted. But can I ask why?'

Sharpe removes the cloth I've draped across the man's forehead and refreshes it in cold water. 'I've been in the Prince's service for a long time. We grew up together. It's important to me that he's happy and, I confess, I had misgivings about him allying himself with anyone related to the Viper. But I was wrong. You have proved you are nothing like your father.' He gestures to the man lying before us. 'No Snake would waste their time and energy to ease the passing of a dying man as you have. Not when it serves them no purpose.'

His honesty is so genuine that I soften towards him. 'Believe me, I have no intention of hurting Torin.'

At the mention of Torin's name Sharpe looks away. 'Do you love him?' he says quietly. He immediately seems to regret the question and quickly says, 'I'm sorry, that was too personal.'

There's no reason why I should trust him with my answer, but something about his frankness encourages me to be the same.

'I love him as much as he loves me.'

Sharpe gives a slight smile.

'I barely know him, Sharpe. But I respect him. And I like him.'

How could I not like Torin? He's proving himself to be a good man. An honourable man. I haven't known many of them.

'I don't think either of us imagines this marriage to be anything beyond a political alliance.'

Sharpe makes no reply, but looks satisfied with my answer. I expect him to leave now but he doesn't, instead sitting with me while we wait for death to arrive and claim his victim.

'Tell me about yourself.' This unexpectedly intimate conversation shouldn't be all about me. 'Are you married?'

Sharpe hesitates for a moment, reluctant now he's the one expected to share. 'No. There is someone. But I can't be with them.' He pauses and I have no idea what to say. 'I think marriage for the sake of your country, even to someone you don't love, is better than being alone.'

'It's a complicated thing, isn't it?' I say. 'Love. Doesn't play by the rules.' I'm not just thinking about Bronn, though his absence hurts more with every passing minute. I'm thinking about my father.

He is undoubtedly a monster: foul, evil, loathsome. For everything he's done, for everything he will do, I hate him. And yet, despite this, some part of me still loves him. He is my father, after all.

Complicated doesn't even begin to cover it.

Before Sharpe can answer, my patient stirs in his deep slumber and starts to cough, his cracked lips splitting under the strain. We try to lift him up to prevent him from choking, but the exertion has exhausted him, and one last breath marks his end.

271

I feel only relief that his suffering is over.

'Let me deal with this,' Sharpe says, resting his hand on my shoulder. 'You should join the others.'

I'm so tired; all I want to do is sleep. But this man's death – his unjustifiable suffering – is why I have to go after my father. He has to be stopped before more innocent lives are lost. And so I thank Sharpe and make my way through the maze of tunnels until I reach the great cave.

Torin sits at a round table that has been positioned in the middle of the standing stones. With him are Grace and his half dozen advisors. I know none of them personally, but all of them by reputation. At one time or another they each served the King and fell out of favour before disappearing from the court. Judging by the looks they give me, my father had orders to kill more than one of them. This must be the only place where so many important people could disappear in the Eastern Isles, and the fact that Bronn knew of its existence and never told my father reminds me where his loyalties have been all along. His absence is a gaping hole at this gathering.

'I'm sorry I'm late,' I say as Torin stands to greet me.

'How is the patient?'

I shake my head in reply.

'I'm sorry,' he says quietly. 'Come, there is much to discuss.'

Torin introduces me officially to his advisors and after a decidedly frosty reception I take my seat beside him at the table.

We waste no time getting to the order of business. It's established that the King has been willing to sacrifice his Fleet to concentrate on protecting the only island of any importance to him – the First. All other islands, including this one, are slowly falling to the bandits who work for my father, and they won't be safe for much longer. Meanwhile, Torin reveals that almost half of the King's Fleet has been destroyed by the Viper, and half of those left remain loyal to their loathsome king. The others have pledged allegiance to Torin. Right now, control of the Isles hangs in the balance.

'I'm strongly in favour of summoning what's left of the Fleet,' says an old council member called Enoch. 'Attack Captain Adler now before he can inflict more damage.'

'He won't let you find him,' Grace says.

'He's too powerful at sea,' I say in agreement. 'I admit I once thought as you do, but Grace is right. My father can make the *Maiden* invisible. And while we're all chasing our tails, leaving the islands unprotected, he'll create carnage.'

'This is not a new plan,' Enoch says, puffing out his chest. 'We haven't all been sitting idly by waiting for you to join us. This is something we've been working on for a while. United, we will hunt him down and destroy him.'

'You'll fail.' I do not appreciate his patronising tone.

Enoch and his supporters bristle at my response.

Torin steps in quickly to diffuse the tension. 'So what do you propose?' he says, gesturing at Enoch to let me speak.

'He's weaker on land. It would even the odds somewhat.'

'They'd still be in his favour.' Grace is in an unusually pessimistic mood.

Torin ignores her. 'And how would we get him on land?'

'Use me as bait.'

Finally I've said something the advisors can get behind. They positively light up at the suggestion of risking my life.

'No, it's too dangerous,' Torin says.

'What part of this war do you think isn't?' Frustration makes my temper flare. I look around at them. 'You know nothing about my father. I do. His drive to punish me will outweigh everything, even his desire to control the whole of the Eastern Isles. It will make him careless and we can take advantage of that.'

'We won't have the numbers.' This time it's a woman called Lora who objects to my idea. 'They're trained assassins, we'll fail in hand-to-hand combat.'

'Probably. But it's the only way we'll even have a chance.'

'Your Highness, this is madness,' Enoch says, turning to Torin. 'We've spent years debating how best to be rid of this madman. Are you really going to trust the word of his daughter? For all we know she's a spy.'

'Want to say that again?' Grace growls the warning at him.

'He's trying to kill me,' I say, really not liking Enoch one bit. 'Trust me, I want to stop him more than you do.'

'What's the matter?' Grace asks Enoch. 'Worried that if we draw him on to land he'll finally carry out the kill order on your head?'

'Enough,' Torin says. 'We mustn't fight among ourselves – the Viper's our enemy.' He turns to me, apology written all over his face. 'But I admit I'm reluctant to meet him on land.'

His lack of support is disappointing, but I'm not ready to give up just yet. 'Lure him to the Fifth; it's not an island he has much advantage on. Spring a trap.' Mist Island would be an ideal place to stage an ambush. The island's own microclimate would act as a veil of concealment. 'Yes, there'll be losses, but what war doesn't have some?'

'It's suicide,' Enoch protests.

'Perhaps there's a compromise?' Torin says. 'Bronn is working with some of the Fleet's best sailors to make one of my ships a force to be reckoned with. He knows the *Maiden*'s weaknesses and will strive to exploit them. I propose we wait until he's done and then launch our sea attack as planned, but with a higher chance of success.'

His idea is met with enthusiasm from his advisors and silence from Grace and me.

'How long will that take?' I say, exasperated by their apparent lack of urgency. 'How many more islands can my father destroy before then? You think he'll stop at the Fourth?'

Silence has fallen round the table as my anger grows.

'He only started there because he knows it was important to me. He'll burn them all to the ground if he has to, don't you understand? He wants to hurt me and every minute I evade him he grows angrier. We have to stop him now.'

'You have a Snake's recklessness,' Lora says.

'And you have a politician's cowardice.' I no longer care about manners.

'We should take a vote.' Once again Torin tries – and fails – to calm tempers.

'I didn't come here to vote,' I say, frustration getting the better of me. 'I came for your help, not your hindrance.'

Torin sighs. 'We have a council for a reason,' he says, and he sounds so weary. 'My father rules with an iron fist, making hasty and ill-advised decisions, and look where it's led us. I don't intend to make the same mistakes. Here, we vote.'

And so we do. I lose. It's decided we wait for Bronn, then mount a mass attack on the stealthiest ship in the water.

'You're making a terrible mistake.' My warning falls on deaf ears, the council already leaving the cave. Torin tries to mollify me, but I shrug him away and storm out. How many death sentences did we just sign?

Grace finds me in the medicine room, grinding mettleroot with such ferocity it's now little more than dust.

'What do you want to do?' she asks, sitting on a pile of sacks.

'What can I do? I need help, Grace. The two of us can't take down the *Maiden* by ourselves.'

She flashes a wicked grin. 'We'd do pretty well, though.'

I put down the pestle and mortar, laughing at the awfulness of it all because otherwise I might cry. 'He'll be preparing another strike.' I sound as helpless as I feel.

'I know.' Of course she does. It's only those naive advisors who don't understand how my father works.

We sit quietly for a while, both of us lost in dark thoughts. Eventually I break the silence. 'Tell me about the Western Isles.' The change of topic is entirely deliberate. I don't want to dwell on what's to come any more. 'Are they really as awful as everyone says?'

Grace smiles, a smile that says she knows she's slowly winning me round to believing her. 'I don't know.'

I frown. 'But you said you were a Westerner?'

'I did and I am. But my brother and I were separated from my parents when we were small and taken east, to the Fallow Island, where we were trained by a respected Guardian.'

That's a lot of information to process. 'You have a brother?'

'A twin. His name is Jax. I haven't seen or heard from him in years.'

I stare at my friend, realising how little I truly know about her. Or the sacrifices she's made for her cause. 'Are there other Westerners living in secret in the East?'

'Yes, but I couldn't tell you how many. We're only told what we need to know. The man who raised and trained me is called Ibner. He's my uncle. There were four other children living with us, my cousins, and from the moment we could walk we learned how to fight. The Guardians take their duty very seriously.'

'But why come to the Eastern Isles? Couldn't you stay at home? Could your parents not come with you?'

'Perhaps there's the answer to your original question. The West wasn't considered safe enough for those who needed to protect the bloodline. So my parents decided to send us away, while they continued their search for your mother.'

I flinch inwardly at such casual mention of the word 'mother'. But I brush it aside, wanting to focus on her story, not mine. 'What happened to Jax?'

'He returned to the Western Isles, as most people believed the lost princess would be found there. But I decided a different path was necessary. To broaden our horizons.' She pauses, picking at a loose thread on her cuff. 'For years I've wondered if I should try to find Jax somehow. Tell him about you.'

Her reluctance is confusing. 'But you don't know where to start?' Surely finding her brother would be a wonderful thing.

'I'm sure if I tried I'd discover a way to communicate. It's not that.' Now she meets my eyes. 'I just fear what they might do to you if they knew.'

The familiar sense of impending doom swells inside me. 'What do you mean?'

'I'm afraid they will try to put you on the throne. Whether you wish it or not. And what I do know of the Western Isles is that they're lawless and dangerous. I have no reason to doubt the talk of wild magic that shrouds them in mystery, nor do I think it foolish to fear the Western waters.'

I remember the nights Grace would thrill me with tales of magic and realise they weren't stories at all. She was telling me her history. Despite everything, excitement spikes my insides. Until I recall one of the more alarming aspects of her tales. 'You don't think water raptors actually exist, do you?'

She shrugs. 'Legends always stem from fact.'

'But no one's ever seen one.'

'Not for a long time. But the stories have passed down through generations. They must have come from somewhere. I was taught all this as a child. In fact . . .' She trails off, suddenly reluctant.

'What? Go on.'

'Well, according to legend, the water raptors only disappeared from the seas when the Western royalty were assassinated. Some people believe they will return when the crown is restored.'

She's deadly serious, and out of respect I don't laugh. 'Then that's a very good reason for me not to claim the throne. Creatures that breathe water so venomous it melts your flesh are best left to the depths. Or to legends.' I try to ignore the way my heart is beating faster at the prospect of seeing such beasts, the unnerving flurry of desire to have them rise.

She smiles, oblivious to my thoughts. 'It's not a future I would wish on anyone. Unless you're certain you want it, tell no one else about this.'

'But Torin knows.'

'I don't believe he'll betray you.'

The more she speaks of the Western Isles, the more confused I become. I realise I'm starting to truly believe her. Somewhere along the line I've subconsciously accepted that my father fell in love with a woman, not knowing her true identity, and unwittingly continued the generational line of the lost Western royalty. It's so far-fetched I feel foolish for believing it. And yet my attraction to the Western waters, the ill-advised swell of excitement at the mere mention of water raptors . . . it would all be explained if what she says is true.

I reach into my pocket and pull out the compass she gave me. I like to keep it close – I find running my fingers over the shells comforting. 'This is from the Western Isles, isn't it?'

Grace smiles sadly, but I can tell she's pleased I've figured it out. 'Yes. It's one of the few relics my ancestors were able to salvage from the palace ruins, relics that were entrusted to Guardians for safekeeping. The truth is, I should have handed you over to the Guardians the moment I realised who you were. To fulfil my duty. But the longer I spent with you . . . Well, I grew to love you. You don't belong to the Guardians, or to anyone else. We exist to protect you, which is what I've done. Returning the compass was my way of releasing you from the Guardians' hold. Your life is entirely yours to live.'

I nod, biting back the tears, moved by her loyalty and affection. Every time I dig, a little more is revealed. I'm not sure it's a good idea to keep digging.

There's a light knock at the door. 'Can I come in?' It's Torin.

My earlier anger has turned to weariness, and I like Torin far too much to stay cross with him. 'Of course.'

When he enters the room his relief is visible. Clearly he'd expected me still to be fuming. 'Thought I might find you here. I wanted to apologise—'

I hold my hand up. 'No need. We disagreed. It might be the first time, but I'm certain it won't be the last.'

'Good, after all we both only want what's best . . .' He trails off as he catches sight of my compass. 'Where did you get that?'

'Grace gave it to me.' I frown at him. 'You recognise it?'

I hand it to him, and he traces his fingers over the painting in the lid with undisguised wonder.

'The royal family crest. From the West. This must be the only thing of its kind left.' Torin is mesmerised.

'The royal crest?' I had thought the 'V' stood for Viper, but now I'm certain it doesn't. I take the compass back from him, running my thumb over the ornate letter. 'What does this mean?'

He smiles at me, though it's tinged with sadness. 'It's for the house of Vultura. Your family's house.'

The name resonates in a way I cannot fathom, unleashing a deep yearning I don't understand. It's like the word itself has reached out and claimed me as its own.

I clear my throat, pushing down the rising well of emotion. 'How do you know so much about the West?'

'It's a long story,' Torin says. 'I hardly know where to start.' He looks from Grace to me, before untucking his shirt and lifting it. On his right-hand side, slightly below his ribs, is a birthmark. A semicircle.

'You have one too?' It hadn't even occurred to me the Eastern royalty would carry their own symbol.

'The mark of the rising sun. That's how I recognised your moon, because I carry its opposite. But there's more I want to show you.'

Fortunately he doesn't remove any more clothing, but instead asks us to walk with him. Torin guides us down tunnels that twist and narrow as we move deeper into the cavern, collecting a torch from the wall to light our way. We stoop as the roof grows ever lower until we arrive at a heavy wooden door, which Torin unlocks with a key I hadn't noticed was hanging round his neck. Before he pushes it open he hesitates. 'Grace, would you mind giving us a moment?'

I can see Grace does mind – having walked all this way her curiosity has got the better of her – but she merely nods her head. 'I'll be right out here,' she says before adding, 'in the cold. And the dark.'

The last I see of her she's resting back against the hard stone wall, arms crossed but alert nonetheless, and then Torin lights the chamber we've entered and I forget about Grace entirely.

18

The room is cramped, dark and airless. And full of ancient books.

'What is this place?' The atmosphere is positively alive with history.

'This is how I know so much about the West.' And Torin smiles at me. 'You of all people should read these manuscripts.'

'How do you have these?' I turn to search his face. 'Who are you?'

He laughs. 'Grace isn't the only one descended from people who care about the Western Isles. My ancestors may have murdered the royal family, but through the generations others in my family have devoted their lives to making amends.'

I look at him now and realise the true purpose of this fortress. It's a sanctuary to contain the truth that's been so conveniently lost and a symbol for restoring hope. That's why there are the twelve standing stones; that's why it's on the island closest to the West.

'You want peace for the Twelve Isles. Not just the East.'

'Of course,' he says. 'Shouldn't we all?'

'Why? We've managed perfectly well on our own for years.' But the moment I say the words I realise how untrue they are.

Torin sits on an uncomfortable-looking stone slab and watches me carefully. 'Do you believe in magic?'

'I've seen no evidence of it.' I don't know why I lie, and as the words come out of my mouth I have to try hard not to think of what I saw with Tomas, the very real magic that spun right before my eyes, or of the magic in the earth that Joren once opened my heart to – before my father scorched it from existence.

'Well, I do,' Torin says. 'And everything I've read in these accounts confirms that belief. The healing potions we have now are nothing compared to what we once had. Magic was synonymous with the whole of the Twelve Isles, not just the West, and Mages were the true advisors to all the royalty. And we destroyed it when we turned on ourselves. We lost a valuable part of our essence.' His voice is raised, such is the passion of his convictions.

'How did we destroy it?'

'I think you need to find out for yourself. What I will say is this – unity is essential for magic to exist in our lands. And we haven't had unity of any kind for the longest time.' Torin pauses before he fixes his beautiful eyes on me. 'But I think you are something of an alchemist, am I right? You're drawn to the little magic that remains, wherever it lurks?'

I'm shaken by how well he reads me when he is still such a mystery to me. 'I can make the odd tonic.' It's all I can bring myself to say.

'Read the books, Marianne. Learn your history, then – and only then – decide what your future should be.'

'All right,' I agree. 'But I'm promising nothing.'

'I wouldn't ask you to. I've spent my whole life trying to free myself from someone who told me what to do and how to behave.'

The sadness that so often surfaces in him is so palpable it hurts. 'Your father is a coward,' I say, reaching to touch Torin's arm. 'You are far stronger than he is.'

Torin's hand covers mine. 'Perhaps. But when I was a child he beat me to stop me crying and bullied me into believing that caring was weakness. He taught me that love was a flaw, that compassion was a failing, and that kindness was irrelevant. I've been a disappointment to him in every way, and though I have no regrets about who I am, sometimes that truth is hard to bear.'

I squeeze his fingers. I know exactly how the conflict tastes. 'You will convince him to abdicate, Torin, and you will rule the East justly. And as your wife and the Viper I will be there to support you every step of the way.' I pause, trying to ignore the twinge of sadness I feel pledging myself to him this way when I love another. But it hurts to breathe when I think of Bronn, and so I force myself to carry on. 'There will be unity once more. We don't need the West to achieve our peace.'

A tear slides down Torin's face as he brings my fingers to his lips. 'And as your husband and ally I will be proud to rule by your side.'

I spend the next few weeks buried in the manuscripts. Grace keeps me company from time to time, but she knows I prefer solitude and so often comes just to bring me food and water.

At first I read nothing new. But then I discover one tome with diagrams of anatomy – human anatomy – which fill in some of the blanks from my own research. I get entirely distracted by drawings outlining the differences between veins, arteries, tendons and nerves, the fibrous web spun inside us. Someone has taken the time to dissect a heart, describing it in such visceral detail that it's easy to imagine the ink is the very blood that once flowed through it. Birds, rats, she-wolves – none of them are quite the same as seeing these sketches of the inner workings of humans, which further my understanding of healing.

But this is not why I'm here, and I have to tear myself away to focus on learning about the West. The more I read, the more secrets I uncover buried within the pages, secrets that tell a different story to the lore I've been taught. And the more I learn, the more incensed I become.

We've been lied to.

When people tell tales of the past they all say the same thing: that the wicked Westerners abused the strength of magic and made it a weapon, a means to harm others – while the peaceful Easterners relied on magic for medicine and maintaining the balance of nature so crops would flourish. That was why the West's attack on us was so villainous, so violent, and why such extreme measures were taken by our king to defend us when the West came to steal our resources for themselves. It's what we've all been told.

These books are filled with documents and accounts that expose that story for what it is: an appropriation of history by the East to hide its own sordid past. A twisted piece of propaganda to conceal its crimes.

The books tell a different story, one of powerful Mages from West *and* East, who fought alongside one another for centuries, against threats from the Largeland in the north. Magic united all twelve islands, and though few were able to harness it, those who could advised kings and queens from both of the royal families, and balance was kept.

But there was one difference between Eastern and Western royalty. The Western bloodline seemed to possess a natural proclivity towards magic, whereas the Eastern bloodline did not. And the Eastern King grew jealous.

Fifteen generations ago, Torin's ancestor was a monster. It wasn't Gormand of the West who was the destroyer. It was Davin of the East.

Davin became enraged to the point of madness that he was not the most powerful man in all the Twelve Isles, resentful that he was not chosen to be gifted with magic. He became obsessed with the idea that Gormand and the Mages would rise up to overthrow him. And so he purged the Eastern Isles of all magic.

Those in the East with a magical inclination were rounded up and slaughtered, preferably burned alive to ensure the thorough elimination of any lingering magic, though a lucky few escaped and fled to the West. But then Davin sent his Viper to kill the Western royalty and the West fell. The remaining Mages hid in the ruins of the West, while Davin was content that in his Six Isles, at least, there was no one left to challenge him. He had proved he didn't need magic to be powerful, that the Mages were no threat to him. And the magic has remained dormant ever since, with no one left to harness it.

The West didn't start the war. The East did. It is nothing short of a betrayal that the truth has been buried in this way. I'm not sure what destroys me more: that the East has been deprived of its magic for so many centuries, or that the West has been so demonised by the side ultimately responsible for it all.

Re-educated, the next things I discover among the ancient texts are the books about magic. When I first pick one up and realise what I'm holding in my hand I hesitate. Somehow I know they are waiting for me to find them. And that if I open them, everything will change.

Terrified and thrilled, I start to read, desperate to immerse myself in knowledge.

With the same urgency that I delved into the she-wolf for answers I devour book after book, searching for the key to harness the power I long for.

Because if I can unlock the magic I've known runs in my veins since that day on the Floral Island, I might just stand a chance. My father is powerful, almost impossibly so. But this . . . this could even our odds, could enable me to protect people . . . to avenge people.

There is so much I can't translate or understand, but I drink in whatever I can. Book after book mentions the water raptors, and how they were used in the distant past to protect the Twelve Isles. The more I read about them, the more intrigued I become. There are many passages devoted to how they can be summoned, some that I can translate, others I can't, and whole sections explaining how the Mages struggled to control these dangerous creatures until they became more of a liability than anything else. I'm beginning to think that Grace is right, that the raptors were somehow linked to the royalty, and that it should have been the king or queen who commanded the raptors, their royal blood a more powerful bond between land and sea than anything the Mages could conjure.

And if I'm right? If I can accept what Grace and Torin say, that I am royalty . . . could I one day wield such creatures to wreak my own revenge?

On and on I read, the chamber providing a never-ending supply of material to fuel my growing desire. Every new snippet of information, every hint of magic exhilarates me and feeds my appetite for knowledge, the desperate longing to harness the ability to make me strong.

I am entirely bewitched.

After several days, Grace brings me some cold broth and tries to persuade me to leave the cave for a while. 'I think Torin's beginning to regret showing you this place,' she says, only half joking.

'I just wish I could make more sense of this,' I say, thrusting a page into her face. 'Can you understand any of it? I think it's an ancient language used by the Mages. I've worked out some of the words, but if I could translate it all . . .'

'It's history,' she says, her voice sharp. 'Informative it may be, but there is no more magic and you are no Mage. I understand the desire to escape your reality by losing yourself in this place, but don't forget who you are. And what your fight is.'

I put the book down, feeling the truth of her words sting. I have been more than willing to forget everything outside these walls, have been seduced by the temptation within, and shame pinks my cheeks.

'I heard from Bronn,' Grace says, her voice softer now. 'He asked after you.'

'And what did you tell him?'

'The truth. That you're miserable.'

I stare at her, wondering again at her perception. For all my excitement at discovering the ancient texts, she has seen the deep unhappiness buried within me. A bleak bloom of grief and fear. 'You shouldn't have. He'll only worry.'

Grace sighs. 'Perhaps he should. I do. I've barely seen you since you've had your nose in these books. I thought you wanted to stop your father. I thought that was why we were here?'

'It was!' I'm suddenly angry with her. 'But they want to wait, Grace! They want to bide their bloody time and I can't bear to just sit with them and their stupid smug faces while my father plots his next atrocity.' I take a breath, trying to calm myself. I know I'm being unreasonable. 'Anyway, I thought you'd be pleased I was learning all about my Western heritage.'

'Don't mistake me for a fool,' she says. 'It's the magic you're interested in, always has been. Maybe it's my fault, feeding you those stories, but I know why you trailed

Milligan around all those years and why you smuggled dead birds to your cabin. I'm not blind, Marianne.'

I'm so surprised she knows all this that I splutter out my reply. 'I wanted to learn how to heal . . .'

'Exactly! You wanted to learn *how* to heal, not to *be* a healer. Not all healers became Mages but all Mages started out as healers, and it's a Mage you've always longed to be. You just didn't know it.'

I have no idea what to say, I'm stunned by her words.

Grace sighs as she comes to sit beside me and takes my hand. 'There's nothing wrong with wanting to learn about things you don't understand, and maybe one day you will become the first Mage of a new era, but right now we're still at war. I need to know if you're in this fight with us, or if I've lost you to a dream.'

I close my eyes and take a deep breath. I swear there's magic in this room, an enchantment that's taken hold of me, whispering to the darkest corner of my soul. But of course Grace is right. Now is not the time to lose sight of what has to be done, no matter how much I wish to avoid it. 'I'm still in this fight.' It's barely a whisper.

Grace clasps my hand tighter. 'Really?'

'I'm still in this fight.' The words are more certain now and Grace's eyes sparkle once more.

'Good. Because we can't do this without you.' She pauses. 'We need you.'

I know Grace well enough to know what that really means and lean over to pull her into a tight embrace. 'I need you too.'

The door bursts open with such force that we both jump. Sharpe is there, out of breath, his eyes wide. 'Come quickly.'

Grace and I are already on our feet, running with him through the gloomy passage.

'What is it? What's happened?'

'There's been another attack.'

Damn my father. Though I might have been happy to forget about him, he certainly hasn't forgotten about me.

'Which island?'

Sharpe turns to look at me, and the fear is written all over his face. 'This one.'

By the time I arrive in the great cave Torin has already assembled his men. An injured woman sits slumped against one of the standing stones and I run over to check if she's OK.

She's not. Blood slowly ebbs out from her abdomen, her hand that once held pressure on it now flopped to the side. There's nothing I, or anyone else, can do for her. But her eyes are open and she's muttering under her breath.

'It's all right,' I say, taking her bloody hand in mine. 'You're safe.'

'The Viper,' she says in a fragile whisper. 'The Viper.' She's repeating it over and over.

A hand rests on my shoulder and it's Torin, ready for war. 'Come. You can't save her.'

'Where are we going?'

'Out to the settlement.'

I'm on my feet. 'You think he's still there?'

Torin nods. 'This woman spoke of an attack on the main settlement. She fled almost immediately, but not before receiving her injuries. We must go to their aid.'

Grace is thrusting a knife into my belt and a pistol into my hand. Fear is spiking adrenaline around my body, but this is what I wanted. A chance to face my father on land. And I'm ready. Ready to end this.

As I join the King's Guard making their way quickly out of the cavern, I realise Torin isn't with us and glance back to see him with Sharpe. They are having a heated conversation, clearly arguing about something and it ends with Torin raising his voice so that I can hear it even from this distance.

'That's an order!'

Sharpe looks like he's been slapped. Wounded, he backs down, and Torin strides over to join me.

'Everything OK?' I ask, even though it's clearly not. In fact, I've never seen Torin so riled.

'I told him to protect the council.'

No wonder Sharpe was annoyed. A skilled soldier, he's wasted being left to mind civilians, and I wonder why Torin's made that choice.

My silence must reveal my confusion because Torin adds, 'Someone has to stay behind.' He's being defensive, and I put his mood down to anxiety. Knowing the Viper is slaughtering the people you've sworn to protect is enough to put anyone on edge.

There are no horses to ride here, the terrain in no way compatible with livestock, and so we run as fast as we can towards the settlement, my guilt prickling as it reminds me I'd forgotten all about these desperate people struggling to pick up the pieces of their ruined lives. While I've been reading, my father, like a bloodhound, has sought out the weak, the vulnerable, and has come to finish them off.

The sun is beating down on us and I'm sweating long before we come upon the scene of carnage. The settlement is a battleground. The members of the King's Guard that Torin assigned to defend the civilians are fighting valiantly, but their numbers are badly depleted. Bodies are strewn everywhere, and screams claw in my ears as unarmed men and women try in vain to save themselves.

Our fresh regiment swoops in, targeting anyone in Snakes' blacks. My eyes look around for my father, desperate to find him before he finds me. But a cry for help distracts me and I run to where a young woman is lying on the ground. It's immediately clear her wounds are fatal; she's bleeding all over but somehow is still alive. I crouch beside her, anxious to be fighting, to punish my father for this savage butchery, but unable to ignore my instinct to heal.

'My son,' she whispers, as if all her remaining breaths have been used to summon my aid. 'Help him.'

I look to the child beside her. The frail body has already emptied itself of blood, and lies motionless beside her. I think of Tomas and grief burns my throat so fiercely I could scream.

'Help him,' she begs.

What can I do? Though we're surrounded by violence I move to kneel beside her dead son and press my hand to the wound at his neck, as if somehow I can reverse what has been done. I offer her a false smile, something to reassure her that he'll be OK now, that she has saved him, and I hate myself for it.

'Don't let him die,' she says, a tear spilling down her cheek.

'I won't,' I say, the lie coming far too easily. 'He's safe now, you both are.'

The woman nods, her breathing slower, and I just have to wait, keeping up this pretence until she dies. But I don't stop looking. Looking for the man responsible for all of this.

The longer I look, though, the longer I sense something's not right. It takes a while to figure out what it is. The way the Snakes are moving is wrong. The way their faces are covered. A horrible wave of uncertainty spreads through me as I desperately hope I'm not right. The moment the poor woman dies, I remove my hand from her son, and silently offering them my apologies I race to the nearest fallen Snake and pull his mask down.

I have never seen him before in my life. It's possible my father's taken on new recruits, so I run and check another one. And another one. And another one until there's no doubt.

'Grace!' I scream her name as I search for her. 'Torin!'

My eyes finally rest on Grace, who is bludgeoning her enemy in his gut, and I sprint over to her. 'Grace, they're bandits! They're not Snakes.'

She pauses as it takes a moment for my words to sink in. 'What?'

'I don't recognise any of them.'

'But why would . . .' She trails off, looking at their clothing in confusion.

'He wants us to think they're Snakes. He wants us to think he's here.'

It's finally getting through to her. I can see the dread building in her eyes.

'We have to find Torin.'

Torin is triumphantly defending a huddle of unarmed people, our 'victory' almost complete, and he's not expecting our frantic appearance as we tell him the awful truth.

But Torin doesn't understand the extent of my father's cunning. 'Why would he do this?'

'To flush us out. To discover where we've been hiding.'

The blood drains from his face. 'We have to get back to the castle.'

He barks orders at his men, for some to come with us, for some to stay and continue the fight, and then we're running again. My heart pounds against my ribs, desperate to escape its torment. Because I know what we're going to find. I know we're going to be too late.

It's deathly quiet as we reach the castle, but the main door is open, an ominous welcome home. It's only when Sharpe appears from the darkness that I'm certain something terrible has happened. I can tell he's injured from the way he stumbles out, and Torin sprints towards him.

I hear Torin's cry of anguish before I can see the cause. Sharpe's pointing towards the great cave as he drops to his knees, his head flailing about. He turns, and dark hollows glisten from where his eyes have been gouged out, blood dripping down his face.

Momentarily I'm too stunned to move, simply watching as Torin clutches Sharpe tightly, but as nausea rises I force myself forward towards the cave. Whatever my father has done it is meant for me. I have to know.

I'm greeted by a macabre tableau. Six of the standing stones have a body tied to them. Torin's advisors. All have had their throats slit. Enoch's has been sliced so violently his head lolls at a strange angle, practically severed, so that the gaping hole reminds me of a ludicrous grin.

Two of the other six standing stones bear a message as well – the fourth and the sixth both have a cross marked on them, scrawled in blood.

The meaning is immediately clear. Two islands down, four to go. My father is just getting started.

Grace is beside me now, taking in the awful scene.

'Cut them down,' I say, my voice breaking.

'Where are you going?'

'To help Sharpe.'

There's nothing I can do for the council, but Sharpe must be in agony and while I can't restore his sight, I can relieve his pain.

Torin is guiding Sharpe into the great cave and I run to wrap my arms round them. 'Let's get him to the healing room,' I say softly to Torin, whose eyes brim with tears. He nods and together we manoeuvre Sharpe along the passageways. About halfway there he loses consciousness. I'm prepared to drag him the rest of the way if needs be, but Torin stops and scoops Sharpe into his arms, not putting him down until we reach the table in the healing room.

I grab jars, searching until I find handfuls of barkweed and coralpine and mash them into a paste. Drawing on something I've read in the old manuscripts, I add a dash of wildroot and a pinch of dirt. If what I've read is true, this will quicken the healing process. As soon as the consistency is right, I smear the concoction on to Sharpe's empty sockets, trying not to flinch when my fingers touch soft jelly where eyeballs should be. When I'm done, I wrap a strip of muslin round his head to keep the wounds clean, before finding a bottle of tonic that will help soothe Sharpe's mind while he sleeps, and tip it gently into his mouth.

Throughout all this Torin doesn't move from Sharpe's side. He holds his hand, their fingers entwined. I see now where his heart lies.

Once there's nothing more I can do for Sharpe I sit down opposite Torin.

'This is my fault,' he says.

'No.' I bite back my tears. 'This is all my father's doing.'

'I should have let him come with us; he wanted to stay with me.' Torin raises his eyes to meet mine, and he looks utterly broken. 'I was trying to keep him safe.'

'Of course you were. You love him.'

Torin nods, acknowledging my understanding, and now his tears flow freely.

I force back the tidal wave of emotion that threatens to undo me. I can't afford to lose my focus now. My time to grieve must wait; anything else would be beyond selfish.

Torin and I sit for the longest time with Sharpe. Grace comes in briefly to tell us how many of the King's Guard have been murdered by my father, but also assures us that the fighting has ceased in the settlement, with the surviving soldiers staying to protect it once more against any further attack.

I don't think my father will be back, though. He would have waited for us to return if he meant to kill me today. No, this was just to teach me a lesson. A reminder that there's nowhere to hide – the councillors' kill orders now complete. He's had his fun here. He'll be moving on to bigger and better things. Which means that time has run out for me.

While I sit with Sharpe through the night, reapplying the salve every few hours and changing the dressing, drugging him so he stays in a deep sleep away from the horrors of consciousness, I formulate my plan. It's a terrible one, full of holes, and highly unlikely to succeed. But it's the only one I have.

And when the sun rises red in the sky, as if it knows the blood that has been shed and the blood still to be spilled, I wake Torin and tell him what I'm going to do.

19

The Sixth Isle never ceases to amaze me with its hostility.
Just when you think a place can't be any more unpleasant
it reveals another sinister corner.

The cove in which Bronn is working on his ship is so
well concealed I would never have found it without a
guide. The mouth to the vast cavern has both stalactites
and stalagmites jutting like teeth, warning sailors away
from entering. The King's Guardsman who accompanies
me rows with great caution through the opening, beads
of sweat on his brow as he risks his life to deliver me.
When I try to ease his fears by mentioning that far
bigger ships have safely navigated this passage he tells
me more have failed than succeeded. And that these
shallows are full of stingerfish, whose venom can
paralyse a man with just one prick of the skin. Which
shuts me up.

It was hard leaving Torin and Sharpe behind. While
I'd explained my intentions to Torin I'd prepared tonics
and lotions for Sharpe's recovery, not wanting him to be
in any unnecessary pain. There's enough pain already
that can't be avoided – for all of us.

Torin had objected to my plan at first. Accused me of
being reckless.

'Doing nothing would be reckless. This gives us a chance,' I'd argued.

But then he'd looked at me, his face etched with sorrow, and I'd realised it wasn't my idea he objected to. It was the prospect of suffering more loss.

I'd taken his hand in mine. 'You once spoke to me of our duty. It never stops following us, and this is mine. I am the Viper's heir. But I am not my father. I will be the Viper the Isles deserve; I will protect them. Whatever it takes.'

His eyes had met mine, and, oh, how I'd wanted to wipe the grief from them. But they were fierce with determination. 'As must I. I couldn't protect the council, couldn't keep Sharpe from harm, but I won't let others suffer as they have. I will do my part, as you ask.'

I'd wrapped my arms round him and held him tight. 'Thank you,' I'd said, and I hadn't just meant for agreeing, but for everything. For existing.

We'd stayed in our embrace for a long time, afraid of what letting go meant, but in the end our destinies had to be confronted.

The last thing Torin had said to me before I left was, 'It will be my honour to fight with you, my friend.'

The warmth of lanterns glows up ahead, bringing me back to the present. Despite everything, a glimmer of something approaching happiness flickers inside me at the prospect of seeing Bronn. I've missed him more than I'd known possible.

The ship looms up ahead, and I look it over, wondering if it will be up to the task.

My guard calls out to the crew as we pull alongside it, and a rope is thrown down for me to climb aboard. As I shimmy up I catch sight of the ship's name. *Avenger.* I hope she can live up to it, because that's exactly what I plan to do. Avenge the Eastern Isles. Avenge Joren, Clara and Tomas. Sharpe. Enoch, Lora and the other advisors. All those who perished on the Fourth. And the Sixth. The list is too long.

Bronn is waiting for me on deck, but greets me with cool formality, his eyes resting briefly on the crystal pendant round my neck. I try not to let it show how much his indifference hurts me as he introduces me to his crew. I fear I've lost him already. But then he invites me to his quarters to discuss matters, and once we're alone, with the door firmly shut, he pulls me to him and I realise he was simply behaving appropriately towards the Prince's fiancée in front of the others.

I want to melt into him, want him to take my pain away, but he can't – no more than Torin's love for Sharpe can fix him. What my father has done, the atrocities I've witnessed, they are my burden. And they give me purpose.

So I pull slightly away from Bronn, moving to sit on a chair. Bronn watches me closely, and perhaps he sees the steely resolve in my eyes because he says nothing about my pushing him away and instead offers me some rum.

The liquid burns my throat, but I ask for another one. Only after I've consumed both do I tell him everything that's happened. His face barely reacts to what I say, but I can see his fists clenching tighter.

'So what are we doing?' he asks when the tale is told. Warmth rushes through me at the word 'we'; I'm so relieved he isn't running this time.

'Is this ship seaworthy?'

I see the glint in his eyes. 'Just about. Depends what you had in mind. She's no match for the *Maiden* yet.'

'I don't need her to be. Can she outrun her?'

He considers this. 'With a good wind? Maybe. For a while.'

'A while is all we need.'

Bronn finally understands what I'm saying. 'You don't intend to beat him.'

I smile sadly. 'Just outlast him long enough to pull him into a trap of our own.'

My plan is simple. I'm still the best bait we have, so we'll take the *Avenger* out to sea, several nautical miles away from the ocean's divide between East and West. My father will think I'm running, fleeing to save my own skin, and will find me, drawn like moth to flame. Then all we need to do is survive long enough to retreat across the border into Western waters. The *Maiden*'s crew will be against following us, will object violently to my father's demand, utterly ruled by their superstitious fears of the Western Sea, but my father will insist that they pursue us.

Once they do, they will no longer have an advantage. The waters are as unknown to them as the rest of us, and it is here that we can put up a fight. We'll lose. But we'll weaken them, and in sacrificing our ship we'll occupy him long enough so that he doesn't see the King's Fleet approaching from behind, led by Torin on his own quest for vengeance. And there's no way my father will get past the entire Fleet in strange waters.

I know I won't survive and I'm at peace with that certainty. My only responsibility now is to stop the Viper and his reign of terror. I will gladly give my life to fulfil that obligation. To keep my promise to Clara.

When I've told Bronn everything he takes my hand gently in his. He knows exactly what I'm saying.

'Make sure the crew know the risks – this is a voluntary mission. I won't ask anyone to come who doesn't want to.' I force myself to look directly into his eyes. 'That includes you.'

Now he smiles, a gesture filled with affection. 'Where else would I be?'

It's so selfish, but I'm grateful. Though the last thing I want is for Bronn to be hurt, in all honesty I don't want to face this alone.

'Besides,' Bronn says, 'if you want this ship to last as long as possible against the *Maiden*, you'd better have the best sailor in the land at the helm.'

'Oh, don't worry, Grace has already agreed to come. She'll be here soon.' I manage to keep a straight face for a few seconds before I break into a smile.

He feigns mock offence, before reaching out and pulling me to him. And for a moment we stay like that, steeling ourselves for all that lies ahead. Then, resting his chin on my head, Bronn sighs. 'We should go,' he says. 'We'll be setting sail soon.'

And there's plenty to do before then as I discover when I leave the sanctuary of his cabin. Sails and rigging all need to be checked, oakum has to be placed between the seams of planks to keep them watertight, and I spend most of my time using pitch to patch up some forgotten holes. The *Avenger* is hardly in the best shape.

Almost all of the crew elect to stay aboard and I'm humbled by their bravery. These are men and women from the King's Fleet that my father has terrorised for months. They trusted him, considered him an ally, and he attacked them without provocation. The mere fact they're prepared to fight with Bronn and me speaks volumes about their courage and belief in their duty. I'm proud to make this final stand alongside them.

Bronn introduces me to Ana, the boatswain, a woman whose skin has suffered from years of salt water and wind, but whose eyes dance with excitement. She welcomes me with the warmth of a long-lost relative and though I'd hoped not to form any attachments with the crew I instantly like her.

The same is true of the quartermaster, Rynce, a man who always has a smile at the ready, and of Harley, the experienced sailing master, who doesn't mince her words – when it comes to our predicament or anything else.

'Your father's a sea-devil,' she says, even as she shakes my hand. 'Hope you're forged from strong steel.'

'I guess we'll find out,' I say with a half-smile.

'Want me to navigate us through uncharted waters, do you?' She bores into me with her sharp eyes. 'Through oceans even the Snakes fear? With creatures so deadly they'll tear the strongest ship to shreds in seconds?'

I shrug with casual indifference. 'If you think you can.'

Harley's laugh has a deep booming quality. 'I like you. Slightly mad. All the best sailors are.'

By the time Grace joins us we're about ready to weigh anchor, and tension is beginning to rise at the prospect of negotiating the treacherous passage out of the cave.

The masts practically reach its roof and, to be honest, I'm amazed they got the ship inside in the first place.

While the last preparations are being made I take the opportunity to speak quietly with Grace.

'How are they?'

Her face softens at my concern. 'Sharpe is doing as well as can be expected. Your tonics are seeing to that. And I've never seen Torin more focused. He has plenty of friends in the Fleet and will round up as many as he can before he's on our tail. He wants to end this as much as we do.'

Torin intends to take Sharpe on his ship with him, unwilling to leave him behind again. I can understand that. I glance over at Bronn. None of us wants to die alone. And all of us know how this is likely to end.

When the anchor is raised barely a sound can be heard. All attention is focused on assigned duties to get us safely out on to the ocean. We don't want this mission to end before it's even begun.

Harley is at the helm; her knowledge of these passages is unrivalled, and witnessing the way she sails the *Avenger*, as if bending her to her will, makes me wonder what she could do with a ship like the *Maiden*. I can tell Bronn is impressed too – he's never been one to miss the opportunity to learn from those more accomplished than him, even if those opportunities are few and far between.

The ship seems to breathe in, squeezing through the gaps in the massive dripstone with defiance. Only once we're clear do the crew relax slightly, glad to be out in the open again, with fresh air to renew our lungs.

Harley sets the *Avenger* on a westerly course as Ana barks the order to drop sails. They work with efficiency, and I wonder why my father has always held the members of the King's Fleet in such contempt. Everything I've seen so far indicates exceptional skill and talent.

Rynce issues a strict duty schedule, allowing everyone sufficient rest while we're not yet in battle. He makes it clear to me that until my father shows up, he and Bronn are in charge of the ship. Once the Viper appears I'm to take over. And so I'm assigned a lot of rest time now because soon enough I'll get none.

My cabin is small, but I'm grateful for it. Most of the crew have hammocks strung up on the gun deck, but Rynce insisted that my authority be marked by having my own quarters.

I ask Bronn about the crew one night, while we're sitting together on my floor, nibbling sea biscuits that are already so hard I can't imagine how our teeth will manage them in a few more days. 'Why doesn't my father have any respect for the King's Fleet? If you ask me, they're more impressive than half his Snakes.'

'Well, this lot aren't officially in the King's Fleet,' he says.

'What do you mean?'

'Apparently Torin has a habit of picking up waifs and strays. Most of this crew are sailors who failed to meet the King's irrational standards, or those who were discharged for minor infringements. Some are reformed bandits, who wanted to atone for their sins. In fact, most of this lot wouldn't be out of place on the *Maiden*.'

I find this revelation oddly comforting. Like we're surrounded by our own kind.

When we've finished our unpleasant dinner Bronn stands up to leave. 'Suppose I should get some sleep.'

I'm exhausted too, but I don't want to be alone, don't want the light he brings with him to go. 'You can have my floor if you don't mind sharing a room.'

He gives me a sideways glance. 'You don't think that would be improper? You are engaged to another man.'

'I think Torin would be pleased to know I have a personal guard.'

Bronn snorts. 'You don't need protecting.' But he picks up a blanket and throws it on the floor.

I smile to myself as I climb into my hammock, relieved he's chosen to stay. I wasn't sure he would.

Bronn snuffs out the lantern before he settles down. The silence that follows is filled with unspoken longing, this stolen time together so precious.

When he speaks his voice is soft. 'Will you let me teach you?'

I'm confused. 'Teach me what?'

'You fight well; Grace has done a good job. But to defeat the Captain you'll need to be faster. Smoother. We should practise while we can.'

'I seem to remember I kicked your ass back at the palace.'

He chuckles to himself. 'True. But I wasn't really trying to hurt you. And there's always room for improvement.'

I blink, the horrible reality of what lies ahead intruding on my temporary happiness. Bronn still believes we can survive this, which is comforting. But to do so I'll have to confront and kill my father.

'You think I'm capable?' It's barely a whisper.

'I know you are.'

And when I reach my hand down into the darkness he takes it firmly in his and doesn't let go till sleep delivers us from our burdens.

The voyage towards the West takes several weeks. It's been days since we saw another vessel, our route taking us far away from land, fishing channels or trading lanes. But we've made no effort to hide, leaving breadcrumbs for my father to find and pick up our trail. And he will. Sea vultures have been dispatched carrying messages we want him to intercept. The trick is to be far enough from the invisible divide not to arouse his suspicions – but close enough that we won't be destroyed before we can draw him into Western waters. But between them Harley and Bronn seem to have a good plan.

We've been lucky with the elements. A few storms, but nothing the ship couldn't weather, even in her far from perfect state. The only brief moment of possible danger was when we encountered a giant serpentshark off our port bow. Though our ship is larger than their usual prey, you can never underestimate the damage a serpentshark can inflict. Fortunately it had no interest in us and was content to swim in our wake for a time before disappearing once more into the secret world beneath the waves. I was far happier to see the swirlseals playing on the edge of a small whirlpool, spinning in the gentle downdraught before diving for fish. They're notoriously shy and not often seen, so I treasured the chance to watch their magical dance.

Hours have been spent training with Bronn. Every day we've sparred, occasionally joined by Grace, and he's shown me how to use my speed to compensate for my slight build. All our work has paid off. My reflexes are quicker, my body nimbler, and as a bonus I'm now proficient with a blade in each hand.

Now that we're as close to Western waters as we want to be without my father in pursuit, it's simply a matter of waiting. We've been sailing in gentle circles for three days with no sign of him. Once I thought I saw Talon hovering above us, but it's possible I was mistaken. Everyone's on edge, knowing we're in the eye of the storm and anticipating the carnage. But we're well prepared and just need to hold our nerve.

Bronn and I have been sparring as usual, only today we've kept to my cabin, wanting to be alone. We've grown closer over the past few weeks, the hours spent together restoring the intimacy of our youth, and at times I've laughed so much I've almost forgotten our plight. At this point I don't need to learn anything more, but we both know our time is running out and we train mostly as an excuse to be together.

It's difficult to move much in the confined space, but we're making do, locked in a long exchange of blows. We're both competitive with each other, not wanting to be the one to lose, and today I use the lack of space to my advantage, backing him towards the wall until he reaches my hammock and falls into it. I laugh, but he's already grabbed me and pulled me with him so that in an instant I'm lying on top of him.

Now we both laugh, but then it doesn't seem funny any more. We're breathing hard from our exertion; I can feel his chest rising next to mine. I drink in his beautiful face, so lived-in, so familiar. I've loved him for ever and I'm tired of pretending otherwise.

I kiss him. His lips are soft, his breath mingling with mine, and we're both hesitant, knowing we shouldn't, knowing we will, and then he's kissing me back harder, one hand in my hair, the other on my waist, and I melt into him.

He pulls away, holding my face in his hands, looking at me with such tenderness it hurts. 'I love you.' It comes out as a promise.

'I love you.'

Vows of our own, ones that mean far more than any binding ceremony.

And then we're kissing again, our bodies entwining with the urgency of two people who know they're on the eve of death and want to make every last second count. In this moment there is only the warmth of his skin, the taste of his lips, and the sense of belonging I've sought my whole life.

Then the ship lurches violently and we almost fall out of the hammock. The spell that had entranced us shatters. That was our time. It's over.

'What was that?' I'm sitting up, adrenaline surging through my veins.

'We just veered hard to starboard. I think we have company.'

We look at each other for a moment, knowing this is it, and I see my own sorrow reflected in his eyes. He presses a deep kiss on to my forehead.

'Ready?'

I'm not. I don't want to die, don't want to lose this man I love so much, don't want to condemn these sailors to a watery grave. But stronger than all those things is my determination to do what's right; I cannot let my father continue his massacre of the Eastern Isles.

I meet Bronn's eyes, fire stirring in my belly, and nod. 'Let's end this.'

20

The crew are frantically preparing for our flight, dropping full sails, and the moment Harley sees us appear on deck, she waves us over to the helm. Despite our circumstances, she has a twinkle in her eye as she gives us a knowing wink.

'Making the most of your final day, are you?'

My blush must be visible because she holds her hands up and says, 'Not judging, after all your prince is devoted to that commander. He'll not be plundering your treasure any time soon.' She laughs at her own coarse joke, but when I don't join in, mortified beyond words, she puts her hand on my shoulder. 'Your secrets are safe with me. Probably be at the bottom of the ocean soon enough anyway. Don't think the fish will care too much.'

Her teasing over, she turns to Bronn. 'All right, let's see what this girl's got.'

I'm not needed here and search for Rynce, but before I can find him my eyes fall on the *Maiden* looming in the distance and heading directly towards us. From this vantage point her fearsome reputation makes sense in a way it never did before. She's massive, her black sails an ominous threat on the horizon as she seems to gain on us every passing minute.

But I also never appreciated how beautiful she is. The way she glides through the water, like a sea vulture soaring through the air, is breathtaking. She was my home and I'm struck by a strange sense of pride at her approach. And an unexpected sense of longing.

Grace snaps me out of my reverie. 'They're closing in on us too quickly. At this rate they'll be in firing range within the hour.'

I look at her in surprise. 'That soon?' I'd never realised she could fire from that far away. 'Will we even be in Western waters by then?'

Grace presses her lips tight together. 'We'd better be. If we want to last more than five minutes.'

Rynce finds me, unrolling charts on the top of a barrel for us to study. They're very old, taken from the room in Torin's castle. No one really knows how accurate they are, but they're the best we've got.

I look at the mark several miles over the border, the place where Torin will meet us to finish what we've started. It suddenly seems a long way away.

'Will we make it that far?' I ask Rynce.

'Harley will get us as deep into Western waters as she can,' is all he says. Not really an answer. But before I can push it he's already turned to Grace, pointing to the Western island closest to the border. 'What land is this?'

'The Eighth Isle,' she says, and seems pleased at his

genuine interest. 'It's the smallest, least populated of all the Western Isles.'

I leave them talking. There's no point thinking about islands I won't live to see. It may be the closest land, but it's still miles away.

We're making good speed, despite the wind direction being unfavourable. The ship's tacking, zigzagging through the waters to reach our destination, and all the while my father maintains his pursuit.

We keep our lead for some time, but the gap continues to close. Nerves are pressing in on me. 'How far are we?' I call over to Bronn.

'Almost there.'

'Then slow down.'

Everyone turns to look at me in surprise.

'What?' Harley puts her hands square on her hips.

'If we just sail straight over, he's going to suspect it's a trap. But if we've taken a beating and retreat to save ourselves, then he won't be able to resist the scent of blood.'

Rynce looks at me as if I've lost my mind, but I can tell Bronn and Grace agree.

'How much damage can we sustain and still reach our mark?' I ask anyone who can answer.

It's Ana who replies. 'As long as the hull isn't breached, I can patch most things up, even in battle conditions. I'd rather we kept the masts too.'

Now I turn my questions directly to Bronn and

Grace. 'How far away will the *Maiden* need to be to wound but not kill us?'

It's Bronn who fields this one. 'They can fire with reasonable accuracy from half a mile away, so she can halve the current distance between us, but no more. We don't want her anywhere near us.'

'Fine. The minute we need to flee, do it.' He nods. I address the others. 'Prepare for attack.'

Harley slows the ship, just barely so as to not draw attention, and the *Maiden* grows ever nearer. She starts to unleash her cannons on us long before they're in range, my father sending a message that he has ample ammunition, enough to waste on a showy display, and that he means to destroy us.

Like we didn't already know that.

When we're inevitably in range and the first cannon fire hits, the *Avenger* shakes from the explosion. It takes a chunk out of our starboard stern, and I can hear the cries below deck with horrifying clarity.

'Report!' Rynce shouts.

'Minimal damage, sir.' Ana is already sending crew down to make repairs.

'Incoming!'

The second cannon shot sideswipes us, grazing the side of the hull without penetrating. But the vibrations shudder through the wood, reminding us how little there is between us and the sea we sail on.

Though chaos surrounds me I'm suddenly flung back inside my dream, my nightmare. Underwater, sinking, the ocean determined to devour me.

A third cannonball tearing through the ship jolts me back to the current and very real danger. It sends splinters flying, injuring those in its path. But there isn't time to think, or react, they just keep pummelling us with blow after blow and then the *Maiden* almost seems on top of us. Any closer and it'll be too late.

'Bronn?' I call out as I turn to look at him. He's cutting this fine.

He's standing at the wheel, his beautiful face set with brave determination, holding his nerve while the rest of us give in to fear. I feel a fierce rush of love for him. Valuable seconds pass, his order seeming to take for ever to come, but in those moments I'm not afraid. I see only him and all he is. And I'm so grateful for every second left at his side.

'Now!' Bronn shouts, and sets the *Avenger* free, spinning so hard to starboard that the ship's very fabric creaks in protest and I have to grab the rigging to stop from falling.

Though bruised, the ship yields to our demands, and once she's straightened herself makes good speed west.

My heart is racing as the divide approaches, and the excitement that's been building inside me as we've sailed closer to the West reaches its peak. My whole life I've been taught this is not a line to cross, have witnessed men who feared nothing tremble at its mere proximity, but I have an unnerving sense that I'm finally going in the right direction.

Bronn reaches for my hand. 'Last chance to turn round.' He's as nervous as I am.

'I wouldn't give him the satisfaction.'

Bronn grins. 'Adler's afraid. You can already see them hesitating.'

He's right, the *Maiden* seems to have frozen as they realise where we're going. Several more cannons are fired, but we've put just enough distance between us to avoid being hit, and they merely pepper the water.

My surprise is matched only by my relief. 'It's working.'

I don't know what I'm expecting when we sail into Western waters, perhaps immediate death, or to sink without trace, but nothing happens. The *Avenger* is undisturbed as she drags her breaking body away from her attacker, bleeding a trail of debris for my father to follow if he dares.

Which, of course, he does. It takes him longer than I would have expected to force his crew to comply, but eventually the *Maiden* continues her pursuit, never one to run away from a fight.

Two hours pass and we maintain our lead. The crew make essential repairs, while I tend the wounded. But we can't outrun the *Maiden* for ever, and when I check how far apart we are, my heart sinks to see my father's growing ever nearer. At this rate we won't make it as far into Western waters as we'd hoped before he catches us.

'Land ahoy!'

My head whips round to look at Bronn, who meets my shocked gaze. There must be some mistake. We should be nowhere near land. I run up to the bow and my blood freezes in my veins.

There on the horizon, beyond any doubt, is the faint outline of an island.

'How is that possible? I thought we were days away from the Eighth Isle?'

Grace is beside me looking as confused as I am. 'We should be.' She snatches the chart from Rynce, who's examining it in disbelief. 'This doesn't make sense.'

'Is it the charts? I mean, they're ancient, aren't they?'

'It's the waters,' Harley says, in an ominous way that commands our attention. 'The Western Sea don't take you where you want to go, but where you need to go.' When we all stare at her she shrugs. 'Why do you think everyone's so afraid of it?'

If she's right and the magic of the islands extends to the ocean, then there's a chance Torin might not find us and all of this will be for nothing.

'Ana, when will the ship be ready for combat?'

The boatswain bristles with pride. 'Whenever you need her.'

'Drop anchor,' I say. 'We can't risk going any further. If Torin's going to have a chance of catching up with us, then we need to do this now.'

A strange hush falls over the deck. There's a difference between saying you'll sacrifice yourself for a cause and the moment when the sacrifice actually arrives – a moment when every member of the crew seems to be searching deep inside themselves for the bravery that got them here in the first place.

And then the spell breaks and everyone gets to work, arming their stations. Bronn brings the *Avenger* about, and our cannons are prepped for use. We have less than half the number of cannons my father does, with a vastly inferior range and considerably weaker cannonballs, but it's better than nothing.

Then we wait, watching the *Maiden* grow larger like she's somehow expanding in size, until she's close enough to unleash her weaponry on us with devastating accuracy.

The first shot penetrates the hull, obliterating everything in its path and causing screams to come from below. We can't return fire yet – it won't reach the *Maiden* and we don't have anything to waste – so we sit tight while we sustain damage.

'Will she hold?' I call to Ana.

'As long as I have breath she will.'

Her team are fixing the ship even as it breaks, but as the *Maiden* grows closer the impact from every blow becomes worse.

Chain shot flies through the sky, the two half balls chained together smashing our masts and ripping apart the rigging. The foremast shatters, causing mayhem as it swings down, flinging two men overboard. I help some others try to secure it before it can do more damage.

But then another shot rips the hull at the waterline and the ocean begins to invade our lower decks.

We finally launch our attack before there's no time left. Cannonballs fly across to seek revenge, but barely scratch the pitch-painted sides of the *Maiden*. I can hear her crew laughing, jeering at us, and soon they'll be close enough to throw their grapple hooks over and board. They'll be planning to slaughter us all – quickly and without mercy. Apart from me. My father will want to punish me first.

I stand with my knife clutched in my fist. I plan on taking as many of them with me as I can.

But still there is no sign of Torin and the Fleet. If we die now, my father will escape. He will win again and will never be held to account for his atrocities.

I want him to die. I want him to suffer.

The thoughts in my head are born from rage. Maybe the Western waters hear the battle cry of my heart and whisper their answer.

I read enough in those ancient books to know there is a weapon beneath the ocean that could offer such a death. I could finally make him pay for everything he's done. To the islands. To the people. To me.

All the longing I've suppressed since reading Torin's books is released, and despite staring death in the face I feel alive, my skin crackling with anticipation as I stand at the edge of the ship. Without a moment's hesitation I murmur the words I memorised curled up in my dark cave and they feel familiar on my lips as if I've spoken them before.

'*Arise, dark demons, sleep no more; come unleash hell, come destroy all. Stir to life, waken now, taste my blood and know my crown. Arise, dark demons.*'

And I bring my blade hard across my palm, letting my blood fall into the sea.

I can feel the magic release inside me, can feel it surging through my veins, my darkness forged in hatred rising up to welcome it, the two combining into a dangerous force that leaves me breathless.

From somewhere deep below us a low rumbling reaches my ears, and bubbles race up to the surface. I look round to see if anyone else has heard it, but they're too busy trying not to die.

Stilling my thoughts, I listen carefully. The noise comes again and my heart pounds. It's the sound of the ocean waking up. I don't know how I know it. I just do.

I run over to Grace who's helping Ana plug holes. 'Something's coming.'

Grace looks up at me in surprise. 'What?'

But it only takes her a moment to read my face and know exactly what I'm talking about. She stands up and grabs my elbow. 'What did you do?' Her fear is alarming. I thought she'd be as excited as I am.

We can all hear it now, the ominous hum that thunders from below, and both crews are distracted by it, ceasing their fight against each other to identify the new threat. And then the skies darken, unnatural clouds forming to obliterate the sun, as all the birds in the ocean take flight, screaming out warnings to one another. The air turns cold, as if frosted by winter's kiss, while the wind whips up from nowhere, the sudden storm tossing the ships around like flotsam.

I turn my gaze back to the sea, entranced. 'They're here.'

Grace clutches me tightly to her, simultaneously wrapping her arm round some rigging and shouting, 'Brace for impact!'

There's barely time for anyone to respond before a vast creature explodes up out of the water between the two ships, sending ours hurtling backwards. Waves crash over the deck as a water raptor shakes itself free of the ocean, extending its long neck high into the sky to taste fresh air for the first time in centuries, before unleashing a guttural shriek that sends most of the crew's hands over their ears.

I've never seen anything like it; its body alone is bigger than the *Maiden*, every inch covered in black feathers that glisten with water. Lethal fins run down the length of its spine and on to the seemingly endless tail that disappears beneath the waves. On top of the elegant feathered neck the enormous head has a beak that could swallow an ocean, filled with teeth that would crush through bone effortlessly, and deep-set eyes that have seen all of time. At its side are two pairs of colossal webbed wings that it unfolds with a flourish, oblivious to the two insignificant ships beneath it cowering in fear.

Orders are being screamed, pleas are being issued, but I ignore them all, holding on to Grace as I stare at the water raptor in wonder.

'They're real,' Grace says, her voice trembling with both fear and awe. 'You summoned one.' I've seen the look on her face before. When it was on Tomas's face I felt ashamed. But now? Now I'm proud. I awakened the water raptor, and the sense of power is intoxicating.

And then a second water raptor rises from the sea, calling a greeting to its mate.

Our ship is thrown further away, like we're froth on the surface and we crash back into the water, this time sustaining considerable damage.

A frisson of alarm shoots through me. If they destroy us before they destroy my father, I've summoned them in vain.

I try to reach out to the water raptors, to command them to attack only the *Maiden*. But they do not respond; they ignore every clumsy attempt I make to control them. And slowly it dawns on me that I have misunderstood exactly what I've unleashed, that even the texts I read were wrong.

They're not a weapon – if they were, I could wield them as I would a sword. But they are as wild and raw as the magic coursing through my veins. Untamed and uncontrollable. Beyond my reach.

What have I done?

'The hull is breached; we're taking on water,' Ana says, her confidence wavering. 'Orders, Captain.'

I snap my eyes away from these vultures of the deep. 'Give us whatever time you can.'

She nods, but I can tell it won't be long. The ship is hanging together by a thread.

A cannon fires, followed by an ear-piercing screech that reaches deep inside me and burns so that I scream with pain.

Grace looks at me frantically. 'What's wrong?'

'Did we fire at them?' I can barely say the words.

'No.' Bronn has joined us. 'That was Adler.'

I grab Bronn's arm to steady myself. I didn't expect this. It's as if there's some connection between me and the raptors – my anger breathed life into them, and now we're bound. As long as they're here at my summoning we're joined in life and death. And pain.

I hadn't considered there would be a cost to using magic. I was so seduced by the power of it, I failed to acknowledge the sacrifice it required.

Now I know.

The water raptors don't enjoy the pain any more than I do, and have their own, far more effective response to Adler's attacks.

A torrent of burning water blasts from their mouths, which pours wildly in all directions. We dive for cover, and I feel drops of it burning through my clothes, hear the screams of those who've been covered in the acidic poison. Men and women plunge into the sea, desperate for relief from the venom, but there is none. The skin peels from their bodies and their screams increase before dying away for ever.

Screams of accusation. Because their agonising deaths are my fault.

Deafened by guilt, I'm dimly aware of the *Maiden* retreating, as the female water raptor flaps her four wings and attempts flight. Through our connection I can tell she cares nothing for our battle, for sides, for duty or morality – she cares only for freedom. As she lifts from the ocean two long legs emerge, followed by clawed toes. Massive talons fasten on to us and she lifts the ship up with her as she pulls free from the water.

I snatch at anything and everything not to get thrown off as she flies clumsily through the air, crushing the *Avenger* in her grip, before crashing back into the water, her first flight failed, her wings still weak from her long sleep.

There's nothing left of the ship, only shreds, and I clutch to planks of wood keeping me afloat in the sea, staring in horror at the carnage I've unleashed.

'Bronn! Grace!'

I search for them, but they're nowhere to be seen. I call out again and again but no answer comes.

Other voices reach me, though, other crewmembers struggling to stay afloat in these unexpectedly icy waters, and I push my concerns for Bronn and Grace aside. Biting my lip to stop shivering, I assess our situation. The water raptor has brought us a lot closer towards land and for the moment she's creating a barrier between us and my father.

If we don't get out of the water, we'll all die from the cold, so there's only one thing for it. We need to brave a Western Isle.

'Get to land.' I'm struggling to breathe, let alone project my voice, and the words come out far too quietly. I try again. 'Swim ashore!'

I'm so close to my nightmare coming true. I can feel the ocean's grip tighten round me, claiming me as its own, but I fight back. There simply isn't time to be afraid right now, so I force my reluctant limbs to move me towards safety, trying not to look at the lifeless bodies still clinging to flotsam, nearly choking when I see Rynce's partially melted face staring blankly at me from where he lies draped over a barrel.

So many deaths and no one to blame but myself. And my arrogance.

It soon becomes clear the force with which we were dropped has scattered debris over some considerable distance, so it's more than likely there are survivors heading for the next cove further round the island. Bronn and Grace must be with them. They must.

And then I see it – the *Maiden* limping towards the island, her damage obvious even from a distance. She may not have been demolished like the *Avenger*, but she won't be able to get far in her current condition. Which means it's only a matter of time before my father and his crew head to the Eighth Isle too, seeking means to repair.

Right towards where I'm certain my friends are.

The shores of the Eighth Isle sparkle. Light reflects off what looks like crushed diamonds in the sand, which dazzles all the way to the dune forest where giant marram grasses tower ten feet high and stretch like a jungle as far as the eye can see, until imposing snow-peaked mountains dominate the skyline.

Though I feel more tired than I've ever been, though I'm bruised, bleeding and afraid, I cannot get over the beauty of this place.

When I first collapsed on to the beach I'd sunk my hands deep into the sand, its grains so tiny and shimmering that they looked like shards of luminous glass, and my fingers tingled with an unnerving familiarity as I felt the texture on my skin. Like I'd been here before. Like I'd been summoned back by something. Or someone.

Now I'm running through the forest, trying not to read anything into that unexpected first impression, or into the tangible sensation that I know where I'm going. I don't stop to think – I can't – I'm just following a path that should take me close to where my father will land.

I'm trying not to think about the rest of the *Avenger*'s crew. A few other survivors were scrambling up the sands as I'd left, and I'd checked they were OK before leaving them. I'd avoided the bodies that had washed up on to shore before I arrived, the tide carrying them quicker than it carried me. I'm certain Bronn and Grace must be alive; they're indestructible. And Harley? Nothing could stop her, surely. What about Ana? The panic and guilt rise and I run faster. I have to find them before my father does.

The forest is just as mesmerising as the beach; thick dunes anchor the giant grasses that, now that I'm close up, look more like bamboo, the gentle breeze causing them to sway so they emit a hollow ring that dances on the air. The forest floor is carpeted with lush foliage, and flowers sprout up through the sand, none of which I can name, all of which entrance me. But as I continue to run, the pretty tune in the wind begins to sound like an eerie drone and I realise the impressive marram grass could be providing dense cover for predators. I've yet to see any wildlife, but am aware of its presence, have heard the scuttles as creatures flee my approach.

A striking blue plant catches my eye and I skid to a halt. I've passed it before. I'm sure I have. Panting hard, I look round and my heart sinks as I recognise the terrain. The gnarled marram plant to my left, with its stem peeling away. The broken cane up ahead, snapped in two, which I jumped the last time I went this way. How is it possible to have gone in a circle? There's nothing for it but to keep going, but when I pass the distinct foliage again I scream out loud with frustration. I don't have time for this.

Abandoning the path, I weave my way through the grasses, sprinting towards the cove, but it doesn't take me long to realise the sound of waves breaking on the shore is growing quieter, the smell of salt fainter. I'm heading away from the sea.

My sense of direction is not this bad. Something else is happening.

But I'm not abandoning my friends, so I press on, running until my chest burns and my legs barely support me.

I'm truly exhausted by the time I push through some dense thickets and see five wooden huts perfectly concealed by the forest. I'm hit by an immense wave of clarity: that I've finally reached where I'm supposed to be. The air in the clearing is sweeter, the smells sharper, the light brighter. It is familiar and strange all at once, as if a fragment of a forgotten dream. All the immediacy of danger is gone, replaced with a peculiar serenity.

Lost in a trance, I hardly notice at first when the door of the nearest hut opens and a woman emerges, her shawl pulled up over her head.

Skin creased with age, back stooped from withered bones, the woman is clearly old, but her opalescent eyes are bright, burning with a keen intelligence as she fixes her gaze on me. She's pale, so very pale, and I wonder when she last saw the sun. Maybe the last time her grey wiry hair saw a comb. I recognise her, though I can't possibly, and for a moment I'm too startled to speak. Then I collect myself.

'Please, can you help? I need to get to the beach.' But even as I say the words I feel no urgency to them. They don't belong to right now.

She raises a bony finger to her lips, before pointing at me and beckoning me closer.

She's been expecting me.

Perhaps trusting a stranger is the last thing I should do, but somehow it feels the most natural thing in the world. She gives me a knowing smile as she turns to hobble back into her hut and after a moment's hesitation I follow.

The hut smells of earth and moisture, and another sickly scent I can't identify. A small fire burns in the corner, the pot hanging above it boiling. The old woman staggers over to it, removes the pot and pours its contents into two filthy mugs before handing one to me.

A cloying sweet smell is emanating from the concoction, and the last thing I want to do is put this in my mouth, but the woman ushers me on, gesturing with her hands that I should drink up. Taking a deep breath, I pour the rancid liquid down my throat. It leaves a foul aftertaste, but warmth spreads through my aching bones, the crushing weariness slowly melting away. The old woman watches me with a penetrating gaze and I thank her as she refills the mug.

There is little furniture in the room, but every inch of the walls is covered in shelves, filled with row upon row of old jars containing dried plants, fragments of bone, scraps of pelt, among other less desirable contents. Even from a distance I'm sure I notice hearts and eyes preserved in some, and animal foetuses in others. Everything's covered in layers of dirt as if it's not been touched in years.

'Please,' I say. 'Can you help me?' Even as I say the words, I'm not sure what kind of help I'm asking for. I know there's something I have to do, somewhere I need to be, but my thoughts are lost behind a veil.

'More than you know.' With difficulty she lowers herself on to the floor and only when I settle opposite her does she continue. 'I know your face.'

'I've never been here before,' I say. 'I'm from the Eastern Isles.'

She chuckles to herself, though I fail to see what's funny. 'You think I'm old, but I don't forget.'

She must be wrong, our paths cannot have crossed before, and frustration makes me irritable. 'I don't have time for riddles.'

The woman considers me for a moment. Then she struggles to her feet and makes her way to her shelves.

'Impatience is your enemy. You must listen if you are to defeat him.'

That gets my attention. 'You mean my father?'

The woman considers me for a moment. 'You plan to kill the Viper.'

The flicker of hesitation is unmistakable in my gut. 'Yes.'

'And yet you're reluctant.'

I sigh, swallowing a mouthful of foul fluid to avoid answering. 'I want to preserve life, not end it. You're a healer, surely you feel the same?' It was the answer I always used to give. I can't remember when it stopped being true. It certainly feels a long time since healing was what I loved.

She gives a wry chuckle. 'I never said I was a healer.'

'Who are you?'

'I'm Esther. And your presence here is no coincidence, Marianne. It's been many years, but finally you've returned.'

I swallow hard, now certain I'm in the embrace of magic. It brought me here and since I entered the grove I've fallen under some kind of bewitchment, one that's stilled time. Somehow it doesn't surprise me that Esther knows my name.

The foul jars. The potions. The enchantments. I'd assumed all the Mages were dead and gone. And yet here I sit with one. The magic I'd unleashed inside me the moment I'd called forth the water raptors claws its way up to my chest and rests there with a sense of expectation. Like attracted to like. And for the first time I see Esther properly. She is not as old as I thought; time has simply been unkind to her. Or magic has altered her in some way.

Or disguised her.

If Esther senses my magic, she gives no sign. Instead she takes something from the shelf and passes it to me. My heart skips a beat. Even filthy, this brooch's similarity to my compass from Grace is obvious. And when I rub it clean it reveals the same pink scallop and cowrie shells set in gold, the 'V' embroidered in what was clearly once the finest thread. They're too alike to be coincidence.

'She wore it every day.'

It suddenly occurs to me that when she said she knew my face, perhaps she meant she knew one similar to it. My heart begins to race with excitement as I think of my mother.

'Did this brooch belong to someone who looked like me?'

'Yes. I took it from her body before I buried her. Your mother.'

As quickly as my heart had raced it now stops, crushed by the weight of unexpected grief, and for a moment I can't breathe. I hadn't realised how much I'd hoped my mother was still alive until confronted with her death again. It was the best part of believing Grace's story and Esther's words have extinguished my dream entirely.

'Will you tell me about her?' My voice is small. Like it doesn't belong to me, but to the lonely child I once was, who wept at night aching for her mother's safe embrace.

Esther's eyes glisten with sadness. 'She was kind. A heart full of love. Especially for her child.' She nods towards me. 'She was my friend.' She sighs, a sound that shakes with sorrow. 'She lived here. Now no one does. She was scared. So scared. She was right to be afraid. I found the bodies.'

'Bodies?' I'm confused.

'She was murdered.' Esther gives me a look filled with pity. 'I'm sorry, but the truth will bring you pain.'

I clutch the brooch tightly in my hand. Pain is no stranger to me. The truth is.

'I need to know.'

Esther nods. 'They lived in the hut next to mine when they first married. Not long after, the baby arrived. A beautiful little girl. And they were happy.'

She pauses, and I wish with every fibre of my being that she could finish there, but know there will be no happy ending to this story.

'The first trip to the sands is an important moment for any island child,' Esther continues. 'All islanders must learn to hear all that the land and sea have to say, but this was more special as this was no ordinary island child. They laughed a lot, the baby's parents, happy as they made their way home from the sands, playing as they took the winding path through the dune forests. The towering trees made for perfect hiding places and the man would run ahead to conceal himself while the woman asked the girl where her father had gone and when they came upon his tree he would jump out, causing the child to giggle with relief.

'But then there came a time when he did not reappear, and the woman became afraid. Clutching the baby tighter she ran deeper into the forest, and perhaps sensing she had gone too far, turned round. Her husband was there, motionless, pinned in his hiding position by a knife penetrating his throat. His mouth was open as if he were about to call out a warning, his eyes still bright with fear, the blood dripping down his neck like red tears of sorrow.

'She ran. But she knew she could not hide, knew whoever had killed her husband was hunting her too. So she did the only thing she could. She placed her child among a dense patch of grass, hoping to spare her from the same fate, leaving her with nothing but a kiss on the head and a solitary tear before she fled. She never came back.'

'You think I'm that child?' My voice is a whisper.

'You are that child.'

'What happened to the woman?' I think I know, but I need to hear it. Have to be certain.

'When the men came for her she fought. She killed one and plunged a dagger through the eye of another before they tore her down. All to protect the baby she loved.'

'The man she stabbed in the eye? He didn't die. Did he?'

'No. I watched him carry you away.'

And then he raised me as his own.

Anger flares inside me. 'You saw this? Why didn't you help them?'

She hangs her head. 'It wasn't that simple. But I knew one day you'd return, and now that you have I will help you.'

I wipe away the tears spilling down my cheek, furious at everything: the loss of my parents, the betrayal of the man I thought was my father, the thought of the life I could have had.

'It's time you knew your true name, the one your parents gave you on your first trip to the sands, the one bound in meaning.'

'My name?' I'm struggling to understand why Adler would have changed it.

'Yes. You are Mairin. Star of the Sea.'

Something deep inside me stirs, an old familiarity that confuses rather than comforts me. My Western name recognises itself, and the power it contains.

'Do all names in the West have a meaning?' I ask, trying to understand.

Esther shakes her head. 'No, not all. It's an ancient royal tradition. It was only fitting that my gift to you at your birth was to enchant your name. You, the true child of the islands. The last of the Vultura line.' She sighs, lost to the memory. 'Adler wouldn't have wanted you to know it,' she continues after a moment. 'Wouldn't have wanted you to know yourself.'

'But why?'

Esther presses her thumb to my forehead and my mind is thrown backwards to my earliest memory, to nearly drowning as a child. Only this time I see Adler push me in, and watch over me as I struggle and fight, before pulling me out and dumping me on the deck like a piece of old rag.

I open my eyes and stare at Esther. 'He wanted me to be afraid of the water. To keep me imprisoned on the ship.' To control me as he always has, as if I were nothing but a doll for him to play with.

She nods sadly. 'Had he called you Mairin, you would never have been afraid of the ocean you were born to love. The name would have empowered you as your parents intended. To be at one with the water as surely as you are one with the land.'

Just another thing Adler took from me.

'There are always impossible decisions to make,' Esther says quietly. 'Once made we simply learn to live with them. Nothing more. But many are coming your way and you must confront them.'

'What if I can't do it? What if I can't stop him?' Desperation almost destroys me.

'Why do you doubt yourself?'

She draws the honesty from me like poison from a wound. 'There is darkness inside me. I could become just like him, a cold-blooded killer, and it terrifies me. What if I lose myself to the cruelty I know I'm capable of?'

'Your mother was like you, with peace in her heart. A gentle soul. But she fought for you. This is a violent world. Defending those you love, defending yourself, does not make you the same as those with murder in their hearts.' She reaches forward to brush the brooch in my palm. 'You alone can stop Adler. You know him better than anyone. Use what you know and you can end this.'

'I thought he was my father. I don't know him at all.' My chest aches with the betrayal.

She smiles sadly. 'Yes you do.' She hesitates. 'As did I.'

I wipe the tears from my cheeks, knowing I'm not going to like what she's about to say one bit.

'I was his lover.'

I stare at her, disbelieving, the implication of what she's said sinking in.

Esther looks sadly back at me. 'It was because of me that he discovered your parents. And you. The power of your true name. My friendship was their death sentence.'

She pauses, but I say nothing, waiting for her to revisit a past that hurts her as it hurts me.

'I was going to leave with him,' she says with a rueful smile. 'Start a new life on his ship as his wife. But then he came to me carrying you in his arms, blood seeping through the cloth he'd wrapped round his wounded eye. He told me a story of bandits, an ambush, but when I touched your cheek, I saw the horrors as clearly as if I'd been there, and my world fell apart. Knew I had shared too much with a man I should never have trusted, had allowed love to blind me to the truth. Knew my friends' blood was on my hands as much as his. He wanted me to raise you with him. When I refused and tried to snatch you from him, he stabbed me and left me for dead.'

She pulls back her top to reveal a faded scorch mark on the left of her chest. 'My potions saved my life, even if they couldn't heal my broken heart.'

'You're the maiden,' I say, my voice nothing more than a whisper. I finally understand why she looks familiar – I've seen her likeness every day of my life at the front of our ship.

'No doubt Adler felt my refusal was a betrayal. But I'd seen the monster he was and couldn't join him, though perhaps it would have been kinder to you if I had. He wouldn't recognise me now, I think.'

'Why?' Our eyes meet. 'Why did he kill them?'

'For the girl with the crescent moon. His greatest prize. For him to call you his own there could be no survivors.'

I turn away from her and close my eyes. It all started here, in this place, and I know now this is where it must end. A strong sense of purpose grips hold of me.

My parents were murdered. My life stolen.

The next time Captain Adler and I meet, I'm going to kill him.

And for the first time I really mean it.

I want to leave immediately, but Esther persuades me to rest while she brews another potion. Her enchantment is slowly wearing off and, as it does, the urgency of Bronn's and Grace's plight returns to me. I'm anxious to resume my search for them, but I do as I'm told, knowing I'll need all my strength if I'm to defeat Adler.

Nothing is as I thought, my whole life based on a lie. The man I called Father stole me from my murdered parents. He knew who they were, who I was. Which means I've been nothing more than a powerful card for him to play at the right time. Did he mean to kill Torin once we were wed? Once he'd removed the King? A Western princess with the Eastern throne. A puppet whose strings he could pull. He isn't just after control of the Eastern Isles – he wants the West too. Total domination.

In time I will grieve for all that has been lost, but not today.

When Esther finishes the potion she's working on, she pours it into a flask and passes it to me along with a warning: 'Whatever happens, do not drink this.'

I take it, confused. 'Then why give it to me?'

'Because you'll need it.'

There's no point doubting her, and so I simply thank her.

For all her magic she can't hide the tears in her eyes. 'Stay alive, Mairin.'

She makes to brush my cheek, but her hand stops before it reaches me, the saddest smile on her face. She lost the right to comfort me years ago. 'Now go.'

I feel what remains of the enchantment lift instantly, the panic and urgency of my mission flooding back with such intensity it's almost overwhelming. I hurry out of the hut, pausing only briefly to glance back at Esther. If I survive, I'm certain I will see her again.

There is no wind now, the marram grasses silent as I hurry through them. I'm finally able to head north from where I landed, searching frantically for the cove that can't be far away, desperate to find Bronn and Grace. I run fast, my body sustained by the grim medicine Esther gave me, and as I'm nearing the sea I hear my name being called. At first it's just a distant murmur, barely audible on the wind, but as I chase after it the sound grows louder, as does my fear.

My 'father' is calling me to him.

My view is obstructed by the forest until I near its edge and then, hiding behind a thicket of stems, I take in the scene before me.

The *Maiden* is anchored close off the coast, looking like she suffered substantial damage to her hull during the water raptors' attack. On the beach is a large group of her crew, including the man who murdered my parents. And either side of him, restrained and gagged, are Bronn and Grace. I'm too late.

'Marianne!' Adler sings my name out as a taunt. 'Come and join us.'

Does he know I'm close by? Or does he just hope?

'Show yourself, Marianne. You're not a coward, are you?' He's clever, this man. None of this has gone according to his plan and his crew will be close to mutiny. Killing me is his last hope of regaining control, and what better way to entice me than with Bronn and Grace?

'I'll make a trade. You for them.' He prods Grace's temple with his pistol. 'I think I get the better deal, but still.'

I don't know what to do, panic rising like bile as I cower in my hiding place. It's a trap, of course it is, but what does that matter?

'Marianne! I know you're on this wretched island. Give yourself up or they die, starting with her.' This time he presses the pistol hard against Grace's head, so that even from this distance I can see her flinch. 'I'll even count to ten. One.'

Everything I'd resolved on – to avenge the Eastern Isles, my friends, my family, to make Adler pay – disappears in a heartbeat. Grace *is* my family and I will not let her die.

'Two.'

I take a deep breath to steady myself. This is it. I walk out towards them. 'Let her go, Adler.'

I see it – the brief flicker of confusion on his face at my use of his name. But then it's gone, and he smiles instead, as if he had known all along I'd come.

And then he shoots Grace in the head.

Her beautiful strong body crumples to the ground even before my scream echoes through the air.

I collapse to the sand, stumbling, shocked, reaching out for her as if somehow I can bring her back from such a death. Then sorrow is eclipsed by rage and I struggle to my feet and race towards her. Adler's men try to seize me but I roar as I make my own assault, burning with hatred, tearing and scratching, my nails like claws gouging the flesh from cheeks and arms. I lash out, holding nothing back, and I'm dimly aware of bones breaking beneath my blows. More hands grab at me as I writhe and kick, wanting to kill them for what they've done – all of it – but Adler's voice cuts through the noise.

'Enough!' He sounds caught off guard. He didn't know half what I was capable of. 'Or I shoot him too.'

I look up to see Adler holding the pistol to Bronn's head and instantly I surrender. As my arms are bound with ropes I hold Bronn's gaze, silently sending a thousand apologies for arriving too late, seeing only relief that I'm alive reflected back. Then I'm pushed in front of Adler whose face is spattered with Grace's blood.

'You know,' he says, as if this isn't the first time we've seen each other in months, 'caring is your weakness. Always has been. Makes you vulnerable. Makes you bleed.'

'I was handing myself over; you didn't have to kill her.' I choke on my own anger.

Adler tilts his head in mock sympathy. 'She betrayed me. So yes. I did. I just wanted you to see.' He gestures to his men. 'Gather our things. We're taking them back to the *Maiden*.'

Adler pulls the gag off Grace's body and puts it on me. It tastes of her blood and it's cloying and suffocating and I want to weep. With pistols at our heads, Bronn and I are roughly marched to the rowing boats and forced on board. As we travel to the *Maiden* I stare back at Grace, lying on the beach, left behind without even the dignity of burial. The sand around her is stained red as she soaks into the fabric of the island and part of me drains away at her loss.

The jeering starts the moment the crew on board catch sight of us and doesn't stop until we're dragged on to deck, given a general beating and thrown at Adler's feet.

'Look who I've brought home,' Adler says victoriously to his men, who cheer at his offering. 'It's good to have you back, Marianne.'

I try to reply but the sound is muffled through the gag.

Adler cups his ear with his hand. 'What was that? Can't hear you.' And he leans forward and yanks the gag down.

I spit a mouthful of blood on to his boots, having bitten my tongue when I was punched in the face, before raising my head to look at him. 'I said, "I can't say the feeling is mutual."'

Two men pull me to my feet and hold me tightly while Adler squares up to me. 'I must say, I was worried that you'd end up getting killed without me there to watch, but this has worked out perfectly.'

'Do it then,' I say. If I am to die, let it be over. But I will not show my fear. I will not give him that power. Never again.

Adler laughs and his crew follow suit. But as I look around I realise it's not everyone. In fact, unless I'm imagining it, some of the crew look distinctly uneasy. Maybe killing his own flesh and blood is a step too far from their captain? Or perhaps they've just lost their appetite for the fight since the water raptors.

'Marianne, Marianne,' Adler says with amusement. 'You know how important you are to me. A quick death won't do for a special guest like you.'

I think of the gruesome display in his quarters: reminders of his special guests. I wonder what part of me he'll put in a jar. 'Lucky me.'

'Milligan's missed you, would you believe? I think perhaps you should pay her a visit to help you settle in. And as for this piece of scum,' he says, kicking Bronn, 'how about a keelhauling, lads?'

The crew cheer, but I'm definitely not imagining the lack of fervour this time. None of them seem overly enthusiastic about torturing Bronn. He was well liked on this ship.

We stare at each other, Bronn and I, as I'm roughly escorted away, neither of us speaking, just silently saying goodbye. We both know what awaits us will be painful and deadly. I watch Adler smile in sadistic pleasure as I'm pushed down into the lower decks. If he ever loved me, those days are long gone. But I also catch sight of Ren, who isn't even bothering to hide his displeasure. I try to make eye contact, hoping to communicate something to get us out of this, but he's staring firmly at his feet.

Milligan is clearly expecting me, and I suspect the moment Adler had me in his grasp, word was sent down here to prepare for my arrival.

My guards undo my restraints and push me hard against a wooden pillar, before landing a punch on to my already bruised ribs. As I choke for air they leave, wishing Milligan luck as they go.

Before I have the chance to regain my breath Milligan ties my wrists roughly behind the beam, followed by my ankles, so I'm going nowhere. She lines up her tools of choice: a hammer, rusty nails, a gully knife, a cleaver. In the fire a poker flashes red ready for use, and I can't help but notice the array of saws hanging on the wall, dried blood still encrusted in the teeth.

I've heard the screams come from this room too many times, and know Milligan is immune to pity or pleas for mercy. I won't give her the satisfaction of that.

'It's a shame really,' she says when she's ready. 'I always thought you had potential.'

'What makes you think you were wrong?' I try to keep her talking to delay the pain. Because I'm terrified. Utterly and completely terrified.

'Cos you're tied up here, and about to be missing a few vital parts. That's what.' She leans in close to nibble my ear, her hand running down my body until it reaches my belt where it lingers too long and too low before she removes my flask. When she steps back she leers at me. 'Tasty.'

I watch her take the flask and am willing to bet it's not rum Esther put in there. She warned me not to drink it and so I silently urge Milligan to take a swig.

Milligan places the flask on the bench and picks up a pair of pliers, examining them carefully. 'It's always good to remove the fingernails first. Remember me teaching you that?'

'You taught me nothing of value,' I say, desperate to stall, hoping any interruption will drive Milligan back to my flask.

It doesn't work. Instead her smile fades and she reaches for a blade. 'You left before I had even begun.' With a sudden rush of anger she moves quickly over to me, so her face is in mine. 'What was the matter? Didn't have the stomach for it?' And she presses the dagger down my cheek, reopening the healed wound that Cleeve inflicted on me. I bite my lip hard to stop from crying out, and soon taste the warm blood that trickles into my mouth. 'Well, the good news is you're back, so I can resume your instruction. The bad news is, I'm going to demonstrate on you.'

She steps away from me, and I'm shaking with fear. She's not going to drink Esther's potion. There's no escape from this. I know exactly what's about to happen to me and I'm helpless to stop it.

'Now, now, you know you're not to start without me.' Adler is striding into the room, not looking too pleased to find me already bleeding without having had the pleasure of witnessing my pain.

'Was just warming her up,' Milligan says, equally unhappy to be chastised.

As Adler takes a seat, I stare at him. Is he seriously going to watch Milligan torture me?

He smiles back. 'Don't worry,' he says. 'I haven't forgotten about your dearest Bronn. He's being prepared for a keelhauling as we speak. But I thought I might wait till Milligan's done with you, so you can come and watch. Wouldn't want you to miss all the fun.'

'You're a coward. So pathetically jealous of Bronn that you have to kill him? And not even brave enough to challenge him face to face because you know Bronn's ten times the fighter you are.'

Adler's eye narrows but he doesn't reply, and instead switches his attention to Milligan. 'Hurry up, woman, I haven't got all day.'

Milligan nods with anticipation. 'Yes, Captain. Now where were we? Ah, yes, fingernails.'

She walks behind me to where my hands are tied, and she strokes my fingers. 'Which one first? Let's try . . . this one.'

A searing pain shoots through me, crippling me, and I cry out despite myself.

Milligan laughs. 'Like that, did you? Good, because there's plenty more to go.'

And she yanks out another one. This time I manage not to make a noise, but it takes every ounce of control to bottle my pain deep inside, far from her reach.

This displeases her greatly. Where's the fun if she can't hear my suffering? Her eyes flick over to Adler. I can see she wants to impress him, but he remains emotionless, merely an observer of her work. Milligan walks round to examine me and reconsiders her method of torture. 'Perhaps I underestimated you. Maybe we'll try something else. Broken toes or broken fingers? Which would you prefer?'

There isn't really a good answer to that question so I say nothing, just watch as she tosses the hammer around in the air, catching and spinning it with the skill of someone who uses it a lot.

'Toes,' Adler says, making the decision for me. 'Break her toes.'

I didn't think there was much left inside of me to destroy, but he just managed to find it. Even after everything he's done I can't believe he's directing my suffering with such casual indifference.

Milligan smiles. 'Toes it is.' She twirls the hammer one last time and is squatting to the ground when Toby rushes into the room, breathing hard from his sprint.

'What?' Not wanting to be disturbed at such a moment, Adler practically bites the poor boy's head off, causing Toby to flinch.

'Water raptors, Captain. Sighted off the port bow.'

I wonder if they can feel my pain, if the bond works both ways. Is an attack on me an attack on them?

I see Adler's conflict. He doesn't want to miss my suffering, but equally he doesn't want his ship shattered into pieces by the water raptors. He swears at Toby before making his decision.

'Carry on,' he says to Milligan. 'I want her screaming by the time I get back. And as for you,' he adds, turning to Toby, 'stay here and watch. About time you grew a backbone.'

I can see Toby about to protest, which only angers Adler further. 'Or perhaps you'd rather come with me and be fed to the raptors?'

Toby shakes his head, staring at his feet, and Adler gives him a look of disgust before turning to me. 'Don't have too much fun without me.'

And then he's gone, leaving me alone with Toby and Milligan.

'Sit down, boy,' Milligan says. 'And don't interrupt my work.'

Toby does as he's told, avoiding looking directly at me.

Milligan doesn't bother disguising her contempt for him. 'Never thought there'd be someone on this ship more useless than you,' she says to me.

'If you think I'm so useless, why not untie me? See if you're still able to butcher me then.' With Adler gone I try one more time to drive her to the potion. Because if I can't get her to drink, my feet are going to be shattered.

'Must hurt,' she says, not taking me up on my suggestion, 'having your own father want to punish you like this.'

'It might, if he actually was my father.'

Confusion clouds Milligan's expression. Apparently Adler hasn't shared this information with his crew.

'Didn't he tell you? Maybe he doesn't trust you enough with such things.'

Her response is to punch me hard in the stomach, winding me so I'm unable to speak. I'm not going to get a better chance.

'Water?' I gasp at her, coughing for air.

She smiles at my plea and reaches for my flask, just as I hoped she would. 'Thirsty, are you? Me too. Hard work this.' She taunts me with the drink. 'Don't mind if I help myself, do you? Seeing as we're in no hurry.'

I don't mind at all. In fact, for the first time since Grace died, my fight to survive stirs inside me.

I watch Milligan as she opens the flask, taking an appreciative sniff before guzzling its contents, glancing sideways at me as if taking my rum is another way to torment me. I feign desperation so she doesn't suspect anything, and it drives her on until she's drained it dry.

Milligan wipes her mouth with her sleeve and belches. With a cruel smile she picks up the hammer once more, ready to resume my torture, but almost immediately concern appears on her face. And then she's retching, tearing at her throat as if somehow she can pull the poison back out.

Milligan reaches towards me, her eyes screaming for help, but I'm tied up and can do nothing – even if I wanted to. As she falls to her knees she gives me one last look of disbelief before slumping to the floor.

I take a deep breath. Esther has given me a chance. But my ropes are tied fast and there's still someone in the room who could kill me.

Toby has grown since I left the *Maiden*, stretched as if put on the rack. He's pulled out his dagger, and looks nervously at Milligan lying on the ground, before stepping towards me.

'Toby . . .' I have absolutely no idea what his intentions are.

He's still as quiet as ever, saying nothing as he moves to stand behind me, and I think I've forgotten how to breathe when I feel the cold edge of the blade against my wrists. Seconds later, the rope is sliced in two, and then Toby releases my feet.

He gives me the smallest smile as he places the knife into my hand and then walks silently out of the room.

Sneaking through the *Maiden* poses no challenge for me. I've been doing it since I could walk, though never with the urgency I have now. But as it happens there's barely anyone around. The only two Snakes I meet on the way are familiar to me, and so when we fight I choose my blows carefully, stunning them rather than killing them. Pain blazes on the raw skin once protected by fingernails, despite having wrapped them in cloth before leaving Milligan's torture chamber, but I push through it. I won't let anything stop me now.

When I cautiously lift the hatch to peer on to deck I see why my journey up has been so quiet. The water raptors loom in the distance and are definitely heading this way, so all hands are working on getting the *Maiden* moving again. Bronn's tied to the mizzenmast, his keelhauling temporarily delayed, while Adler shouts orders to his crew as if somehow this mortal peril they're in is all their fault.

Even from here I can see Bronn's been beaten and can't tell whether he's conscious. Angling my blade, I catch the sun and direct the glare on to his face. His eyes open, looking for the source of the annoyance, and when he sees me, his relief is visible.

I climb from the hatch and walk with confidence

across the deck towards Adler. Most of the crew are too frantic to notice I'm there, but those that do stare at me in disbelief, too stunned to react. When Ren sees me he holds my gaze before giving me the briefest of nods and a rare smile. I've earned his respect.

'Adler,' I shout to the man I used to call father, 'it's time we ended this, once and for all.'

Now every head on deck turns to look at me, and no one is more surprised than Adler himself. He hadn't thought me capable of this.

A couple of deckhands rush forward to capture me but Adler bellows out to them, 'Leave her!' The crew shrink back as though he'd struck them. They can hear his fury as well as I can.

'Milligan's losing her touch,' Adler says, casually stepping towards me as if two lethal water raptors weren't pursuing us.

'Drinking always was her weakness.'

He nods in understanding. 'So here we are, Marianne. Just like old times.'

'Not quite. Then I would have done anything to make you proud.'

'Apart from complete your Initiation?'

'I may have wanted your approval, but I never wanted to become you.'

'And yet, you already have. Killing Briggs the way you did? Couldn't have done better myself.'

'I am nothing like you.'

'Keep telling yourself that,' he says with a smile. 'But you have blood on your hands and I couldn't have asked for more from my daughter.'

'You are *not* my father.'

There's a slight murmur of confusion through the watching crowd, and I can tell Adler would have preferred them not to know that particular piece of information. But he recovers quickly.

'Something you should be thankful for. Your real father was a coward. Died without any fight. Your mother on the other hand?' Adler gestures to his missing eye. 'Now she showed spirit.'

He's trying to get under my skin and it's working. It's taking every scrap of self-control I have not to rise to his taunts.

'If you like spirit so much, why did you try to kill Esther?'

He narrows his eye, processing the information. All this time he'd believed Esther was dead.

'Didn't you know? She's alive, despite your best efforts. If it makes you feel better, I think she might hate you even more than I do.'

'Alive?' In that one word there's more emotion than I've ever known him to express. For a second I see he was once capable of love, albeit in his own twisted way. But then it's gone, replaced by anger. 'Well, thank you. Now

I know. Once I'm done with you I'll go and finish the job.'

'You loved her!' I shout, furious with myself for putting Esther in danger. 'You carved her into your figurehead! Why would you want her dead?'

'Because she betrayed me. And I don't forgive betrayal.'

'Nor do I.'

He raises an eyebrow and laughs. 'You think you can kill me? Marianne, even if I thought you had the guts, do you honestly think you're good enough?'

I look him dead in the eye, hoping my confidence masks my terror. 'Try me.'

His smile fades. 'I had hoped it wouldn't come to killing you. I'd far rather you join me. Give me the Western Isles and I'll extend my protection to you. When the East falls I'll let your prince live. I'll even take Bronn back despite his duplicity.'

'I would rather die than join you.'

'Then allow me.' And with no warning Adler dives at me, his dagger ready to strike.

He pushes me to the deck and I'm forced to drop my own dagger in order to grab both his wrists, desperately resisting the blade's progress towards my throat. He's ridiculously strong and for a moment I remember these arms reaching down to pick me up as a child. I felt safe in the hands that are now trying to kill me. But they never held me with love. I was nothing more than a trophy to display, to be polished, to remind him of his greatest kill and his highest prize. With a surge of blind fury I bring my knee up into his groin and he releases his grip just enough for me to roll away.

Before I'm even on my feet he's standing in front of me, cutlass in one hand, dagger in his other, while I have nothing. He lunges in my direction and I have to dodge swiftly out of the way, snatching up a length of broken chain left forgotten on top of a barrel, and holding it taut to block his relentless strikes. Sparks fly as steel hits steel, and I can hear Talon circling above us, shrieking out objections to this disturbance.

'You're a disappointment,' Adler says as I struggle to fend off his attack. 'Grace taught you nothing.'

The mere mention of her name causes my hatred to flare up towards him and in the split second he takes to move his arm back for momentum, I release one end of my chain and swing it diagonally from side to side. Now Adler's the one blocking the lethal metal as it whips across in front of him.

'She taught me enough to destroy you, you lying, treacherous, murdering, manipulative bastard,' I say, and with that final word I lash the chain down to knock the dagger from his hand.

A glimmer of uncertainty crosses Adler's face, and then he clicks his fingers. I sense the approach behind me and duck just in time to avoid a cutlass being brought down on my head. Apparently Choke hasn't forgiven me for besting her at the palace and she attacks with ferocity. Adler bows out from the fight, unleashing three more of his Snakes on me, and I dance with them, gliding, kicking, striking and weaving to attack then defend as required.

'Didn't expect me to play fair, did you?' Adler laughs, but I don't waste my energy answering, focusing entirely on my opponents: their body placements, their shifts of weight, the angle of attack, their weaknesses. Two are easily dispatched – a broken arm and a sharp jab to the throat – but for each I take down Adler adds two more until I'm fighting half a dozen people and, though I'm holding my own, I'm not sure how I'll be able to beat them all – especially if Adler keeps ordering others into the fray. I'm outnumbered.

And then I'm not alone. Two cutlasses join my side, quickly removing Choke and Turner from the equation. Bronn and Ren stand beside me, challenging anyone to keep coming for us. The others pause and it's as if someone's temporarily frozen us all.

'Ren?' Adler says, the betrayal an unpleasant surprise.

'I'm sorry, Captain,' Ren says. 'Your time has come to an end.'

Adler laughs. 'Three against fifty? I don't like your chances.'

'Four.'

Adler turns to stare at Toby who's hovering at the mizzenmast, clearly having cut Bronn free as he did me. Adler's laugh now borders on maniacal. 'Oh, well, if they have *you* on their side, then I surrender!'

But though some of the crew join him in mocking Toby, not everyone does. The tension becomes razor-sharp and I can almost taste the mutiny in the air.

I need to convince the rest of the crew to join me, need to prove that I'm worth switching allegiance for. If I am to be their captain, I can't just win their respect. Right now they have to fear me, more than they fear Adler.

'There may only be four of us, but have you stopped to consider what I've done?' I'm looking at Adler, but I'm addressing the crew. This is my pitch, and it'd better be good.

'You think we're here by mistake? I lured you into these waters. You're here because I wanted it. Time and again you have underestimated me. Briggs, Cleeve, Milligan – all dead because of me. And still you have failed to see the truth before you.' I pause for effect, before gesturing out to sea. 'The raptors didn't just appear, that was no coincidence. They have to be summoned, called from their dark depths by magic and blood. You should surrender. They'll be here in minutes and will destroy us all. Because it was my magic, my blood. They are here at my command.'

The intake of breath is audible and the atmosphere shifts again. Nothing frightens these sailors like magic and myth.

'You're lying,' Adler says. 'Even you wouldn't be foolish enough to summon creatures that would ensure your own death – imagining for a moment you were even capable.'

'I am more than ready to sacrifice my life if it means the end of yours. It was always my plan. I do not fear death, Adler. Do you?'

He glares at me; I see a brief glimpse of doubt in his eye before he blinks it away. 'I would rather die than hand myself over to a girl like you.'

'Good, because I would rather kill you than let the raptors have the pleasure.' I don't wait for permission. This time I strike first.

In one swift movement I've stooped for the knife he dropped and I fly at him. Chaos descends on the ship in an instant as almost half the crew attack the rest. Ren wasn't lying when he said there were others willing to defect, and my speech has persuaded many that I'm worth backing, but I have eyes for only one man.

We both know this is personal; every strike is intended to kill, and his blows come hard and fast, so that it's all I can do to parry them, every ounce of his hatred towards me channelled behind each swing of the cutlass. He smashes through barrels, pallets and even the boards of the ship itself as he pursues me around the deck. I draw on every move Grace and Bronn ever taught me to survive the onslaught, swerving and twisting my body to narrowly evade his every swipe. I see a grappling hook and snatch it up, slinging it to block his blade even as it's already slashing down towards me. My deflection knocks Adler off balance and gives me a spare second to regain my footing. It's all I need to bring my knife up under Adler's chin, leaving a deep gash.

He pauses, looking at me with incredulity, as if he can't believe I dared to do it.

'Scared?' I say, wanting to taunt him.

'Of you, Marianne? You don't have what it takes.'

My foot rests on a cutlass that's fallen from a dead man's grasp, and I flick it up and catch it, holding it in my left hand. Now I'm the one with two weapons. 'My name is Mairin of the house of Vultura. Star of the Sea. And I have exactly what it takes.'

And then I launch myself at him and show him everything I've ever learned about swordplay. Moving with a speed both Grace and Bronn would be proud of, I slice and hack with a blade in each hand. Adler parries me well, but then I manage to strike his fingers with my dagger and he drops his cutlass. As he falters I kick him hard in the chest, sending him reeling backwards on to the deck. This is it. My chance to kill him.

But I hesitate, the conflict I thought I'd resolved flooding to the surface. He's all things evil, but there was a time when I loved him and some small part of me hasn't forgotten that. Is he worth it? Worth becoming an assassin for?

There's no opportunity to redeem my wavering resolve, because at that moment a furious water raptor slams into the side of the ship, tilting the *Maiden* violently to her port side. I'm almost thrown down, but quickly thrust my blade into the deck and hold on tight until the *Maiden* rights herself.

When she crashes back into the water my eyes scan for Adler, but he's disappeared. The fighting has changed now, the crew not certain which is a more immediate threat to their lives, each other or the sea creatures. While some continue to fight among themselves, most turn their aggression to the two water raptors circling us.

I search for Bronn – he's locked in an exchange with a Snake I don't recognise and I call out to him. He turns at the sound of my voice, simultaneously knocking out the man he was fighting, and we run towards each other.

Before he can reach me, the female water raptor swings her massive head across the deck, scattering crew into the water like flies, and demolishing the foremast in her wake. Chunks of wood crash down over us, and Bronn has to retreat to avoid getting hit.

'Marianne!' he shouts over the chaos. 'We've got to get out of here.'

'Reach the helm. I'll join you there.'

Bronn nods and then he's gone, while I try to find a different way through.

I don't get far before my path is blocked, but not by debris. The water raptor has come about, and I have to dive out of the way as she opens her mouth wide and pours a torrent of poisoned water over the deck. The screams that follow are awful, and I only survive by leaping on to dangling rigging that keeps me out of harm's way.

I swing from the rope and clamber through to the other side of the ship, desperate to find Bronn, but he's not by the helm and panic sets in. I race towards the quarterdeck, and that's where I see him.

He's lying on the deck, his body covering Toby's to protect him from the venom, his arm and side badly burned.

'Bronn!' I run towards him, but I'm distracted, not focusing, and feel a blade slip into my abdomen with astonishing ease before I see, too late, that Adler's stepped directly into my path.

The air seems to flee my body and as I hit the deck my eyes meet Bronn's, our faces at the same level. I thought I was ready for death, but the sadness that consumes me is more painful than my wound.

I roll over, pressing the gash hard as if I can push my blood back in, and stare up at Adler, whose shadow blocks out the sun as he stands over me.

'You know, I've enjoyed this,' he says, kneeling down so he doesn't have to shout. 'All this defiance you've shown has made taking the Isles so much more satisfying. The King really wasn't making it a worthwhile game. Shame my ship has been damaged, but she can be fixed. And I'll return home more feared than ever – the man who killed both the water raptors and the girl who summoned them. So thank you. Truly, thank you. *Marianne.*' He uses the name he gave me as one final display of control, of ownership.

I want to respond, want to retaliate, want to leap to my feet and slice his villainous neck, but all I can do is gasp for air, like a fish torn from the water. Adler laughs as he stands up and leaves me to die.

I watch as he climbs the ratlines up the mainmast and realise with horror that he plans to release the harpoon at the raptors. Despite their size, one perfect shot through the heart should be enough to destroy them. And he's the Viper. He'll make the shot.

He's going to win. Again. By killing me, by killing the raptors, there really will be nothing to stop him destroying what remains of everyone and everything I love. He'll slaughter anyone who's helped me, plunder the islands of every resource, and steal all the beauty from the world.

No. I simply won't abandon the Isles to such a monster. Not while there's breath in my body. Dragging myself across the deck feels like it takes for ever, but I only need to be faster than Adler and he's slower on the ratlines than he used to be. The knife that lies discarded not ten feet away is all I need and, clawing my way with my fingers, I inch closer to it, smearing a trail of blood behind me, until finally my fist closes round the heavy handle.

Breathing is almost impossible, but my head tells me that the fact I'm still alive means he's missed my vital organs. I have time. I can do this. I roll on to my back and twist so that I can see Adler high above me, already on the platform and aiming the harpoon at the water raptor as she approaches for another attack.

Using every last inch of my remaining strength I throw the knife.

No more conflict.

No hesitation.

It lodges squarely in his heart and for a moment he just stands there as if he's sustained nothing more than a bee sting. And then his eye finds me, and he knows. One final moment of understanding passes between us before he falls, plummeting down, his body breaking on impact with the deck.

It's done. I am free of him. And even though I ran a long time ago, I finally feel the noose slip from my neck.

I lie back, exhausted. In the end I didn't kill him in the heat of anger or with a violent heart. It wasn't revenge that gave me the strength to throw that knife. It was the need to protect. Just like my mother. It gave me no pleasure, but I have no regrets. Adler killed hundreds of people, many of whom I loved.

A strange hollow sensation is creeping through me.

'Captain Adler is dead!' Ren's voice penetrates the air and the fighting breaks up. 'All hail our new captain.'

A new captain who's bleeding out all over the deck.

'Incoming!' A desperate voice shrieks out as the water raptors make a fresh attack, and they smash into the ship as though it were paper-thin.

My captaincy may not last long, but while it does the crew are my responsibility. Many of them have risked their lives to give me allegiance and so I will not fail them. I should never have unleashed the raptors, should never have abandoned myself to the powerful, dangerous lure of magic. It may already be too late to put things right, but I have to try.

Getting to my knees seems to take hours. I clutch desperately at my side, not even certain what I intend to do until the words leave my mouth.

Releasing my wound, I raise both hands high and direct my command to the water raptors, this time with only peace in my heart.

'*Stop, dark demons, cease and flee. Return to sleep, return to sea.*'

The female water raptor breathes one last watery shower, but this time into the ocean, and then slowly, as if not entirely willing, they both disappear back under the waves, leaving only stunned silence behind them.

I remain on my knees but return my hands to stem the bleeding. I'm aware that everyone's staring at me, shocked by what they've just witnessed. Their old captain is dead and their new one just commanded the water raptors to leave us alone, and even though I said before that I had summoned them there's a difference between hearing and seeing. The crew know everything's about to change. The ship is silent with anticipation, with fear, the only sound coming from Talon, who squawks as he swoops down, landing on my shoulder, gently pecking my ear in approval. Well, his loyalty was easily won.

'Adler was a traitor and a thief!' I say, my voice horribly soft but thankfully carrying on the wind nonetheless. 'He killed my parents and raised me as his own, before making me his enemy. It's been many generations since the name of the Viper was won through conquest, but Adler is dead by my hand. By rights, I am your captain.'

Ren steps forward and crosses his arms in salute. 'And we pledge to you our fealty.'

I nod in appreciation. With both Bronn and me injured I'll be testing his loyalty soon enough. 'It's time the Viper became a symbol of protection once more. We will be feared, yes, but only by those who wish to harm others or take what does not belong to them. We may serve the King, but more importantly we serve the islanders. Adler's reign of chaos is over. The honour of the Viper shall be restored.'

The crew who fought for me cheer and offer a salute, which I return as best I can. The blood loss is making me dizzy.

I beckon Ren over to me, and barely whisper my orders to him. 'Secure all the Snakes who chose to ally with Adler. I'll decide what to do with them if I live long enough.'

He rests his hand on my shoulder. 'Consider it done. We'll get you help.'

I lie down and listen to Ren issue commands, securing the ship for me, and then close my eyes. I've done my part.

Someone shakes me awake. Bronn is beside me, dressing my wound. His own look fiercely painful but he doesn't flinch as he tends to me.

'Don't you die on me,' he says as he pulls a strap tight round my waist. 'Do you hear? If I have to live, so do you.'

I manage a weak smile. 'Sounds fair.'

'That was a hell of a shot,' he says. 'Grace would have been proud.' And Bronn kisses me firmly on the forehead before attending to his own injuries.

I blink tears away as the wind whips through my hair, carrying with it the pungent smell of saline, the coming of rain, the promise of a storm. A sense of belonging settles over me. I'm not done with life yet, far from it. Adler's reign may be over, but mine is just beginning. Today is not the day I die. I'm the Viper. And I have work to do.

The spot I've picked for Grace's grave is in the shade of an ashblossom tree overlooking the sea. It's beautiful; I think she would have liked it.

We're stuck on the Eighth Isle until we can finish repairing the *Maiden*. As soon as she's seaworthy I plan to leave the Western Isles to regroup with Torin and begin to undo the devastation Adler caused. Sea vultures have been sent and received – Torin and the Fleet never even made it into Western waters, an unnatural storm forbidding them from crossing the divide, as if the West knew they weren't part of Adler's and my unfinished business. Now they've returned to the Eastern Isles, where Torin will put forward a motion that his father abdicates immediately.

Several survivors of the ill-fated *Avenger* have been found, including the indomitable Harley, who seemed invigorated by the ordeal, and the ever-resourceful Ana. All of them have elected to join my crew, much to my delight. It's a comfort to have them on board when many of the Snakes who switched their loyalty to me in the face of defeat have yet to gain my trust.

When the time does come for us to leave, I'm uncertain if I'll ever return to the West. Though I now know I'm descended from the lost royalty, when Adler took me from my parents he also took that future. Now I want to make my own.

I've decided to keep the name I've grown up with. Though Adler may have given it to me, over the years it's become part of who I am, and so I have chosen to keep it for myself. My true name will stay tucked into my heart along with my love for the parents I never knew, my link to the life I could have had and will never know.

Esther seems to have found a kind of peace now she's told her story and justice has been dealt. My recovery has taken a while, but once I was strong enough to leave the ship I found my way back to her grove to tell her of Adler's death. She made a tonic to aid my healing and offered to teach me all she knew if I stayed. I was tempted, more than I'd like to admit, but much to Esther's disappointment I declined. I told her – and myself – that I had duties to fulfil. And I do. But we both know that's not the whole truth. I fear the part of me that rises with the magic. The darkness I cannot dare to unleash again. If one day I change my mind and decide to return, Esther's made it clear she'll be waiting. So perhaps the West isn't quite done with me just yet.

At the sound of footsteps I turn to see Bronn coming over the brow of the hill, the evening sun turning his black hair copper. Though I was able to heal much of the damage he sustained, I couldn't prevent him accumulating a few new scars from the burns. Water raptors' venom is incredibly potent.

He sits beside me on the dry ground and rests his shoulder against mine.

We don't speak.

We weren't expecting still to be alive, and while it was one thing to give in to our desire when we had nothing to lose, now everything's changed. Or rather returned to how it was.

I am betrothed to another man. A man I will marry for the sake of the Eastern Isles. A good man.

The man by my side is my opposite and my reflection. The dark to my light. The light to my dark. And everything in between. But I'm not sure either of us could survive the heartbreak of being together yet being apart. Love is not enough.

As the last birds go home to roost, Bronn breaks the silence.

'So I've been meaning to ask, do I call you "majesty" or "captain" now?'

'I think . . . both.'

He laughs. 'You'll want me to salute and curtsy next.'

'But of course.'

While I'd recovered I'd told Bronn everything about Adler, about my parents, about my ancestors. My secrets are safe with him. He knows restoring the Eastern Isles is all that matters right now.

'What will happen to us when we return home?' he says, serious now. 'When you marry Torin?'

I turn to face him, wanting to comfort him, but I can't. I only have honesty, and it's not always kind.

'I don't know.'

He nods, a shadow falling across his face. It wasn't what he wanted to hear, but he knows anything else would be a lie.

'Then I'll wait for my orders, Captain.'

He salutes me, his eyes lingering on mine, before he turns and leaves me alone once more.

I stay there a while longer, looking out over the ocean. I know tomorrow will bring its own troubles; there will always be new battles, fresh fights to win, but for now, in this moment, at least I'm at peace with myself.

A gentle breeze stirs across the sea from the East and I close my eyes. Let the wind bring what it will. I'm ready for anything.

ACKNOWLEDGEMENTS

This book simply would not exist without the support and downright hard work of some outstanding people, all of whom I am endlessly grateful to know.

Firstly eternal thanks to my powerhouse of an agent, the wonderful Davinia Andrew-Lynch, whose unwavering belief in both me and this book has meant the world to me. I cannot believe how lucky I am to get to navigate these publishing waters with you by my side – there just aren't enough superlatives to describe you. You're a true warrior queen.

Infinite thanks to the amazing Lena McCauley, editor extraordinaire. Thank you so much for seeing Marianne, understanding her and giving her the opportunity to set sail into the world. I feel utterly privileged to have the opportunity to benefit from your knowledge and wisdom. It's been an absolute joy working with you on this book, from start to finish.

To all the team at Orion and Hachette – you are beyond incredible. Thank you for welcoming me into the fold so warmly. Huge special thanks to Samuel Perrett for designing a cover more beautiful than I dared dream for, to Jennie Roman, my copy-editor, to Emily Thomas, my fabulous publicist, and to Naomi Berwin for her marketing prowess.

Massive thanks to Allison Hellegers, for your perceptive input and support. Thank you for everything you've done and continue to do.

A humongous thank you to Fiz Osborne, for all your insight and advice over the years. I cannot tell you how much I value your help, your friendship and your general awesomeness.

To my beautiful friends, to each and every one of you who has stuck by me through the years, listened to my tales of rejection, and never once suggested I give up – thank you. There have been ups and (more) downs, but you've kept me going with your encouragement, and I'm so grateful to you all. You know who you are, lovely ones.

My family are, fortunately, nothing like Marianne's. There are so many of you, it would take another novella to mention everyone by name, but thank you to all of you, for just being you, for being in my life. I love you all. Extra special thanks must go to a few people though. To John, Yu-Chiao & Lorna, for reading an early draft and giving me feedback. To Bea for your beautiful drawings of Marianne's compass. To Eddie for helping me out over the summer when I really needed it. To Aunty Gill, for always cheering me on from the sidelines (and for the most gorgeous book deal gift!).

A great big thank you to my dad, for being my biggest

fan never to have actually read anything I've written! Thank you for coming to my rescue numerous times so that I could focus on my writing. You're such a huge support and I love you lots.

Where do I even start thanking my mum, who has read every draft, taken every anxious phone call, comforted me at every rejection and encouraged at every turn? I would never have dared to dream so big without knowing you were right behind me, wouldn't have been brave enough to keep going without you picking me up and dusting me off. I love you so much.

To my amazing husband, Joe; thank you for never once doubting me on this long journey. Thank you for being beside me the whole way as I've followed my dreams. From the very first draft you've pushed me to find the truest path for my characters and could spot a plot hole a mile away. I couldn't have done any of this without you. Lovings.

And to my beautiful daughters, Kara and Odette. My very favourite people ever. Thank you for not complaining too much when I shut myself away to disappear into another world! It makes me constantly happy that you both love books and reading as much as I do – what a gift to be able to share with you. I am so very proud of you both and love you for ever. Thank you for being the best girls in the world. Thank you for making all of this worthwhile.

TURN THE PAGE FOR A SNEAK PEEK
OF THE NEXT BOOK IN THE

ISLES OF
STORM & SORROW
TRILOGY

VENOM

It's a beautiful night for a wedding. The moon is radiant, offering its shimmering light as a blessing on the union and the stars shine bright in celebration. The gentle breeze scatters delicate pink petals from the trees like confetti.

The room I'm in looks down over the gardens of the summer palace, and I rest my head against the cool glass of the window. Not moments ago, I was surrounded by people, fussing over me, preparing me, filling the air with laughter and excitement. Now I'm alone. Waiting.

I am dressed for midnight. The only colour on my person is the scarlet thread woven through my corset. Otherwise I'm entirely in black as befits the Viper, though for one day only I'm in an elaborate gown, rather than my fighting garb. I slide the dagger gifted to me by my crew into my boot and immediately feel more myself. A bride I may be, but I have plenty of enemies who would love to use this day to their advantage.

There's a soft knock on the door. It's time. A flock of nerves takes flight inside me, fluttering in my chest. With a deep breath, my chin up, I meet my future head on. Two chambermaids greet me with a smile, before placing a heavy velvet cloak on to my shoulders and fastening it with a bejewelled brooch at my throat. The hood is lifted carefully over my hair and I'm escorted from my chamber.

The ceremony is taking place outside, in a courtyard

lit by a thousand candles and filled with islanders who have congregated to watch this historic event unfold. A hush descends over the crowd at my arrival, every head turning to watch me make the long walk to where the priestess waits to mark our vows. My heart is beating fast – too fast – though I'm comforted to see members of my crew standing either side of the aisle.

And then there he is. My eyes lock on him like a needle on a compass. Bronn. My eternal north.

His face remains as impassive as ever – he's had years to practise concealing his feelings – and though I'm still not always able to read him, today I have no doubt what's going through his mind. Reluctantly I pull my gaze away from him, moving my focus to the man waiting for me just feet ahead.

Torin. He is dressed in the finest cloth, trimmed with velvet and sparkling with fragments of crystal. He has never looked more handsome which I didn't think was possible. He smiles at my approach – a wonderful, genuine smile because Torin can't give anything less – but I glimpse his conflict nonetheless. I'm not the only one forsaking love in the name of duty today.

In a few steps I'm beside him, trying to block out the rest of the world as I listen to the priestess's words, making my vows with as much honesty as I can. I promise to honour Torin, swear to defend him with my life, and pledge to remain true to him above all others

– until death parts us. This last oath is by far the most difficult to make, but I force the words out. At least both of us know the truth. And as I'm not deceiving Torin in any way, there's no guilt.

Behind Torin, standing just close enough to be in my peripheral vision, is his new bodyguard, Braydon. I haven't got used to him yet; he seems to trust me as little as Sharpe did to begin with, but while I eventually won Sharpe round, I feel Braydon's dislike for me might be harder to overcome. I can feel him scowling even as I become his Princess.

My eyes dart over to Sharpe, standing off to one side. The loss of his sight meant he had to be reassigned, and though he remains Torin's aide, his misery these past months has been obvious. He looks as though he wants to be here as much as Bronn does.

Our vows made, Torin and I are instructed to place our wrists together, as we did during our binding ceremony so long ago. But this time, rather than red-hot metal, silk is wrapped round our scarred skin, and we turn to face all those who have assembled to witness such a momentous occasion.

The crowd cheers, and my crew salutes us, before Torin leans over to kiss me gently on my lips. It's all part of the act, I know, but I can feel the colour rise to my cheeks. His skin is soft where Bronn's is rough; his touch is ice where Bronn's is fire.

He is my husband. I am his wife.

When we walk back down the aisle, still bound together with the silk, I manage to avoid looking at Bronn. It takes me a few moments to realise I'm holding my breath, and exhale. The worst, after all, is over. I force myself to relax, even going as far as to acknowledge the crowds of people who are cheering our departure.

It's then I see him. The stranger. There's nothing extraordinary about him but that's exactly what makes him stand out. He's dressed a little too normally. He's blending in a little too much. He stands exactly like a man who doesn't want to be noticed.

I look away, not wanting him to know I'm suspicious, but keep him in the corner of my eye – I don't want to lose sight of a potential threat. Torin must feel me tense, because he looks over, concerned.

'What's wrong?'

I give him the brightest smile possible, so that to the crowd I will seem merely like a happy bride talking with her new husband. 'Behind me, towards the wall. Black hair, tied back. Tall. Do you see him?'

Torin returns my false smile with one of his own and leans towards me, giving the impression of whispering sweet nothings into my ear, while really looking past me to see who I mean.

'Yes. Who is he?'

'I was hoping you might know.'

'Want me to have him removed?'

I shake my head. 'The last thing we want to do is cause a spectacle.'

When we reach the end of the aisle, Torin searches my face. 'We did the right thing, didn't we?'

I squeeze his arm with my free hand. 'Of course we did.' Though I do wish the night was over. I would rather not have to endure the coming celebrations.

I've had no say in this wedding. I didn't want it here, in the summer palace, deep in the heart of the First Isle. Set atop a mountain peak, the palace is bleak and isolated and a long way from my ship, which makes me feel vulnerable and uneasy. I didn't want an extravagant feast and dancing, when the islanders are still struggling to fill their bellies. But it's all been arranged by someone else.

The King.